EARTH SHOUT

BOOK 3 IN THE EARTH SONG SERIES

NICK COOK

ABOUT THE AUTHOR

Somewhere back in the mists of time, Nick was born in the great sprawling metropolis of London. He grew up in a family where art was always a huge influence. Tapping into this, Nick finished college with a fine art degree tucked into his back pocket. Faced with the prospect of actually trying to make a living from his talents, he plunged into the emerging video game industry back in the eighties. It was the start of a long career and he produced graphics for many of the top-selling games on the early home computers, including *Aliens* and *Enduro Racer*. Those pioneering games may look crude now, but back then they were considered to be cutting edge. As the industry exploded into the one we know today, Nick's career went supernova. He worked on titles such as *X-Com*, and set up two studios, which produced

Warzone 2100 and the *Conflict: Desert Storm* series. He has around forty published titles to his name.

As great as the video game industry is, a little voice kept nagging inside Nick's head, and at the end of 2006 he was finally ready to pursue his other passion as a full-time career: writing. Many years later, he completed his first trilogy, *Cloud Riders*. And the rest, as they say, is history.

Nick has many interests, from space exploration and astronomy to travelling the world. He has flown light aircraft and microlights, an experience he used as research for *Cloud Riders*. He's always loved to cook, but then you'd expect it with his surname. His writing in many ways reflects his own curiosity about the world around him. He loves to let his imagination run riot to pose the question: *What if?*

ALSO BY NICK COOK

Prequel to the Multiverse Chronicles

The Earth Song Series (The Multiverse Chronicles)

The Fractured Light Trilogy (The Multiverse Chronicles)

For all the talented creators of the visionary sci-fi movies from the 50s and 60s. They helped to sow those first seeds of wonder that I carry within me to this very day.

CHAPTER ONE

IT SEEMED as if at least half the population of Eden had crammed into the huge underground cinema to watch the launch. Every one of the thousand seats had been filled. The rest of the crowd thronged the walkways, some standing, many sitting on the steps. Despite the almost party atmosphere, there was an underlying concern visible in many of the faces around me and we were all collectively holding our breath. The next ten minutes were going to be critical for the survival of our planet.

I sat in the front row with Jodie and Mike on one side of me. They were squeezing each other's hands as we watched the live streamed broadcast from Cape Canaveral. The fact that it was a night-time launch only added to the drama of the event.

Jack sat on the other side of me, drumming his hand on his leg to each tick of the countdown. Meanwhile, I was doing my best to resist biting my fingernails.

Ruby, the latest member of our team and a skilled sniper, sat away from our group with her security buddies in their grey uniforms. Laughter kept punctuating the tense atmosphere as

Ruby shared some joke with them. And judging by the way she kept glancing across at me, it was probably at my expense.

She hadn't come out and said she had a problem with me in charge, but it certainly came across in her attitude. Every opportunity she got, she seemed to choose her mates in the security team rather than be anywhere near me. With a considerable number of ex-soldiers in their ranks, they were obviously her natural tribe as opposed to a bunch of civilians. Though Jack was an exception, no doubt because he was ex-military too. I still had no idea how I was going to win Ruby round.

In front of the audience on the five-storey-high IMAX screen, spotlights bathed the huge SpaceX rocket that Sky Dreamer Corp. had partnered with for the launch of our precious payload. The cover story was that this launch was part of a mesh internet grid that would be used by future missions. But of course the truth was very different. SpaceX's Starship rocket actually contained TREENO, The REines Experimental Neutrino Observatory. This consisted of a large cluster of CubeSats that were going to be essential to us speeding up detection of any future waking micro minds. An ancient race of aliens called the Angelus had visited Earth in its early past, hiding a series of tetrahedron crystals. These were the micro minds, fragments of an AI consciousness that we now called Lucy. She believed that when we finally found all these micro minds, they would help our world defend itself against the coming threat of an alien invasion. But how Lucy's micro minds could defend us from them, even she didn't know – and wouldn't until we'd found the last fragment of her consciousness. That was why this launch was such a big deal.

'Twenty, nineteen, eighteen...' the male commentator began, his voice booming out in the theatre.

Vented liquid oxygen began to billow freely from the rocket as it got ready to launch.

I sat up straighter as the countdown reached ten seconds. You could almost taste the tension in the room. A thousand people leant a fraction further towards the screen.

I turned to Mike and Jodie. 'Good luck, guys.'

'Thanks,' Jodie said, looking sick.

Mike chewed the quick of his thumbnail. 'If that rocket blows up...'

'It won't,' I replied. 'SpaceX launches are usually as reliable as clockwork.'

'Usually,' Jodie replied worriedly.

I patted her arm. Then I cast a look over at Alice sitting in her wheelchair to one side of the IMAX screen. Despite the drama of what was about to happen she had a distinctly distracted look, as if she was somewhere else in her head. That probably had everything to do with Tom still being out of contact.

Tom was in charge of intelligence gathering at Eden. I'd first met him on a car ferry heading for Orkney. At the time he was wearing a full-blown disguise, pretending to be an old Scottish guy who had a taste for whiskey. He had gone AWOL after a deep-cover mission and none of us knew where he was. Alice in particular seemed to be taking his disappearance very badly. I'd learnt from Niki, our head of security, that Alice and Tom went way back.

'Five, four, three, two, one... We have go for launch.'

The impressive surround-sound speakers thundered as the Raptor engines roared into life, ear-splittingly loud. I could feel the vibrations passing through my abdomen. Yellow and golden fire billowed out of the base of the SpaceX rocket. Then, just like that, the rocket began to lift off from the launch pad on an expanding blossom of fire and cloud.

Cheers erupted in the theatre, hundreds of instant celebrations. Jodie threw her arms round Mike and kissed him. In stark contrast, Jack high-fived me. But we hollered with the best of them as the rocket cleared the tower and started to rise into the sky. I caught Alice allowing herself the briefest smile as the rocket's Raptor engines turned night into day over the Cape Canaveral launch pad.

The camera cut to a long shot as the rocket streaked upwards on its needle of light. The ongoing commentary was barely audible over the continuing whoops that filled the room.

Jack leant in towards me as the clapping faded away. 'Isn't that a spectacular sight?'

'It really is,' I replied. But despite my sense of awe, there was also a constant worry gnawing away at my insides. Another longer countdown was ticking down in Eden, on dozens of displays that had been mounted around the underground base. They were intended to keep all our minds tightly focused on the time we had left until the arrival of the Kimprak, the alien species who would destroy all life on Earth if we didn't find a way to stop them. We had roughly four years left until they arrived in our solar system.

I noticed Alice had disappeared. Was she thinking about the longer countdown too? In my case at least part of the reason was personal and had everything to do with the man that I was sitting next to, Jack.

'Max-Q,' the commentator announced.

'That means the maximum pressure is on the launch vehicle,' Jodie said. 'When there's the biggest danger of the rocket blowing up.' She squeezed Mike's hand so hard it left red welts on his fingers.

I gradually felt the tension slacken in my jaw as the critical seconds ticked passed.

Then one of the flight control team over the live feed from Cape Canaveral said, way too calmly, 'We have confirmed booster separation and second-stage ignition.'

Light flared around the pinprick rocket being tracked on a

highly magnified camera. It showed the SpaceX Super Heavy booster separating from Starship and beginning its return to Earth.

The thunderous applause became deafening and the looks on the faces around me were exultant. But the longer I stayed here, the more I felt like a spectator. If I was to hazard a guess, that was probably exactly how Alice had been feeling just before she'd left.

I bent my head towards Jack. 'I'm heading up top to the jungle to look at the stars.'

Jack gave me a surprised look. 'Not going to the party in the Rock Garden? Leroy got you some Highland Park especially.'

'No, I just need a bit of fresh air.'

'Oh, OK...'

Something passed through Jack's expression that I couldn't quite read. I turned away rather than trying to explain myself. I didn't want to get into it right then. Yes, he had a lot to do with my current downer, but I wouldn't tell him that. I began squeezing my way through the people sat on the steps.

The room behind me erupted with more cheers as the commentator called out something else. The doors swung closed behind me, cutting off the sound of the celebration. I headed away to attempt to find some peace from my own troubled mind among the stars.

CHAPTER TWO

Jᴀᴄᴋ and I entered the silo from the access lift to find Alice peering up at an inspection panel in the chrome belly of Ariel. This antigravity saucer-shaped craft had been at the centre of a maelstrom of effort for months now.

'How's it going?' Jack asked as we approached.

Alice turned her wheelchair to face us. 'We're getting closer, but the magnetic gravity disruptor still isn't stable. The good news is we've been able to make great progress with the vectoring supersonic nozzles round the edge of the craft.'

'The *what?*' I asked.

'They provide direction propulsion for Ariel,' Alice replied. 'We've also just finished the cockpit. You should have a look at it before Lucy gets here. It really is quite something.'

'It's OK to poke around in there then?' I asked.

'Just as long as you don't touch anything on the flight deck. You don't want to find yourself airborne and not able to control the ship.'

Jack held his hands up, smiling. 'I'm not touching a thing.'

We headed from the landing pad up a ramp into the craft. What we encountered as we entered the cockpit was the last thing I'd been expecting. Inside was a spherical room about ten metres wide, with a circular metal grid platform within it, connected by rotating gimbals to two rings. It looked designed to rotate like a gyroscope. Hexagonal darkened monitors lined the cockpit round the platform, almost giving it the look of honeycomb.

'This so wasn't what I was expecting,' Jack said.

'Me neither,' I replied as we climbed up a short ladder to the platform. On it were six flight seats arranged in a petal formation that faced out towards the monitor screens. One of the seats had what appeared to be flight-like controls built into the arms. In the seat next to it was a large semi-circular glass screen with a HUD containing information.

'That seat looks like the command information centre system from the Armadillo,' Jack said.

'The CIC is certainly based on it, although right now Ariel doesn't have any armaments,' Alice said to us through the open ramp. 'There's another important addition. That seat with the controls built into it is for the pilot.'

'You mean you're not going to let the Delphi AI system fly this?' I asked.

'Oh, don't you worry, Delphi will still be there for backup and to make sure the various elements of the flight system play nicely together. However, the primary control will be down to the pilot as this is a completely new field of aviation for us. We've obviously tried to anticipate as many aspects as we can. For example, the spherical cockpit is designed to keep the flight-deck platform level as Ariel effectively rotates around it. With the exception of the TR-3B Astra, the experimental gravity reduction craft of the US military, this will be unlike any other aircraft our world has created. We're going to be facing the unknown with Ariel on her maiden flight – it's going to be difficult to anticipate everything that might be thrown at us.'

'So you're going to use a test pilot?' Jack asked.

'We most certainly are,' Alice replied. 'Me.'

'You're not serious?' I said before my brain had a chance to clamp down the thought.

Alice's eyebrows rose up her forehead. 'Good to hear you have such confidence in my flying skills, Lauren.'

'No, I didn't mean it like that...' My gaze travelled to her wheelchair before I could stop it. Bloody hell, I was on a roll today.

'Oh, I see. You think that because I have a spinal injury I can't pilot this craft? Is that about the gist of it?'

'Sorry, I didn't mean to suggest—'

But Alice held up a hand to silence me. 'Please relax, Lauren. I'm really not taking this personally. It's a perfectly reasonable assumption. However, I would have thought you knew me well enough to realise that being confined to wheelchair won't stop me when it comes to the opportunity to fly Ariel.'

'Of course...' I cast a desperate look round for Jack to jump in and deflect the conversation.

He raised his eyebrows a fraction at me before turning to gaze down at Alice from the flight deck. 'So how will you actually pilot this thing? Will you clamp your wheelchair somewhere?'

'Oh, I have something far better than that. The flight seat has been moulded to my body. And to fly Ariel I only need my hands – there's no rudder control to speak of. So you see, this ship is perfect for someone who's a paraplegic like myself.'

'That's great and everything, but surely a test flight is a risky thing anyway?' I said. 'Wouldn't it be safer if someone else took Ariel out for her first flight?'

Alice shook her head. 'It's precisely *because* it's risky that I'm going to do this, Lauren. This craft is primarily my design. There is no way I could just be a spectator whilst someone else puts their neck on the line. Wouldn't you do the same in my position?'

I sighed. 'Yes, I probably would.'

'So we got there in the end. If it's any comfort, Niki felt just the same until I sweet-talked him round.'

'I'm not surprised,' I said. 'You, Alice, are a force of nature not to be argued with.'

'Says Lauren Stelleck, our very own Lara Croft,' she replied.

Jack chuckled. 'Isn't that the truth.'

Before I could object, a warbling alarm filled the landing bay and red light began to strobe on the wall.

'Looks as if we're about to get company,' Alice said.

The sound of motors whirring echoed from somewhere high above us in the launch bay shaft. A round disc of stars slowly started to appear as a cover slid back. A single point of light blazed far brighter than even Venus in the night sky, growing larger fast. Then, without so much as a sigh of wind, the falling star stopped directly over the entrance to the silo. It was close enough to make out its form – a shining six-pointed crystal with shimmering blue energy rippling through its surfaces. The craft, made from two combined micro minds that had fused together, gradually descended into the silo.

'Lucy still takes my breath away when she carves the sky up like that,' Alice said.

'Hopefully with her help it won't be long before you're doing the same with Ariel,' Jack replied.

I felt the usual thrill at seeing Lucy arrive. This would be the sixth time Lucy had made a house call to Eden since our mission in Peru.

As she drew closer, her glowing crystal surfaces cast blue

light across the shaft's rock walls. A strong smell of ozone washed over me as the craft slowed to a complete stop just a metre above one of the vacant landing pads next to Ariel. Its hover was so stable that she could have even landed on solid ground.

Alice slowly released a breath as she gazed with childlike wonder at the micro mind ship. 'It's always so astonishing to see technology so in advance of our own.'

'Don't forget that you're looking at the handiwork of the Angelus, the first sentient species. They've had a few billion years' head start on us,' I said.

'Just so. And what I wouldn't give to know what makes Lucy tick. But, that aside, this will be the perfect opportunity to test out Jodie's Cage experiment.'

'If it works as hoped, it will be quite something to see,' Jack said.

'Oh, that it most certainly will,' Alice said. 'Lauren, could you please contact Lucy and let her know what we've got planned?'

'No problem.'

I took out the Empyrean Key, which I'd grabbed on the way down from one of the acoustic labs where Jodie had been testing it. This was the ancient stone orb I'd originally unearthed with Jack at the Neolithic site of Skara Brae back on Orkney. I also found my tuning fork in the small rucksack I'd slung over my shoulder and struck it against one of the rounded raised faces of the stone. As the clear note rang out, a constellation of icons appeared round the orb. Among us, only I could see this. The Angelus technology tapped into my synaesthesia ability, meaning certain sounds triggered visual effects. That was how I'd first discovered the Empyrean Key was actually a control device that enabled me to interact with Lucy's micro mind.

'Everyone ready?' I asked.

'It's so disorientating, I'm not sure I ever will be, but please go ahead,' Alice said.

I selected the star symbol for the E8 dimension and flicked my wrist forward. At once the world blurred away and a room came into focus round us.

Bookshelves filled the floor beneath a carved wooden roof decorated with tiles. I instantly recognised it as the famous Bodleian Library in Oxford. In E8 Lucy could model whatever she liked. I knew the real-world version contained one of the oldest collection of literary works in the world. Of course, knowing Lucy's attention to detail, this perfectly simulated version did too.

Alice stared slack-jawed at the shelves of books around us.

The first time she'd visited the E8 dimension with us, Lucy had given Alice functional legs. Alice had uncharacteristically had to fight back tears when she'd realised what the AI had done for her. Ever since, Lucy had respected Alice's wishes that she preferred to be in her wheelchair, even when transported over to the higher reality of E8.

'Oh my, this is incredible,' Alice said in a whisper.

'Why, thank you,' Lucy replied from the doorway. She was wearing an academic cape and even had a black mortar board on her head, resting at a jaunty angle. 'But I can't really take the credit – you humans had an awful lot to do with the design.'

I smiled. 'Thanks for that.'

Lucy grinned and held her arms out to me. 'Hello, trouble.'

I crossed to Lucy and hugged her. Now, like always, it felt like the most natural thing to do in the world.

Jack raised his eyebrows at me. Maybe he did have a point about this AI becoming a true friend to me. Things certainly felt easy with her, just as they had with my real aunt, who Lucy was modelled on.

Lucy finally let go of me and shook Alice's hand. 'So how has Ariel's antigravity drive been coming along?'

'Actually, we have a name for it now: the Revolution Field

Drive, otherwise known REV,' Alice said. 'We ran a competition at Eden and that was the clear winner.'

'Oh, catchy, I like it,' Lucy replied.

'And, to answer your question, we've almost got it running smoothly. But there are a few kinks in the system that need ironing out with your help.'

Lucy nodded and glanced at Alice's wheelchair. 'Are you really sure you wouldn't prefer working legs? It's no bother.'

'As I told you the first time, this is my body now and I've come to accept it.'

'You humans are such a tricky species,' Lucy said. Then she turned to Jack. 'Good to see you, handsome.' She kissed him on both cheeks.

'You too, gorgeous,' Jack replied.

I gave him an eye-roll. 'Please don't encourage her – you so know what she's like.'

'Oh, you're no fun,' Lucy told me. 'Anyway, where are you hiding my favourite man?'

'If you mean Mike, he's in the lab with Jodie,' Alice said. 'They're monitoring the systems of the TREENO CubeSat fleet we just launched.'

'Ah yes, I kept an eye on that. So quaint to use a rocket to launch them, but everything seemed to go OK from what I could see?'

'Yes, it was a perfect launch,' I replied. 'Anyway, what have you been up to – apart from spying on our CubeSat launch?'

'Well...' Lucy dropped down into one of the plush velvet seats that had just magically appeared in the middle of the library. She was able to change any aspect of a modelled reality that she liked. 'Even though my sensor array is still severely compromised, I've been able to monitor activity over much of your world during orbits across the visual wavelength,' she said. 'Are you aware of the significant increase in the use of the UFO Tic Tac craft since I saw you last month? Most of the activity seems to be centred over the region you refer to as Illinois.'

'We've heard some of the reports about them,' Alice replied. 'There was also an increase in accounts of cattle mutilations across that state too.'

Lucy blew out a puff of air between her lips. 'Oh, that's nothing to do with your alien visitors.'

'We thought as much,' I said. 'It's probably the Overseers conducting another misinformation campaign.'

'They really do love to paint the aliens as the bad guys,' Jack replied.

'Wheels within wheels,' Lucy said, shaking her head.

'I don't suppose you have you any idea what's behind this increased Tic Tac activity, do you?' Alice asked.

Lucy spread her hands wide. 'Right now I have no way of knowing. However, I'm starting to wonder whether the increased sightings might be somehow linked to the flights of the TR-3Bs Astras, in which I've also seen a large increase. On one occasion a fleet of at least ten Astras flew in formation pursuing a Tic Tac. The alien craft only just managed to escape them.'

'It was exactly that increased TR-3B activity that Tom was investigating when he dropped off the radar,' I said.

'There's still no news about him then?' Lucy asked.

Alice looked away and nodded. 'None whatsoever...'

Jack grimaced at me behind her back. I could guess exactly how she was feeling. When I was in charge of a mission it felt as if everything was my responsibility.

'Anyway, back to matters in hand,' Alice said, obviously changing what was an uncomfortable topic of conversation, 'would you be happy to help Jodie to do a test run with her new experiment?'

Lucy pressed her palms together. 'You're telling me the Cage is ready for me to play with?'

'We think so, but we won't know for certain until you give it a spin,' Alice replied.

'Then let's do this thing,' Lucy said with a wide smile.

CHAPTER THREE

LEAVING LUCY IN E8, we went back to our world and stepped through a doorway into Alice's personal lab. With its huge racks of equipment, including industrial 3D printers and exotic-looking tech of every description, it was one of the most highly equipped facilities within Eden. And that was saying something.

The first thing that grabbed my attention, as it always did, was the set of large information displays that Alice had mounted in her lab. They showed a star map, with one on the right highlighted with a yellow box. That was Tau Ceti. To the far left of the screen was a blue dot, Earth. And linking the two was a white line. It was solid leading away from Tau Ceti until it met a red dot a short way along. That was the current position of the Kimprak asteroid ship. Ahead of it the line leading to Earth was dashed. Jodie had run the numbers and this was what the simulation had revealed.

A quick glance told anyone looking at it that the alien ship had already travelled fifteen per cent of the distance towards Earth, but now it was accelerating, since its solar sail had brought it closer to the speed of light. To ram that message home, at the top of the screen was a countdown timer that currently read *4 years - 33 days.*

Alice knew exactly how to keep everyone completely focused on the coming threat, especially as this display was mirrored throughout Eden's labs and workplaces. The social areas thankfully got a pass – even she realised that people needed some time away from the threat hanging over our heads.

Jodie and Mike were sitting before a bank of monitors, champagne glasses in hand. Behind them was the experimental Cage. This was an AR – augmented reality in a soundproofed room. But rather than being a metal barred structure that the name might have suggested, it was actually a transparent glass-walled cuboid room. The Cage's interior surfaces had been lined with small clear pyramids that pointed inwards. These were acoustic structures that Jodie had designed to modulate the sound waves within the structure to trigger my synaesthesia. A domed camera had also been mounted in the ceiling next to a speaker panel.

'Hey, shouldn't you guys still be celebrating your big success at the party?' I said as we approached them.

'Trust me, this is our idea of a good time,' Jodie said. 'There is nowhere we'd rather be than watching the first data roll in from the TREENO fleet.'

'Amen to that,' Mike said, clinking his glass against Jodie's.

'So how's it looking?' Alice asked as she peered over their shoulders at the screens.

'All systems are in the green and the CubeSats are performing as expected. We haven't lost communication with a single one yet.'

'That sounds like great news,' Jack said.

Alice smiled at him as she wheeled her chair up to the control desk. 'It really is. None of this would have been possible without Jodie and Mike's efforts.'

'Oh, it's been a blast, especially when I get to work alongside my favourite scientist,' Jodie replied.

She and Mike exchanged goofy grins with each other. They were always so cute together.

'So, in another day of firsts, are you ready to give your Cage a go, Jodie?' Alice asked.

'Oh, damned right I am,' Jodie replied, her Swedish accent thickening as it did whenever she got excited. 'I've been itching to do a test run now the calibration techniques are complete.'

'This could be another big moment for us,' Alice said. 'If this works, it's going to speed up development of the REV drive tenfold, especially if Lucy is able to consult on its design on a daily basis.'

Alice's enthusiasm was infectious and my worry about the Kimprak lifted a fraction.

Jodie spun her chair towards me. 'Do you want to strut your stuff and see if this actually works?'

'No problem.'

With the Empyrean Key in hand I opened the door of the Cage and stepped inside. Alice wheeled her chair in behind me and pulled the ten-centimetre-thick acrylic door closed behind us. A slight hiss came from the airlock as it hermetically sealed itself into place.

Alice pulled an AR headset on to her head. I wouldn't need anything apart from my usual synaesthesia to see Lucy. But if this all went according to plan, then Alice – plus the others viewing the remote monitors – would be able to see Lucy in our world for the first time ever.

'Powering up the systems now,' Jodie's voice said from a speaker in the ceiling.

Through the clear pyramid-covered walls we saw the fragmented image of Jodie crossing to a control station. She began toggling various options on the screen.

'I have to say I have been so looking forward to this,' Alice said.

'Me too,' I replied.

A loud screeching came out of the speaker, making us wince.

'Sorry, my bad,' Jodie said. 'The synaesthesia carrier tone will settle down, Lauren.'

'Thank god for that,' I said, holding my hands over my ears.

A moment later the whistling subsided to a gentle humming tone. Icons immediately erupted all over the Empyrean Key in my hand as my synaesthesia kicked in.

'Wow!' Alice exclaimed, staring at them through her visor.

'You can see them through your AR headset?' I asked.

'Like you wouldn't believe. So this is the world as you experience it, Lauren?'

'It is – at least what my synaesthesia allows me to see with the Empyrean Key.'

'Well, it's very impressive. And what a remarkable system for a computer interface.'

'Don't let Lucy hear you call her a computer.'

'Oh, don't you worry, I wouldn't dare,' Alice replied with a smile.

Through our prismatic view of the rest of the lab we saw Jodie and Mike high five each other. I could also see a live feed from the dome camera displayed on a large monitor. That view showed the icons over the Empyrean Key, just like in here. Mike, Jodie and Jack were staring at it with rapt attention.

'Welcome to my world, everyone,' I said, gazing up at the camera and spreading my arms wide. I bowed slightly like a ringmaster welcoming the crowd into the circus. 'OK, now we know that everything is checking out from our side, we're ready for the main event,' Jodie said. 'Lauren, could you give Lucy a call?'

'I'm on it.' I selected the brand-new alien-head icon for the new communication function that had been added, the icon itself

Lucy's idea of a joke, and rotated the stone orb forward to select the function.

A melody of rising notes bounced around the room. A constellation of glowing points of light appeared around Alice and me within the Cage. They began to swirl as if they were being carried on a faint breeze before slowly coalescing into a humanoid shape. As the rolling harmony dropped to a whisper, a person came into sharp focus.

Suddenly Lucy was standing in the room with us.

Her student gown was gone and instead she wore a glittering silver evening dress. Her dark hair had been scooped up and cascaded down in dark swirls both sides of her head. She looked stunning – a perfect look that would have taken me several days to achieve with a garden rake and several tons of make-up.

Alice was staring at Lucy open-mouthed. I saw her image had appeared on the monitor outside too.

'You can really see me?' Lucy said, staring back at Alice and me.

'We certainly can. Welcome to our reality,' I said with a smile.

'This is truly incredible,' Alice said as she extended her hand to shake Lucy's.

The AI reciprocated but their fingers slipped through each other.

Alice shook her head. 'Sorry, you look so real, even though you're an AR projection.'

Lucy laughed. 'It's the same for me. I forgot I had no physicality in your world.'

I gestured towards her elaborate sequin dress. 'You look as if you went to a lot of trouble with your wardrobe choice for this big moment, Lucy?'

She grinned. 'I just wanted to look good for my first appearance in your world. And anyway, where is my favourite man?'

My eyes darted over to Mike. He had visibly paled as Jodie cast him a suspicious sideways look. The two women in Mike's life meeting like this could spell some big trouble for him. Even if one of them was an AI, I was pretty sure Jodie would take a dim view of Lucy's full-on attention towards *her* man.

A cough came over the speaker. 'I'm here, Lucy,' Mike said. He approached the glass room and raised a hand in greeting, casting a slightly worried glance back towards Jodie. She had already crossed her arms and fixed her boyfriend with a quizzical stare.

I caught the look of amusement Jack was aiming at me.

Oblivious to anyone or anything but Mike, Lucy beamed at him. 'Get yourself in here for a hug, handsome. Oh, sorry, I wasn't thinking. We obviously can't do that here. But maybe you can pop over to E8 for a proper catch-up...' Lucy actually licked her lips at him.

The glare that Jodie now gave Lucy was set to kill. I couldn't help but feel sorry for Mike, but only a little. He'd set himself up for this confrontation between Jodie and Lucy because he seemed to be into both of them. Besides, if I was being honest, it did creep me out that Mike had been flirting with a facsimile of someone who was also my aunt, albeit a much younger version.

'If you could stay still, Lucy,' Jodie said with a strained tone to her voice. 'I need to run some more calibration tests. That dress you're wearing is throwing out the optical sensors.'

'Oh, not a problem at all,' Lucy said.

Before I realised what she was doing and could stop her, Lucy clicked her fingers. The next moment she was standing there stark naked, showing off her very shapely figure including full breasts and curving hips. I couldn't help noting the lack of pubic hair. Wherever Lucy was getting information from, that so wasn't my real aunt. I suspected Lucy had probably been referencing too many porn channels as she'd modelled herself.

Alice's hand rose to cover her mouth as she tried to suppress a laugh. 'Well, goodness me.'

I wasn't surprised to see Mike turn several shades beyond scarlet as he gawped at Lucy. Jack by contrast was shaking his head and giving me a *Mike is so much in the shit now* look. I had to bite down on a laugh.

When Jodie's voice came over the speakers again it was Arctic cold with a snowstorm blowing through it for good measure. 'The system is now calibrated, so you can get dressed again...' She didn't say *bitch*, but it was implied by her tone.

Lucy smirked and clicked her fingers again. In the blink of an eye she was wearing jeans and a polo shirt. 'Hopefully this outfit won't mess with your sensors, Jodie.' She pouted slightly towards the other woman through the glass walls.

If I could have grabbed her arm I would have done. She was obviously trying to bait Jodie.

Alice jumped in, clearly attempting to deflect the growing tension. 'Lucy, now we know that the Cage works, are you happy to go through the REV drive design again with me? We're still having a problem stabilising the antigravity field and I could really do with your input.'

'I'd be absolutely delighted to,' Lucy replied.

'Then let's get to it. Jodie, can you project the schematics for the drive system in here?'

'Just give me a second,' Jodie replied in a crisp *I'm not going to drop to her level* voice.

However pissed off with Mike she was, Jodie was nothing but professional when it came to her work. A moment later a rotating translucent 3D model of a torus-shaped device was hovering in the Cage with us.

'This is seriously impressive. It looks as clear as day in my synaesthesia vision, Jodie,' I said.

'And for me in AR too,' Alice said. 'This alone proves how incredibly useful the Cage will be with our future work.'

'Thanks, but I can't take all the credit. The acoustic patterning system is down to Mike.'

I couldn't help but notice the way Jodie's voice tightened a fraction at the mention of his name. I immediately felt sorry for Jodie – and even Mike. Relationships were tricky to navigate at the best of times when you worked together – even non-relationships like the thing between me and Jack.

'I'll leave you guys to it,' I said to Alice and Lucy. 'You don't need me now the Cage is up and running.'

Alice gave me a distracted nod.

'See you later, my little sunflower,' Lucy said.

I let out a groan.

'I mean, Lauren.' She grinned at me.

It was as if the AI had swallowed a Miss-Most-Annoying pill today.

I stepped out and Lucy's form briefly swirled away as the acoustic seal was broken, but then reformed a second later when I shut the door behind me.

Mike, standing next to Jack, looked as if he wanted to be anywhere but in the lab.

'OK, enough of me being a party pooper,' I said, 'who's up for grabbing a quick drink at that launch party?'

'God, yes,' Mike said, as if I'd just thrown him a lifeline as he drowned in a pool of sharks.

'Sounds good to me,' Jack replied.

I turned to Jodie. 'How about you?'

'No, I want to keep an eye on the TREENO data when it starts to roll in. Looks as if it's going to be a late one.'

'I can help you with that,' Mike said.

'No, I've got this,' Jodie replied without even looking round at him.

If she'd seen his hangdog expression she might have eased up on him a bit. But instead Mike sloped away with us, his tail well and truly between his legs. He didn't say a word all the way up in the lift either. Yes, work romances were definitely a bad idea. Maybe Jack and I had it right after all.

CHAPTER FOUR

A WEEK later Mike was singing into the mic as he pogoed his way around the small stage in the very popular Rock Garden, the stalactite-and-stalagmite-filled cavern that had been converted into a bar.

This was karaoke night, a regular fixture of Tuesday evenings in Eden. Mike's song was the closing act and he was throwing everything into it. He needed to, because Ruby's rendition of the Rolling Stones' 'I Can't Get No Satisfaction', along with her full-on body strutting, had driven the crowd wild. Thanks to that she was sitting on top of the leader board. Ruby was as uber competitive in this as everything else that she did.

Despite the enthusiasm of the audience to me singing Coldplay's 'Yellow', it'd been a lame performance, and I'd definitely hit more than my fair share of bum notes. That same audience would have probably applauded a quacking duck. Still, it didn't help the fact I was languishing at the bottom of the leader board.

I wasn't sure what Sid Vicious would think of Mike's effort. Maybe buy him a beer, based on the fact that half the people in the room were jumping up and down like maniacs to the song.

The lights that illuminated the stalactites over our heads pulsed in time to the music as Mike started to swing the microphone around like a lasso.

Niki, sitting opposite me, just shook his head with a look of bemusement on his face. And Jodie, whom I'd finally persuaded to join us, was looking anywhere but at Mike as she endlessly stirred the ice in her third mojito of the night.

Mike screamed barely comprehensible lyrics into the mic.

Jodie allowed herself a brief glance at his rock-god antics on stage. She bit her lip as her attention snapped back to her cocktail.

If I needed any reminder why relationships at work were a seriously bad idea, Mike and Jodie were the poster boy and girl for it. To say that the atmosphere had been tense between them since Lucy's return would have been the understatement of the century. Yes, they were utterly professional whilst working. But they now only talked to each other when absolutely necessary. The tense atmosphere between them had become so bad that the rest of us steered well clear of them when they were within a hundred metres of each other. So quite why I'd decided to sit on the same table as Jodie tonight was beyond me. Probably a misplaced act of sister solidarity.

Niki's hand tightened round his beer glass. It was as if he was imagining the glass was Mike's neck. Maybe he wasn't a big fan of the Sex Pistols?

My gaze flitted over to a table in a cosy corner of the cavern, where Jack was sitting with Alice. I couldn't help but notice how their heads were angled together as they spoke – to the point of almost touching. There had also been way too much eye contact for my liking. It was hard not to feel a little bit jealous at the blossoming friendship between them. I just needed to keep reminding myself that Jack and I'd had our chance with each other but had decided not to go there. And that was the end of it.

The thrash of the instruments on the karaoke track came to a rip-roaring end. Nearly everyone was whooping and applauding.

Leroy, the Rastafarian with a heart of gold who ran the Rock Garden, ducked under the counter and leapt up on to the stage to join Mike. He hushed the audience with his hands and clicked a button on a small remote. The lyrics on-screen behind him were replaced with a curved graph. It displayed a large golden needle that was currently pointing to zero.

'Ladies and gentlemen, do you think we just heard the winner of tonight's karaoke competition?' Leroy called out.

Lots of affirmative cries came back from the audience.

'Well, let's see if it's official. Let's hear your appreciation of Mike's rendition of "My Way" and see what our clap-o-meter says.'

The cavern rumbled with an earthquake of applause and cheers. The needle immediately shot up, almost reaching the very top of the arc. Ninety-two per cent flashed on screen. The clap-o-meter was then replaced by the leader board with Mike's name now firmly at the very top.

Leroy held Mike's hand up in the air like a boxer who'd just won the match. 'We have ourselves a winner, ladies and gentleman!'

I resisted the urge to cheer and punch the air as Niki's frown deepened and Jodie's head bent so far downwards she was almost kissing the table.

'Thank you, guys!' Mike shouted. 'As a sign of my appreciation, the next round is on me.'

The applause became ear-splitting as Mike jumped off the stage. Everyone surrounded him to pat him on the back or shake his hand. Even Ruby gave him a fist bump complete with finger explosion.

Mike started to head towards our table, but, spotting Jodie, he veered away towards Jack and Alice's table instead.

I couldn't help but feel a small victory as he joined them. *Two's company, three's a crowd...*

The furrows on Niki's forehead were so deep now they could have been carved from rock. I had no idea why he was developing such a problem with Mike. The atmosphere at our table desperately needed a different focus and quickly, especially now the ear-bleeding music had finished and conversation was possible again.

I leant towards Jodie. 'So, how is progress with Ariel?'

Jodie's eyes rose to mine and her face brightened. 'Actually, really well, Lauren. The gravity field generated by the REV drive is nearly stable after all the improvements, thanks to the AI's help.'

Although most of Jodie's quiet fury seemed to have been directed towards Mike, it was hard not to notice that she now refused to refer to Lucy by her name. At least *AI* was an improvement over *computer*, which had been her term for her only a week ago.

Niki stopped glowering across at Mike long enough to turn his attention towards Jodie. 'Does that mean you're almost ready for the first test flight?'

Jodie nodded. 'Probably early next week if we keep making progress like we currently are.'

Niki sighed. 'That's what I was worried about.'

I tightened my eyes on him. 'But this is what we've all been working towards. It will help even things up against the Overseers during any mission.'

'Maybe it will, but I'm still not happy about the choice of test pilot.'

'You mean Alice insisting she'll be the one in the hot seat?'

'Exactly. She's far too essential to Eden. But she seems happy to risk the future of this whole organisation on what amounts to a joyride. Especially when the key technology has been supplied by that damned computer avatar.'

I flinched, taken aback by Niki's sharp tone. Jodie had every right to be hostile towards Lucy, even though she did a good job of keeping a lid on her emotions for the sake of getting the job done. But Niki too? And why the attitude?

Jodie shook her head at Niki. 'Actually, even I have to admit that the AI's work is astonishing. The entire science team have been over all the schematics for the new REV drive components with a fine-tooth comb and can't find a single flaw. Whatever else that AI is, she certainly knows what she's talking about. As far I'm concerned, Alice has every right to be confident that the first flight will be a huge success.'

I nodded. 'Jodie's right. When it comes to cutting-edge science, Lucy really does know her stuff. If Jodie and Alice are confident in her – as I am, and the rest of the team, then maybe you should be too, Niki?'

'That's as maybe, but we're talking about a test flight here,' he said. 'You well know those are to shake down any problems, problems that might include the REV drive failing for some unforeseen reason. All I keep picturing is Ariel plummeting out of the sky with Alice on-board. So forgive me if I don't share your enthusiasm.'

Jodie held up her hand. 'Before you get yourself too wound up, Alice and even the AI stated that we need a backup plan just in case that highly unlikely scenario happens. So we have a plan B for that eventuality. We've designed an escape pod system to cover any major technical malfunction.'

'Niki, please relax and stop imaging the worst,' I said. 'Jodie and the team really have got every angle covered.'

But Niki growled in a good impression of a bear waking up with a migraine. 'There's always going to be an element of risk, however good the preparations are. And what if something goes wrong, like a catastrophic explosion in the REV drive and our illustrious leader is killed?'

Jodie pulled a face. 'Well, for your information, Alice has even prepared for that scenario too. She's left a list of key personnel who will take over the running of Sky Dreamer Corp. in her private safe. I happen to know that this includes you.'

Niki didn't reply, but this time made a sound like a bear gnawing on a bone. The person sitting before me seemed like a completely different guy to the relaxed person who'd taught me how to use a weapon properly.

I leant on my elbows. 'Look, Niki, let's face it, Alice is a force of nature. You might as well accept it's going to happen whether you want it to or not.'

The imaginary bone splintered in Niki's mouth as his jaw clamped down, emitting a *humph* sound.

Over his shoulder I noticed that Mike had excused himself from Jack and Alice. As I watched them laugh together, my inner teenager felt something twist inside me, even though I'd no right to feel anything.

My smart watch pinged and I glanced down to see Lucy's name on the screen.

'I need you down in the lab, Lauren,' her voice said from the watch's speaker.

It was as good an excuse as any to get away from this toxic atmosphere. 'Looks like I'm needed elsewhere,' I said to the others.

Jodie peered at me. 'Would you like me to come with you?'

'If I need you, I'll shout, but you should stay here with Niki and chill otherwise. You deserve a break after all your hard work.'

'Not sure this is my idea of a good time at the moment, but OK.'

You and me both, I thought as I nodded towards her.

Niki just raised his chin a fraction at me, quickly returning to staring at Mike's back whilst he joked with Leroy as he topped up his beer at the bar. Yes, the atmosphere in here was acidic and the sooner I got away from it the better.

I entered the lab to see Lucy on the monitors of the Cage at an easel. She was gently dabbing her paintbrush on a canvas that had its back to me. Painting was definitely a new thing for Lucy and I found myself immediately desperate to know what she was working on.

'Hi, what's the emergency?' I asked as I walked towards the AR room.

'Nothing, I just wanted to give you an excuse to get yourself out of that awkward situation. Not to mention it was getting painful watching you smash your heart on the jagged rocks of unrequited love.'

I pulled up short and stared at Lucy as she peered at me over her canvas with a grin. 'What do you mean by that?'

'Oh, come on. I saw those puppy-dog eyes you were giving Jack throughout the karaoke evening.'

'Even if that was remotely true, how could you possibly know that?'

'I got bored working here by myself whilst you guys were off having all the fun. So I hacked my way into Eden's security system. I now have access to every camera in this facility. Now I can keep an eye on my favourite people.'

'Anything to do with Mike by any chance?'

Lucy grin widened. 'Busted. Anyway, I also grabbed the opportunity to link into the communication network. That means you can now talk to me from anywhere within this complex.'

'You do that realise that basically amounts to spying on everyone?'

'Piffle. We're all one big happy family. I'm only trying to help.'

'So you're telling me there'll be no getting away from you now?'

Lucy pouted at me, something I'd never seen my real Aunt Lucy do in her life. 'I could take that personally.'

I put my hands on my hips. 'Maybe you should. But back to Jack. I so wasn't making puppy-dog eyes at him.'

Lucy just raised her eyebrows at me and crossed her arms.

I pulled a face at her. 'All right, maybe a little.'

'That's better. You do know you can be honest with me about these things. And especially if you need a girlfriend to talk to.'

'If you say so.'

'I most certainly do. From all the information I've been able to dig up about the human mating process, I think the nearest comparison is that you're behaving like a hormonal teenager whose got the hots for the captain of the football team.' A smile curled the corners of her mouth.

'Thanks for that flattering analogy, *girlfriend*.'

'Here to help,' Lucy replied, her grin growing ever wider.

'Anyway, you can talk, Miss Let's Objectify My Aunt's Body So You Can Get Into Mike's Pants...if that's actually a thing you can do?'

'Oh, trust me, my homework on human intercourse wasn't just for your benefit.'

'Ewww!' I held out a hand to stop her. 'Whatever algorithm in your code is responsible for your behaviour towards Mike, you seriously need to have a word with it. You do know that you've turned the relationship between him and Jodie into a car crash?'

Lucy shrugged. 'Mike's a big boy. He can look after himself.'

'Maybe he can, but I can't help but feel that you're stirring things up deliberately,' I said as I opened the door to the Cage.

The AI fluttered her eyelashes at me as she briefly faded as I entered. 'What, little innocent me?' She looked back at her canvas and made several dabs on it with her paintbrush.

This conversation was the equivalent of pushing a boulder up hill, so I decided to change the subject. I gestured towards her canvas. 'I didn't know you were an artist.'

'Your species is fascinating in so many ways, but it's your artistic expression that is one of your finest achievements. From music and dance to books and the visual arts, and everything in between, you as a race have really intrigued me. So I thought I'd give it a go myself and try to really understand this form of self-expression.'

'You certainly take your homework seriously. So what are you painting?' I began to walk round so I could get a clear look at her canvas.

'Oh, nothing important,' Lucy said as she grabbed the painting off the easel and placed it behind her back.

However, this billions-year-old AI might have been smarter than the whole human race put together, but she hadn't thought through the fact she was standing inside a reflective glass box. I could see a portrait image of Mike displayed across the transparent prismatic mirrors behind her. It looked as if it was painted in the style of the Pre-Raphaelites, so stunning that it wouldn't have been out of place in the Tate, even if its subject matter was slightly unsettling.

I obviously stared a fraction too long, because Lucy glanced over her shoulder and thinned her lips. 'Damn it!' The canvas dissolved away into particles, her paintbrush along with it.

'I'm not sure what Mike would say if he knew you were immortalising him in that way.'

Lucy wrinkled her nose at me. 'Then it will just have to be our little secret – along with your puppy-dog eyes.'

'That sounds like blackmail to me!'

'No, just girlfriends looking out for each other,' she replied.

'Anyway, I did have a serious reason for getting you down here.' Lucy clicked her fingers and a hologram schematic for the REV drive appeared, floating in the Cage. 'I've made something of a breakthrough with Ariel's gravity-disruptor drive system and we're ready to go. And when I say *ready*, I mean as in a test flight tomorrow ready.'

'Seriously?'

'Seriously. I've downloaded the revised plans to the 3D printers and they will have the new components ready by the morning. After a quick installation, we'll be all set. Bring your popcorn – it promises to be one hell of a flight.'

Despite my irritation with Lucy, a huge sense of relief washed over me. This was the best news we'd had in a long time. And I knew one woman who would be over the moon when I told her, although Niki would be much less so.

CHAPTER FIVE

AFTER ALL THE frenetic activity centred on the Ariel prototype during the last few hours, it was almost eerily quiet in here now. The sense of expectation grew stronger by the minute in the launch silo, almost like the building of static before a thunderstorm. Jodie and the team of engineers were making last-minute adjustments to the REV gravity-reduction drive through an access hatch.

Meanwhile, I stood with Jack, Mike and Ruby, watching the final preparations to get Ariel ready for her first flight. Niki and Alice, who'd positioned her wheelchair on a platform hoist that would raise her up into the belly of the craft, were locked in an intense conversation.

Niki scowled at her as if it were an Olympic sport. 'Look, all I'm saying is that you should let one of our other experienced pilots take Ariel out for her first test flight.'

Alice sighed. 'I realise you have the best intentions, but you need to respect my decision, Captain.'

Ruby winced. 'She only calls Niki that when she is seriously pissed with him,' she whispered.

Our head of security crossed his arms. 'I will, but that doesn't mean I'm happy with it.'

Jodie glanced over at Niki as she finished fastening the last bolt into place. 'Please, you need to take a chill pill about this flight. I've run hundreds of simulations and they have all come up with perfect scores.'

Niki shook his head. 'With all due respect, Jodie, they were still only simulations. We're talking about someone putting their life on the line here.'

Mike whispered to us, 'The problem for Niki is that Alice is the one in charge and she gets to make the rules.'

He obviously hadn't said it quietly enough because Niki's head snapped round and he glowered at Mike. His look was so hostile that for a moment I thought the head of security might actually march over and thump Mike in the face.

But Jodie had already crossed to Niki, placing a hand on his arm and shaking her head. That touch was like someone had hit the off switch on Niki's anger and his shoulders dropped. Mike had a lot to thank Jodie for, since she'd somehow defused Niki's fury.

A voice-clearing cough echoed round the landing bay from the speakers. 'I couldn't help but hear what you were all saying,' Lucy said. 'And I have to say I have a lot of sympathy for Niki's concern.'

Niki pulled himself up to his full six feet two inches. 'At least one person round here is listening to me.'

'Actually, I think you have a point too,' Jack said.

'Aha, so you see, Alice. It's not just me who's worried about you unnecessarily risking your life like this.'

Alice rolled her eyes at Jack. 'I thought you might at least understand. You know how much this flight means to me.'

'Yes I do, but you also know it's risky,' he replied.

She shook her head and then turned in her chair to give me a challenging look. 'And what about you, Lauren. I suppose you agree with Jack?'

I raised my hands. 'Hey, keep me out of this. I can see it from both sides.'

Alice opened her mouth to respond, but another sound of throat clearing came over the speaker.

'Look, before you all kick off another endless round of arguments, I have a suggestion that I think you're all going to rather like,' Lucy said.

Niki's gaze tightened on one of the speakers. 'Go on.'

'I can fly in close proximity to Ariel. Then if there are any problems with the REV drive I can extend my own gravity field to envelop Ariel and bring her safely back down to the ground. Alice wouldn't have to use the ejection pod system. Think of it as me tagging along as an insurance policy.'

Niki's face visibly brightened. 'Now I like the sound of that.'

'However, there is one tiny little catch,' Lucy added.

Jack groaned. 'I thought it sounded too good to be true. What is it, Lucy?'

'Lauren will need to be on board for the test flight. Unfortunately my core flight control protocols, which enable me to alter my gravity field, are handled by one of my compromised systems. In the event of a crisis Lauren would need to manually override the system using the Empyrean Key.'

'What? But I'm no computer programmer,' I replied. 'Wouldn't Jodie be a better bet – at least to accompany us as well?'

'I'd be more than happy to do that,' Jodie said.

Niki stared at her. 'But you can't.'

I glanced between them. Why the sudden overprotectiveness on Niki's part?

Jodie squared up to him, hands on hips. 'Oh, but I can and I will if I want to.'

A sharp clapping sound came over the speaker. 'People, will you all take a moment to breathe? No, Jodie, you really don't need to be on board because all Lauren will need to do is activate an icon with the Empyrean Key. That will initialise my drive override.'

'OK, I guess even I can manage to push a button,' I said. My gaze snapped back to the man-made saucer craft. So I would be going up in that thing. A slight edge of concern crept in, but that lost out to the excitement rising through me. As something of a sci-fi geek this was beyond what once would have been my wildest dreams. Even with everything I'd experienced in the last couple of years, this was going to be right up there with the best of them.

Niki looked between Alice and me. 'Are you both really set on doing this?'

I cast a wide grin at Alice. 'Now I've got my head round it, yes, I can't wait.'

'And do you need to ask again, Niki?' Alice said as she smiled back at me.

He sighed. 'No, not really. But please, Alice, just promise me that you'll take it easy with this first test flight. No loops or whatever it is that test pilots do. Baby steps and nothing more.'

'Of course, Niki.'

'Then I've just got one thing left to say...' He paused a suitably dramatic length of time. 'Good luck.'

Jodie beamed at him. 'I knew you'd see sense.' She stood on her tiptoes and gave the head of security a peck on the cheek.

As a foolish smile filled Niki's face, Mike stared at Jodie's back with a confused look.

A cog turned over in my mind. Seriously? Was this the reason for the captain's barely contained hostility for Mike? Could Niki really be Mike's love rival when he at least seemed to be his late forties?

Jodie spun on her heel and gestured towards Ariel. 'OK, people, let's make this happen.'

I sat in the incredibly comfortable reclined CIC seat on Ariel's flight deck, my sense of anticipation now through the roof. A currently transparent screen hung suspended on a metal arm in front of me. When the weapon systems were added this would light up like a Christmas tree for whoever would eventually sit here, someone like Ruby. But for now it was safe for a rookie to sit in the hot seat. Alice had slid herself out of her wheelchair, now stowed in a locker that had lowered itself into the floor, and sat next to me in the pilot's chair.

Further out around us, on the curved screens that lined the spherical walls of the cockpit, critical system information was displayed. That included the REV drive temperature, showing a toasty 120 degrees Celsius. Another glass screen had automatically lowered in front of Alice when she'd first sat in the chair, displaying flight information, including air speed, currently at zero.

'OK, Eden Control, time to test our transparency mode,' Alice said into the microphone on her headset.

'Roger that,' Jodie replied from the control centre that had been set up in the lab next door to the silo.

Alice pressed a button in the arm of her pilot's chair. The hexagonal screens on the curved cockpit walls were filled instantly with a perfect 360-degree virtual view of the landing bay, provided by a live video feed from multiple cameras mounted on the exterior of Ariel's fuselage and stitched together by Delphi to give us a seamless panoramic view.

I might have been used to what I thought of as the magic carpet mode in the other Sky Dreamer Corp. craft, but this was seriously jaw-dropping. It was as though the cockpit had become a translucent bubble. Over that view a vector outline of Ariel's hull was superimposed and showed the edge of the saucer-shaped craft encircling us.

The landing bay around us was deserted, thanks to Niki's natural overabundance of caution. All ground personnel, including Jack and Mike, had been pulled back to the flight control desk behind a now sealed blast door.

Alice had arranged for a live feed to be streamed to the IMAX theatre so that the rest of Eden could watch our maiden voyage. According to Jack, who'd briefly put his head round the door, it was quite the party atmosphere in there. This test was even being relayed to the astronauts in the Martian mission-simulation cavern. No one wanted to miss out on what was going to be one of the most important moments in the history of Eden.

Lucy's crystal micro mind ship began to slowly rotate on its axis on the cockpit's screens as she hovered above the floor.

Alice gestured towards her. 'Lauren, do you want to check in with Lucy to confirm that your synaesthesia link is working with her OK?'

'Checking now.' I raised the Empyrean Key in the flat of my hand. But rather than use the tuning fork on my belt, I spoke into my headset's mic. 'Delphi, please broadcast carrier tone.'

'Broadcasting carrier tone,' Delphi's voice replied around us.

A soft chime rang out and settled into a single looping note. At once a constellation of icons appeared around the stone orb, including a new teardrop-shaped icon that I hadn't seen before.

'The icon you'll want to know about is that new one,' Lucy's voice said from the same cockpit speakers that Delphi had just used. 'That will initiate a manual override of my drive-control safety protocols – if needed in an extreme emergency.'

'Does this mean you've been spying on us all this time?' I asked, surprised that she was able to see what was happening.

'Only since you activated the Empyrean Key. I've piggy-backed on to Delphi's control systems on board Ariel. And before you start complaining that I'm snooping on you, it means I'll be another pair of eyes keeping a lookout for anything going wrong.'

'That sounds good to me,' Alice said. She turned towards me. 'So are we ready to make history, Lauren?'

'Always.' A swarm of butterflies began swirling in my stomach. This promised to be the experience of a lifetime.

Alice smiled as she adjusted the mouthpiece on her headset. 'Eden Control, are you ready for our departure?'

'Check,' Jodie's voice replied. 'Opening launch bay door now.'

A quiet rumbling sound came from above Ariel in the launch silo. A bright blue disc of sky began to appear overhead on the virtual walls of our flight deck.

Alice flicked a switch and the ladder that led up to the platform retracted into the floor. The clamps locking the flight deck into position were released with a clunk. A slight whir came from the gimbal motors that connected it to the two rings, designed to fully rotate on their pivot points. They spun a couple of degrees as the gyro levelled out the floor on which our seats were mounted.

'OK, I'm warming up Ariel's REV drive now,' Alice said. She flicked another switch and a humming noise came from the cockpit's curved floor.

The temperature on the projected HUD rapidly climbed to 150 degrees Celsius. I felt the pull of gravity within the cockpit release me a fraction. The sense that the world had shifted beneath us freaked me out more than anything else.

Alice peered at the read-outs on the wall screens. 'Plasma acceleration at a hundred-and-fifty-K revolutions per minute. Pressure is two-hundred-and-fifty-K atmospheres. Gravity vortex disruption is an eight-nine per cent of mass. Our REV drive is in the green, Eden Control.'

'Roger that,' Jodie said. 'We're seeing the same figures here.'

'Then we're good to go,' Alice said. 'Eden Control, on my mark.' She placed her hand on the metal egg-shaped device on the right arm of her chair, which was mounted on a gimlet rod that enabled it to be moved in any axis. Alice then rested her left hand on what looked like an aircraft throttle control in the left armrest.

I centred the teardrop icon in the Empyrean Key's holographic display, ready to initiate it at the first hint of trouble.

A quiet whooshing sound came from outside and the excitement ratcheted up inside me. This must have been what it was like for Neil Armstrong, Buzz Aldrin and Michael Collins as they sat on the launch pad in Apollo 11, getting ready to launch and knowing they might be about to make history. But I had a growing sense of fear too. What if we blew up in the launch silo, our bodies ripped apart by the sudden G-force as the REV drive let go and did god knew what to gravity?

I suddenly found it hard to breathe.

'Five, four, three, two, one...' Jodie said.

Alice settled herself in her pilot's chair as the numbers on her display ticked up. 'We have ignition of multimode lift rockets.' She gently raised the egg shape on its control arm and simultaneously pushed the throttle a fraction forward.

The hissing sound became a soft whoosh and Ariel began to slowly rise upwards. My excitement became euphoric as my fear was swept away. Incredibly, this had worked and we hadn't been blown to pieces – so far at least.

As Alice nudged the throttle back and we came to a dead stop, whoops and claps came over our cockpit speakers.

'All systems are functioning nominally,' Jodie's voice said over the noise of people applauding.

Alice beamed at me. 'Not exactly a fire and brimstone launch of a traditional rocket, but...'

She held up her hand.

I leant across and high-fived her. 'This is amazing, Alice. Just think of the possibilities now we know the REV drive actually works.'

'Goodness, yes. Now we've been able to replicate what the Overseers have had access to for years, at last the entire human race can benefit from this technology – not just a chosen few. We certainly couldn't have done this without your help, Lucy.'

'Oh, you are more than welcome,' Lucy replied. 'But you wait until you get this baby outside and use the supersonic vectoring nozzles in combination with the REV drive. After what you're used to flying, Ariel is seriously going to blow your human minds.'

'It's already pretty much blown and we're only ten metres off the ground,' I said. 'The theory is one thing, but the reality of this craft is on a whole other level.'

'Then let's go and see what Ariel can do in the wide open sky,' Alice said.

'Just remember to keep this maiden flight below ten thousand feet,' Jodie's voice said. 'Although you're in a pressurised capsule, let's take this one step at a time.'

'Understood,' Alice replied. She pushed the accelerator forward again just a centimetre and we started to rise further.

The rock walls skimmed past in an almost totally eerie silence, the only sounds the gentle hum of the torus-ring electro-magnets spinning the heated mercury within the REV drive. There was also the background hiss of multimode rockets lifting the remaining eleven per cent of Ariel's weight that wasn't being neutralised by our gravity-disruptor drive.

On the virtual cabin walls I looked down to see Lucy's micro mind ship had now taken off. She floated up beneath us, maintaining a ten-metre separation. Above us the disc of sky was growing steadily bigger, now ringed by trees.

We rose towards the circle of blue like a train approaching the pool of light at the exit of a tunnel. With a burst of sunlight we exited the silo and tree trunks then canopy tops sped past. Ariel had quickly cleared the trees and was steadily rising above them until the jungle stretched away beneath us in a green-carpeted series of hills and valleys.

'Talk about a smooth ride,' I said. 'This certainly puts a helicopter to shame.'

'I agree. Even our electric-powered aircraft fleet can't match this,' Alice replied.

'Trust me, there's no comparison,' Lucy's voice said. 'And to demonstrate just how superior she is, I suggest you bring her to a complete stop. Then try initiating a slow full three-sixty-degree forward roll.'

'That will take me back to my aerobatic days,' Alice said. 'Lauren, are you up for this?'

I gave her a thin smile. 'Just nothing too violent. If I start to look green, please stop whatever it is you're doing.'

'Don't worry, I will. Let's give this a whirl...' Alice gently rotated the control egg on the end of its rod mounting.

The outline of Ariel's nose appeared over the view, although, technically, did a saucer-shaped craft have a nose? She started to dip towards the ground on the spherical screens around us and my brain sort of freaked out yet again. With a gentle hum from the gimlet platform motors the flight deck continued to stay completely level. As the view outside rotated on the cockpit wall screens, Lucy's craft orbited past us like a crystal star as we rolled forward.

'Oh my...' Alice said, her eyes widening.

Ariel continued to rotate until the projected outline of her hull on the screens was pointing straight down. I could just see the open launch shaft as a dark hole in the jungle far beneath us. Even the specks of a flock of scarlet macaws flying over the trees were visible, heading towards a salt lick I knew the birds favoured, having seen them when we'd been training in the jungle. This flight was already far beyond anything I could have imagined.

We continued to roll until the craft was upside down. The contradiction between what my eyes saw and what my body was telling me intensified as the flight deck remained level.

'We're monitoring an elevated heart rate from you, Lauren – are you OK?' Jodie asked.

'I'll live, but this is beyond mind-blowing. Sort of like being in a crazy computer flying sim without any sense of inertia as you sit on your sofa.'

'That's the general idea behind the design,' Jodie replied.

Ariel began to roll back up towards the sky, righting herself, not that there was a right way up in this craft. I glanced around for a sick bag as I fought a swirl of nausea.

'You look a bit green, Lauren,' Alice said as we rotated back to the horizontal again and she killed the roll.

I took in a deep breath and flapped a hand towards the cockpit camera that Lucy was obviously using to spy on us. 'Give me a moment and I'll be fine, but, bloody hell, this is so disorientating. It's absolutely bonkers.'

'And, Alice, how are you doing?' Jodie asked.

'Fine actually. I've had a lot of flight time in aerobatic craft, although this really isn't like anything I've flown before.'

'In addition to the gyroscopic-controlled flight deck, there is also the gravity-dampening effect of the REV drive. With extreme acceleration up to Mach 6 you might pull a couple of Gs, but nothing like you would without the REV drive.'

'Talking of which, I think it's time to experience that acceleration for ourselves,' Alice said. 'Lauren, if it becomes too much just say and I'll back off immediately.'

'Oh, don't you worry, I will.'

'You'll be fine,' Lucy said, cutting in. 'Your brain should quickly adapt to what's going on, Lauren. But if it doesn't, just kill the transparency mode and Alice can use her chair's screens to fly Ariel.'

'Maybe we need a safe phrase, Alice,' I said.

'"I'm going to puke" will work just fine for me,' she replied with a smile. 'So are you ready to see what Ariel's rate of ascent is like?'

'I guess so.' I gripped the Empyrean Key harder and kept my eye on the teardrop icon.

'In that case I'd recommend a maximum of fifty per cent throttle with the vectoring multimode thrusters,' Jodie said. 'Any more than that and you'll find yourself in space before you can blink. And don't forget to keep to that ten thousand feet altitude limit we agreed.'

'Oh, you are so raining on my parade, but all right,' Alice replied.

She pushed the throttle halfway. The acceleration was instant and we tore up in to the blue sky, as if we'd just hit warp speed. But it was gentle too, just the softest pull of inertia pressing me down into my seat. The view on the screens of the outside world was another matter.

'Holy crap!' I shouted as the jungle beneath us dropped away at a mind-bending speed, even though my body experienced what was probably less than a single G-force.

Even Alice's eyes had widened as the blurred world outside came to a stop as she killed the throttle.

Lucy streaked up from the jungle below, halting just beneath us like a sheepdog that had got too far away from its flock.

Alice gawped at the glass screen in front of her. 'Holy moly, according to the read-out we're now at nine thousand feet. We also hit Mach 2.5 in that ascent – over twice the speed of sound and with almost no sense of acceleration. But what happened to the sonic boom we should have caused by ripping through the air like that?'

'You're still thinking of this as a conventional human aircraft, but it really isn't,' Lucy replied. 'As you know, the REV drive's gravity-disruption field also affects the surrounding air, creating a bubble round the craft. You can go as fast as you like through air – or even water for that matter – all without causing so much as a ripple, hence no sonic boom.'

'You're saying we could use Ariel as a submarine too?' I asked.

'Absolutely, although you would need to add impellers to the design. Of course, if this were a fully antigravity ship – with deflector plates for its propulsion system like my ship uses – you wouldn't even need that.'

'Sounds like a conversation for another time,' Alice said.

'I'm afraid not. That level of technology is beyond your species for the moment at least. And that prime directive of mine won't let me just hand it over to you. Anyway, let's concentrate on what your new toy can do.'

Alice nodded. 'Let's try out some gentle manoeuvres.'

Much to the relief of my stomach, Alice pushed the egg control on its mount whilst applying only a tiny amount of throttle. Ariel slid forward like a hot knife through butter. She rotated the egg towards the right and the ship turned gently in that direction. Lucy kept pace, tracking Ariel a hundred metres beneath us.

'Oh, now that's just silky smooth,' Alice said with a wide smile.

'I suggest you try out the lateral controls now,' Lucy said. 'That will be a brand-new experience for you too.'

'Why not?' Alice replied. She gradually slid the egg across to the left and Ariel immediately slid to the right. Only the gentlest tug of gravity pushed my body into the side of my seat.

'That's incredible,' I said as my nausea began to subside, overtaken by awe. 'To think that this technology has been kept secret from humanity by the Overseers. It's criminal.'

'Absolutely,' Alice replied. 'Imagine if this had been in the hands of NASA. We would have been able to colonise Mars and the suitable moons of our solar system decades ago.'

'The Overseers have certainly been responsible for holding your species back,' Lucy said. 'You should have been far further ahead as a space-faring race than you currently are.'

'Well, that's something I intend to put right,' Alice said. 'As soon as we can, I plan to make sure this technology is used for the benefit of all of humanity, not just a few who are desperate to maintain their hold on power.'

I nodded. 'Well said.'

'And heartfelt on my part,' Alice went on. 'So what do you say we begin testing out that thesis right now, Lauren? How about a quick jaunt into orbit?'

'Don't even think about it,' Niki said over the comm link.

Alice winked at me. 'I should have known you'd be still listening in.'

'Of course I am. I know you far too well. Just think of me as your conscience sitting on your shoulder, reminding you to keep safe.'

I snorted. 'Your very own Jiminy Cricket in other words, Alice.'

She laughed. 'OK, fair enough, Niki.'

'Um, guys, I hate to butt in, but I'm detecting something that needs my urgent attention,' Lucy said.

I tensed in my chair and got ready to select the teardrop icon.

Alice peered at the readouts on the glass screen in front of her. 'Is there a problem with our REV drive? I'm not seeing it...'

'No! Sorry, I didn't mean to panic you. I just checked in with some US military satellites that I tinkered with a little when I was last in orbit. I've had them keeping an eye out for any interesting UFO activity.'

'And you've spotted something?' I asked.

'Yes – a Tic Tac is currently cruising through the skies over Illinois. I'll escort you back down to Eden and then I'll go and check it out to see if I can make contact with the aliens piloting it.'

A first-contact situation... This was the sort of thing I'd been dreaming of since I was a small girl, not least after having seen *Close Encounters of the Third Kind* at a very impressionable age. That movie had left an enduring impression on me. And as astonishing as Lucy was, and Sentinel before her, they were still artificial intelligences. What Lucy was talking about was a sentient biological life form.

I turned my head towards Alice. She was drawing her top teeth over her lip and gazing at me.

'You want to tag along too, right?' she asked.

'Of course, but this is just meant to be a test flight.'

Jodie's voice came through the radio. 'Don't for one minute think—' Her voiced hissed to silence.

Alice lowered her hand from the control panel. 'Well, clumsy me. I seemed to have turned our radio off.'

I grinned at her. 'Oops!'

'Lucy, is there any reason we can't follow you?'

'None at all, but this is a test flight, so let's try to at least honour the spirit of what you've agreed with the others. We'll keep your speed below Mach 5. And if you don't mind, Alice, I've slaved Ariel's flight systems to my own. As skilled a pilot as you are, you need more flight time to gain a full feeling for flying Ariel before you're ready to fly a mission like this solo.'

'Understood and agreed.'

'Then get ready for the rush of your lives as I take over your ship,' Lucy replied.

I cast a silent prayer to the patron saint of test pilots and did my best to maintain a calm face as Alice released her hands from the controls.

Data suddenly filled the curved screens, scrolling past rapidly. Then the control yoke and throttle began to move by themselves. Just like that we were blurring towards the horizon at an impossible speed, Lucy racing ahead of us like a guiding star.

CHAPTER SIX

THE COCKPIT SCREENS suddenly went blank as we exited the airspace over Eden, just as always happened in other craft we flew. That was important to maintain the secret location of the underground base. The logic was that if we didn't know where it was, this information couldn't be interrogated out of us if we were ever captured. Alice was an obvious exception to this rule as she'd had the base built. But she wasn't in the frontline...normally, at least.

With a lack of visual clues and the grease-smooth flight characteristic of the REV drive, it felt as if we were sitting in a darkened room, apart from the gentle hum coming from the floor. The only hint that we were flying at eye-blistering speed was the HUD flight information on Alice's curved glass screen, currently showing Mach 2.5.

There was strong new car smell to Ariel that had been scratching at my nose. Not unpleasant, but a distinct whiff of metal, hydraulic fluid and plastic. No doubt that would recede after a few further flights, as new car smells always did.

Alice closed down a diagnostic overlay that she'd projected on to the main cabin walls whilst Lucy flew Ariel for her.

'How's it looking?' I asked Alice.

'Jodie will be ecstatic when she sees these figures. Everything is operating exactly as we hoped.'

'Maybe after she finishes laying into you when we get back, hey?'

Alice pulled a face. 'Oh, don't you worry, Lauren. I'll do my best to hide away from Jodie until she cools down. Thankfully Eden is a big enough place to do exactly that. There are a few hidden rooms that she doesn't even know about.'

'Good plan,' Lucy's voice said. 'Jodie is someone you don't want to upset.'

'Tell me about it – and I'm meant to be her boss,' Alice replied. 'Mind you, it often it feels the other way round.'

I smiled. 'Jodie's certainly pretty fierce when she wants to be.' I glanced at the distance read-out that had reached well over a thousand miles. 'So, Lucy, what's our ETA now?'

'We're about five minutes out.'

'In that case let's power up the external cameras again,' Alice said. 'Delphi, please restore the transparency feed to the cockpit.'

'Affirmative,' a synthesised female voice replied.

At once the cockpit was flooded with light as the cabin's wall screens shimmered into life.

With the view restored the astonishing speed we were moving at really hit home.

Through breaks in the clouds, I could see a vast patchwork of cornfields stretching away in every direction around us. The views of them raced by as we hurtled through the sky, tower clouds like vast mountain ranges whipping past us. Just ahead, Lucy's shining micro mind craft had precisely matched her velocity to Ariel's, so much so that we could have been fixed together by an invisible metal pole.

Alice peered at her screen. 'I'm seeing a faint radar click about ten miles out, Lucy.'

'Yes, I'm detecting it too. That's our Tic Tac and it seems to be in a holding position.'

'Hang on, if we can see it on our radar, can't everyone else too?' I asked.

'Absolutely. You can guarantee there'll already be fighter jets scrambling to intercept it,' Lucy replied. 'So we need to keep this first contact brief and get out of here before anyone else arrives.'

'OK, as time is short, how are we going to handle this?' I asked.

'I suggest we hold off at a safe distance so our actions aren't mistaken as hostile,' Lucy said. 'After all, the last time you ran into one of these guys they were being shot at by one of the Overseers' TR-3B Astra fleet.'

'Then I suggest we close to no nearer than a mile and attempt to make contact remotely,' Alice said.

'That sounds good to me,' I said.

Still under Lucy's control, the throttle moved back by itself. Ariel and Lucy's ship hurtled to a sudden stop. In any other aircraft our brains would have smashed into the fronts of our skulls. But thanks to this ship's REV drive the G-forces that we should have experienced were reduced by eighty-nine per cent. It felt like braking hard in a car.

'I have a steady radar contact a mile ahead of us,' Alice said, peering at her screen.

'Me too,' Lucy replied. 'Here's an enhanced view from my optical display. I'm going to share it with you on your cockpit's screens.'

A pop-up window appeared on the wall in front of us. My heart leapt as I saw what was within it: a magnified view of a Tic Tac craft. The ship glistened in the sun like a giant white polished pill. It was almost completely featureless apart from a couple of spikes that stuck out of the bottom. It somehow looked wrong hanging there, as if it didn't belong in our world.

Alice was gawping too. 'Well, isn't that quite the sight? Is this like the other Tic Tacs you encountered over Peru, Lauren?'

'Exactly the same from what I can see.'

'Most fascinating.'

'Oh, you'll find this interesting too,' Lucy said. 'My sensors are telling me that the ship has a full antigravity drive system. That means we are definitely dealing with a very advanced species.'

'I think we could have worked that part out for ourselves,' I said.

'Good point,' Lucy replied.

'Regardless of that, let's open up a radio channel and see if we can establish contact,' Alice said.

'You can certainly try,' Lucy said. 'But I've already been bombarding the ship with communication protocols across the entire electro-magnetic spectrum. And so far I've received not so much as a squeak back. Of course, you may get more lucky.'

'Lauren, you're the closest thing we have to a first-contact expert on-board,' Alice said. 'Can you handle this?'

'I can give it a go,' I replied.

'Then I'm opening a channel for you now. Just press the green button on your seat's armrest when you're ready to speak.'

I located the button and pushed it. 'Hi, unidentified craft. The first thing we want you to know is –' I glanced to Alice, looking for inspiration, but she just shrugged at me – 'we, um, come in peace.'

Alice didn't quite roll her eyes at me, but only just. This was a hugely historic moment and there was me coming up with a bloody cliché.

A distinct lack of anything came back over the comm channel and who could blame them. They probably hadn't even bothered to look up from the crossword or whatever it was they were doing.

'Keep going,' Lucy's voice said. 'I just registered a small electrical surge within that craft. That suggests they heard you at the very least.'

I cleared my throat and tried again. 'Can you please tell us why you're here?'

Again, there was no audible response.

'Are you registering anything else, Lucy?' Alice asked.

'Just a constant energy signature now, nothing more. But that does suggest Lauren has got their attention.'

'Maybe they can't understand our language?' I said.

'Oh, it's definitely not that,' Lucy replied. 'Any species advanced enough to have a craft like a Tic Tac will also have the technology to interpret human language – and a thousand others.'

'So we're like a salesman ringing the doorbell and those guys are just pretending to not be in?' I asked.

'More likely the Overseers have tried to sucker them in with a similar approach previously,' Alice said.

'That's very likely knowing just how devious that organisation can be,' I said. 'So how about the old shields-down *Star Trek* approach instead?'

'The last time I looked we didn't have shields,' Alice pointed out.

'I know, but what I mean is we could approach the Tic Tac with our own systems running at minimal power.'

'Oh, I see what you're driving at,' Alice said. 'Keeping our power at low levels shows them that we're not initiating any energy weapons.'

'Let me try approaching first,' Lucy said. 'You hang back here just in case they misinterpret my advances towards them as hostile.'

'OK, but the first hint of trouble and we all head straight back to Eden,' Alice said. 'I'm in enough trouble as it is. Niki would be furious if he knew what we were about to try.'

'Agreed,' Lucy said. 'I'm handing primary control of Ariel back to you, Alice. That way you can make a fast exit if necessary and I'll catch up with you.'

'Understood,' Alice replied. She took hold of the egg-shaped controller, her other hand poised over the throttle.

'You have control,' Lucy said.

There was a slight movement downwards before Alice compensated for it. 'I have control,' Alice repeated back.

'OK, I'm going in. Wish me luck,' Lucy said.

'Keeping everything crossed for you here,' I replied.

With a gentle surge Lucy's star-shaped craft began to slowly roll end over end as she headed towards the Tic Tac.

The AI gradually closed the distance between herself and the other craft until she came to a dead stop less than a hundred metres away. Then she began to orbit round it, like a circling sheep dog who had cornered a stray.

'OK, I'm using more obscure communication protocols now, including mathematical formulae and even the value of pi to see if we can get a response,' Lucy's voice said.

Over the next few minutes the Tic Tac remained stock still as though it wasn't even aware of Lucy despite her close proximity. What were the crew in that thing making of all this?

A warbling alarm came from Alice's control panel and a red square box appeared over our cockpit screens to the starboard side.

Alice peered at the glass screen. 'Oh shoot, it looks as if we've got military company and...' She blinked hard. 'Approaching speed is Mach 8.'

'There's only one thing that can move that fast – a TR-3B Astra,' I said.

'Looking at the masked radar signatures, I think you're right,'

Lucy said. 'Guys, you need to get out of here and fast. Whatever propulsion system they are using, it's even more powerful than Ariel's vectoring thrusters.'

'But what about you?' I asked.

'They're almost certainly tracking the Tic Tac craft, which doesn't seem that concerned about hiding its radar signature. So I'll engage full-stealth mode and I suggest you do the same. Then I'll hang around here to see what happens. I'll catch you up back at Eden.'

'Understood and good luck,' Alice replied. She glanced at her monitor. 'Time to engage our chameleon cloak.' She pressed a button on the panel.

A muffled bang came from somewhere beneath us.

Alice stared at her readouts. 'Darn it, we have an overload in the power feed to the exterior-cloaking screens.'

'You mean we can't hide ourselves?' I asked.

'Not until we get it fixed. Delphi, initiate immediate power bypass for chameleon system.'

'Initiated,' Delphi relied. 'Three minutes until rerouting complete.'

Alice frowned at her glass screen as she scanned the displayed information. 'At the speed that bandit is coming in at, we're going to need to forget that ceiling of ten thousand feet if we're going to escape it.'

'Whatever you're going to do, you've got less than thirty seconds until they arrive,' Lucy said.

'On it already,' Alice replied. She raised the egg control upwards and pushed the throttle all the way forward. One moment we were hovering in the skies over the Illinois prairies, the next we were shooting straight upwards at a speed that was enough to steal my breath away.

'Mach 6.2, our maximum speed,' Alice called out.

Even though there was less than one G of acceleration,

thanks to the REV drive, my hands still clawed my flight seat's armrests. But there was also a flip side too. My eyes drank in the astonishing view that only astronauts had previously seen on their way into orbit as the Earth started to curve away beneath us. My lifelong dream of becoming an astronaut was about to be realised. I just wished it was in happier circumstances when our lives weren't suddenly on the line.

Alice shook her head in amazement as she took in the view. 'Well, Ariel can certainly shift her tush.'

'Oh bloody hell!' Lucy's voice said over the comm channel.

'What's wrong now?' I asked.

'It turns out it wasn't *one* TR-3B Astra, but three flying in close formation. They seem to have some sort of tech to alter their radar profiles. And, to make things even trickier, somehow they've detected my presence with a kind of energy-scanning system. They are throwing that beam around like a bloody searchlight. I'm locked into a game of chase with one of them, and I'm finding it hard to shake it off.'

'Have the other Astras engaged the Tic Tac?'

'Yes. The alien ship sensibly got out the hell out of here, but one of them is on its tail.'

'And the third craft?' Alice asked.

'Now to the really bad news. I'm afraid it's on its way up to you right now. It seems they managed to get a visual lock on you whilst you were departing.'

'Understood. We'll take appropriate measure,' Alice replied, her tone suddenly iced-water cool. She glanced across at me. 'I would say hang on, but the gravity-disruption field will deal with most of the G-force. So just pray to whomever or whatever you believe in instead.'

My fingers sought out the Empyrean Key and I clung on to it like a talisman. 'You've got this, Alice.'

'I hope so, for both our sakes.'

She pushed the control egg forward and curved us away as a red box appeared on the cockpit floor beneath us.

We sped down in a steep arc, the flight-deck gimbals compensating to keep us level.

'Hostile craft is closing,' Delphi's voice said calmly from the cockpit speakers.

'Then it's time to shake things up a bit,' Alice said. She yanked the egg control in reverse and we slapped into our harnesses as Ariel jinked backwards. The gimbal motors whined as the ship rotated rapidly around us.

'Oh my goodness, this craft is something else,' Alice said as we hurtled backwards as fast as we'd been flying forward a moment ago.

But the enemy Astra raced up to the same altitude as us, visible on the forward-facing cockpit screens. The red lock box overlaid on them began to grow bigger as they closed the distance rapidly.

'They're beginning to reel us in,' Alice said, her brow ridging.

My mouth grew dry. 'Can you go any faster?'

'I'm already redlining the multimode vector thrusters. If I push them any further, we'll destroy them.'

'That will be academic if they blow us out of the sky. Do whatever you have to do to shake them. And don't worry about me losing my breakfast.'

'In that case it's time to show them just how good we are.' Alice slammed the egg control hard left and we shot immediately sideways. But when I glanced to the left I saw the Astra had almost instantly switched directions to match our change.

Alice began to zigzag through three dimensions, quickly overloading my senses with a blur of movement as Ariel spun round us in every axis. The motorised gimbals whined ever louder as they fought to keep the flight deck level. But whoever was flying that Astra was damned good too. They matched us move for move as we buzzed about the sky like two crazed wasps trapped in a jar.

'OK, if you really want to play...' Alice said to herself. She gritted her teeth, threw the throttle wide open and lifted the egg control hard up. I sank into my chair as we sped upwards into the darkening sky. Pinpricks of stars grew stronger around us as the Earth steadily became a globe below.

We were so high now I could see a large storm system sweeping towards the west coast of North America. We had to be at an altitude equivalent to the orbit of the International Space Station. Unfortunately, even that incredible manoeuvre hadn't shaken the Astra off our tail. Through the floor of spherical cockpit I could see it rising fast towards us.

'Power successfully rerouted to chameleon system,' Delphi announced.

'Not a moment too soon,' Alice said. She threw Ariel back towards the Earth at the same point as hitting a button.

'Chameleon system engaged,' Delphi announced.

'Now let's pray we can lose that hotshot pilot,' Alice said. 'The good news is they haven't opened fire on us yet despite having several clear chances to do so. Maybe they have a weapon malfunction.'

We sped away as the pursuing TR-3B slowed to a stop and a light beam lanced straight out from it, sweeping the darkening sky like a lighthouse lamp.

'Now our cloak is operating again, it looks as if they're using that fancy sensor to try to locate us,' Alice said.

I nodded. 'It looks like that searchlight beam we saw the Tic Tac use back in Peru.'

'Very interesting... Delphi, can you give me a magnified view of the craft?' Alice said.

'Digitally enhancing image,' Delphi replied.

A window on the display opened up to reveal a triangular

craft floating against the stars above us. As it slowly rotated I spotted a red panel in its grey belly, as if someone hadn't yet painted it the black of the rest of the craft. Three round orange engines glowed towards the tips of the ship's belly. In the middle was an inward-facing dome lined with square panels, which was emitting a fainter light, presumably something to do with their magnetic gravity-reduction drive. Unlike the Tic Tac, this ship had a man-made feel to it.

A beam of light lanced out again from the Astra through the sky, just over Ariel.

'Let's make sure we don't get into its path,' Alice said. She tipped Ariel on to her nose and we began to speed straight down towards Earth.

I felt the tension release from my jaw when the Astra stayed put and their sensor beam shot out in the opposite direction.

I relaxed into my chair. 'It looks as if we lost—'

My words were cut off by a warbling alarm from Alice's control console. It immediately lit up with red lights.

Alice began to flick switches. 'No, no, no!'

Intuition was screaming at me that something spectacularly bad had just happened. 'Talk to me, Alice?' I yelped.

'The REV drive is going offline. I pushed it too hard and for too long.'

A vibration shuddered through Ariel and then, as if someone had thrown a switch, gravity suddenly yanked my body from left to right within my seat as the ship went into a flat spin.

'I'm losing control!' Alice shouted, her face ashen as she moved the control egg in every direction to no effect.

Ariel started to tip forward, the leading edge of the craft now pointing straight down. The prototype ship began to corkscrew as it dropped. We were thrown around in our flight seats as the G-force was no longer cushioned by the REV drive. The gimbals were fighting a losing battle to keep our flight deck level – it had begun to pitch violently from side to side like a boat in a wild, stormy sea. This was no longer a computer game where we were passively watching the action on a screen. This had just got far too real.

An altimeter flashed up on the HUD as alarm after alarm joined the first and we sped ever faster. An audible scream of air was coming from outside as there was now no gravity bubble to protect us. The cockpit had already grown noticeably warmer and sparks rushed past on the screens as we re-entered the Earth's atmosphere. I knew enough about spaceflight to realise that the leading edge of the saucer-shaped craft was probably glowing red hot right by now. The sparks faded as the world outside became blue again.

'Alice, we've got to abandon ship and use the escape pods,' I said.

There was no response.

I looked across to see her expression frozen like a mask. Her hand was still clamped on the egg control, unmoving.

The altitude display whipped past 100,000 feet.

'Alice, talk to me!' I shouted.

She was shaking but remained mute, fear etched into her every feature as we hurtled below 70,000 feet. A canopy of clouds rushed up to meet us.

I felt the burn of bile at the back of my throat as Alice's arms dropped away from the controls of her flight seat and she closed her eyes. We were going to die.

CHAPTER SEVEN

THE WHOLE CRAFT shook with a cacophony of groans and screeching metal coming from the titanium airframe around us. Alice and I rose up into our seat harnesses as Ariel plummeted towards the ground. We had at best less than a couple of minutes before we slammed into the rapidly expanding patchwork of prairies beneath us. But my most pressing problem was that Alice still seemed locked into some sort of catatonic state.

'Alice, you have to bloody well do something!' I shouted.

Her lip trembled but she didn't respond. What had happened to her ice-maiden control of only a few minutes before?

I tried to reach across towards her control panel, but I couldn't fight the sharply increased G-force. Maybe voice control would still work?

'Delphi, initiate escape pods,' I said.

'Pilot authorisation needed to abandon vessel,' Delphi replied.

'Bloody override it. This is an emergency and we need to evacuate the ship!'

'I'm afraid I'm unable to do that, Lauren,' the ship's computer replied.

'Oh, don't go all HAL on me!' I forced my head over to stare at Alice. 'Alice, you have to issue the command!'

Alice's expression remained a mask, her eyes locked on to the view of the prairies of Illinois growing larger beneath us.

I needed to grab hold of the woman and shake her out of wherever she'd disappeared to in her shock. But that wasn't physically possible in the negative G-force induced by our rapid descent. It was doing its best to drag my body out of its harness and hurl me up at the ceiling of the circular cockpit and pin me there. But I realised there was one last thing I could try...

'Lucy, we could really do with your help right now. We're about crash and are unable to eject.'

No reply came back. Maybe she was too busy – or something worse had happened.

Shit, shit, shit!

My mouth was glued up with saliva as the altitude indicator sped below 5,000 feet. We were close enough to the ground now for me to see a lone blue tractor kick up a cloud of dust behind it as it trundled along a track. Maybe the tractor driver would be the first on the scene to pull our smashed bodies from the crash site, not that there would be a lot to recover if we hit the ground at our current speed.

There was literally nothing I could do to stop this happening.

Some deep animal instinct took over and something inside me relaxed as my subconscious registered that death was inevitable. And of all things that I could have spent my last moments thinking about, Jack's face filled my mind. How could I have left things as they currently stood? Now he would have no idea just how much he meant to me. I had to leave him a message.

'Delphi, do you have a black box recorder?'

'Affirmative,' Delphi replied.

The black box would record the final data from Ariel before it ploughed into the ground – along with cockpit voice recordings. If anything could survive the impact, it was the black box.

I cleared my throat. 'This message is for Jack Harper...' A deep breath. 'Jack, I want you to know how crazy I am about you, so crazy, in fact, that I didn't trust myself to tell you whilst keeping focused on trying to get the job done.'

I watched as a flock of swallows spiralled over the tractor, but my attention was snatched back as the G-force ramped up and I was barely able to breathe.

Damn it, I needed to tell Jack how I really felt. 'Jack...I... love...you,' I ground out through my clenched jaw. My vision started to go red as the blood rushed to my brain.

'If that's how you feel, then you should tell him in person,' Lucy's voice said from the cockpit speakers.

Before I could reply I spotted a blurring bubble of air that was her otherwise invisible craft speeding up towards our plummeting ship.

'Lauren, you need to activate that teardrop icon to override my drive safety protocols,' Lucy said.

'Got it. Delphi, initiate carrier tone.'

'Carrier tone initiated,' the ship's AI replied.

Barely audible over the rushing air outside, a chiming tone filled the cockpit and the teardrop icon appeared over the Empyrean Key. Fighting the G-force, with muscles cabling in my arm, I moved the icon into the selection window and flicked my wrist forward.

Just like that the world outside hurtled to an abrupt stop. As the negative gravity released, we were suddenly floating against our harnesses in zero G.

'Got you!' Lucy said. 'I've extended my antigravity field and enveloped you with it. Told you I could do it.'

I gulped in a breath. Ariel was now hanging in mid-air,

pointing straight towards the ground that was just a few hundred metres below us.

'I disappear for a few minutes and look at the trouble you get yourselves into,' Lucy said.

With a gentle hum lights lit up all over the control console. Alice slowly blinked and then licked her lips.

'I've also just had a quick tinker with your systems to bring the REV drive back online,' Lucy continued.

Her star-shaped craft came to a gliding stop just beneath us. She was only visible because of the slight distortion in the air that outlined her.

'I'm handing over autopilot function back to Delphi and retracting my antigravity field so you can now fly under your own power again.'

'Affirmative,' I replied.

There was a slight vibration as the shimmering air around us disappeared. Then once again gentle gravity took hold of our bodies and pulled us back down into our seats.

'Thank you, Lucy,' I said. 'I thought it was all over there for a moment.'

'Evidently, if your declaration of love to Jack is anything to go by,' Lucy replied.

'You weren't meant to hear that.'

'It's already forgotten.'

A shaking gasp came from Alice and she placed her hands over her mouth as tears blossomed from her eyes. 'Oh my god!'

I reached across and touched her arm. 'Are you OK?'

She took a shuddering breath and nodded. 'I'm so sorry, Lauren. I'm not sure what happened there. It felt as if my body turned into a block of stone and I couldn't move.'

'That sounds like a freeze response to me,' Lucy said.

'A what?' Alice asked.

'It's a variation of the fight or flight response you humans sometimes experience in a dangerous situation. To quote your medical text books, "in a hyper-aroused state that could threaten a person's sanity", such as ploughing your prototype ship into the ground, for example, "the body secretes endorphins and other chemicals to function as an analgesic". Basically it's your body's way of dialling down the experience and allowing you to disappear into yourself before death. That's the physiological explanation; however, this is way out of character for you, Alice.'

This didn't sound like the Lucy I knew, more like a psychological expert who'd stepped into her shoes for a second. But then again anything was possible with her. She was an AI after all.

Alice breathed through her nose. 'For a computer sometimes you are far too sharp.'

'Hey, I'm multitalented,' Lucy replied, sounding more like her old self again.

I peered across at Alice. 'Is this something to do with an old trauma that triggered you?'

Her eyes locked on to mine. 'And it would seem you're very perceptive too, Lauren Stelleck.' She gestured towards her legs. 'You're both right – it had everything to do with how I did this to myself.'

'You've never spoken about that before, Alice,' I said gently.

'There's a good reason for that. Even today it's too raw. When I lost control of Ariel just now, it took me straight back to the most awful time of my life. You see, I used to live for aerobatics. During an air show, when I was doing an inverted loop, my plane suffered a catastrophic structural failure. Half of the rear tailplane sheared off and my plane, Suzie Q, veered straight towards the crowd. I had a split second to make a decision – either take a forced landing on top of those poor people watching me or try to pull the plane round, back to the airstrip. But I knew the latter would mean I would almost certainly stall the aircraft.'

'And you chose that option, didn't you?' Lucy's voice asked.

'Of course I did. My last-ditch desperate manoeuvre killed what little airspeed I had left and I stalled straight into the strip. I should have died that day, but somehow I survived. It may have left me unable to walk, but I've tried to make the best of it. I've never piloted an aircraft since then – until today.'

'Oh good grief, Alice.' I forced myself to keep my annoyance in check because that wouldn't help anyone right now. Instead, I used the most compassionate tone I could in the circumstances. 'No wonder just reacted the way you did.'

She nodded. 'I wouldn't normally admit this to anyone, but I often relive it in my nightmares, waking up drenched in cold sweat.'

'So why put yourself through flying Ariel after experiencing something like that?' Lucy asked.

'I thought it would be my way back. I even designed the flight controls of Ariel so I could fly her. She held within her my dreams of being able to fly again.'

'You're saying that in the past tense now?' I said.

'Oh, Lauren, do you think I can really take to the air again after this?'

'Guys, I hate to interrupt, but there's a tractor getting closer to us by the second. Even though your chameleon drive is back online, at such close proximity the driver might notice something in the air. We'd better make ourselves scarce before they get here.'

Alice's face paled. 'I can't fly Ariel, not now.'

'If you prefer, I can take over your flight systems again and get you back to Eden, Alice?' Lucy asked.

Alice bowed her head and nodded. 'Please do that.'

Her sense of relief was palpable. But I also knew that if she didn't face this fear down in the immediate aftermath she probably never would dare try to fly again.

The tractor was a only a mile away as I tightened my gaze on her. 'Actually, I don't think that's a good idea. I know you might not want to, but as my actual Aunt Lucy once said to me when I managed to crash my motorbike, when you've been thrown by your horse you need to get straight back in the saddle.'

Alice, that ever confident powerhouse of a person, bit her lip. 'I'm not sure I can, Lauren.'

'What happened to the woman I've never seen back down from any challenge? You, Alice, have been an inspiration to me from the moment we first met.'

'That's wonderful to hear, but to a greater or lesser extent we all have masks that we wear to take on the world. We project how we want to be seen rather than who we really are. The truth is, I'm a damaged soul, Lauren.'

'Aren't we all? I carry so many demons inside me I honestly wonder sometimes how I get out of bed in the morning.'

'It sounds as if you are discussing what is basically the innate conflict of the human condition,' Lucy replied, back in psychoanalyst mode. 'Everyone has things in their past that continue to haunt them. But here's another piece of advice that Lauren's real Aunt Lucy once told her: you become the stories that you tell yourself.'

I blinked and looked down through the floor screens at Lucy's micro mind ship hovering just beneath ours. 'How do you know what my aunt said, Lucy?'

'That's a conversation for another time, Lauren. Anyway, to my artificial consciousness that statement sounds like the truth if ever I heard it. Don't be ruled by what has been, but instead be inspired by what could be.'

I felt as if I was seeing a deeper side of Lucy – certainly not the part of the AI that was causing mischief between Mike and Jodie.

I squeezed Alice's arm gently. 'Lucy's right. So what do you say? Are you ready to get back into the saddle? I promise you, from personal experience, it will help.'

Alice tipped her head back, took a deep breath and slowly nodded. 'You two are quite formidable when you gang up on someone like this.'

'You'd better believe it,' Lucy said.

'Then I give in...' Alice reached forward, hand shaking, and took hold of the controller, slowly rotating it back.

Ariel rolled immediately on her axis until her outline on the curved cockpit walls was once again parallel with the ground.

The tractor was heading ever closer to us along the track.

Alice took hold of the throttle and threw me a faint smile. 'I'm almost inclined to kill our chameleon field for a moment to give that tractor driver the social media shot of the decade.'

I raised my eyebrows at her. 'Or maybe not.'

'Indeed...' She gently pushed the throttle forward and Ariel surged away over the tractor. We were close enough to the vehicle for me to catch the puzzled look the guy in the cab cast up towards the sky. Presumably he'd just noticed a slight shimmer in the air pass over him.

Swallows swooped around us, somehow still aware we were there, even though we were cloaked and almost completely silent. We quickly climbed away into the sky, with Lucy pulling along-side us.

Alice glanced across at me. 'You really should tell Jack how crazy you are about him.'

Lucy's laugh seemed impossibly loud as it bounced back at us in our spherical cockpit. 'Oh, you heard that little nugget too, did you?'

'I most certainly did.'

My face blazed as I strapped myself back into my seat. Oh hell, the cat was well and truly out of the bag.

CHAPTER EIGHT

ALICE, Jack, Jodie and I sat together round the table on the veranda of Alice's house back at Eden for our debriefing after the nearly disastrous test flight. Niki should have been there to lay into us, but had been called away to deal with some security matter. Ruby, on the other hand, had ducked out of endless weapon training to be here – chewing gum and giving me a look I couldn't quite read. Even Lucy was present in the form of a smart speaker, but so far she was keeping surprisingly mute. The other missing person was Mike, who was monitoring the TREENO fleet data. Not that he would have been here even if he could. According to Jack, he was still avoiding Jodie as much as possible.

A calming blue sky was displayed on the giant screens lining the cavern's ceiling, beginning to turn gold as the sun slid towards the western horizon. Unfortunately, the tranquil setting did little to take the edge off Jodie's anger. She rested her elbows on the table and clasped her hands together, both index fingers pointed like pistols at Alice. The president of Sky Dreamer Corp. might have been Jodie's boss, but it didn't seem that way from how the chief scientist had just ripped into Alice.

'I can't believe you would do something so reckless, Alice,' Jodie said. 'You of all people.'

Alice gave her a haunted look and nodded. 'For what it's worth, me neither. I certainly can't begin to apologise enough to you and the others. It was reckless to take Ariel on an extended test flight, especially when I put Lauren's life on the line too.'

I sat up straighter. 'Hey, I was a willing co-conspirator. You've got nothing to beat yourself up about there.'

But Jack, who'd been mostly mute, chose that moment to shake his head, very unhelpfully in my opinion. 'Actually, and I'm sorry to say this, but this is on you, Alice. There was a clear chain of command and the first priority of a leader is to not needlessly endanger someone else for whom they are responsible.'

Jodie nodded, her mouth a thin line. 'Exactly. This was basically an excuse for a joyride that nearly cost both you your lives. We could have dispatched an X101 or Armadillo to attempt to make first contact with that Tic Tac.'

Ruby blew her cheeks out. 'Oh, come on, guys. Any of you would have done the same if you'd found yourselves in that situation. I know I would have done.'

I nodded, grateful for her unexpected vote of confidence. 'With all due respect, Jodie, an electric craft would have taken far too long to reach the Tic Tac. So please stop lecturing Alice about this.'

Alice shook her head. 'Thank you both for sticking up for me, but they're right. The truth is that I got carried away. I could have let Lucy deal with the situation by herself. However, I am determined to learn the lesson from my reckless decision. If nothing else I realise now that Ariel isn't ready for frontline mission deployment yet, no matter how much I would like it to be.'

Jodie pulled a face at her. 'With all due respect, Alice, the only reason she failed is because you pushed Ariel way beyond her performance boundaries.'

'And the reason I had to push her so hard was because those darn TR-3Bs were way faster than her. Somehow we need to increase the performance of Ariel to match, or ideally exceed, those craft. We also need more safety measures, including a redundancy backup system. Losing the chameleon drive due to a power overload at such a critical moment proved that Ariel isn't mission-ready yet – and that's just one example. We were lucky that pursuing pilot didn't open fire on us. Neither of us would be sitting here if they had.'

'Oh, give me strength,' Jodie muttered. 'Do I need to remind you it was meant to be a flight test rather than a shakedown of all her systems? The key takeaway from all this is that the REV drive system proved itself. And the rest we can work on. I also need to add both defensive and offensive systems to her.'

'And I would expect exactly that sort of diligence from you, Jodie,' said Alice. 'Based on what you've just said, it's my decision that until every aspect of Ariel has been triple-checked and improved she is to remain grounded and not be flown by anyone.'

We all stared at her. 'Hang on,' I said. 'Aren't we in danger of overreacting here? Ariel is by far the fastest craft available to us. We might need her in the air sooner rather than later.'

'That's as maybe, but she's still not quite ready for prime time yet,' Alice said.

Jack nodded. 'I'm with you on this, Alice. When the military develop combat aircraft they don't simply push them straight to the front line. Every aspect has to be shaken down first.'

Ruby pulled a face at him. 'Getting Ariel squeaky clean for deployment isn't something that we have much time left for, or have your forgotten the urgency of all this?'

Jack shrugged. 'I realise it's not ideal, but neither is throwing lives away needlessly.'

His eyes flicked towards me and I had the distinct impression there was something he wasn't saying here. But what exactly?

Away from that, an itch of irritation grew inside me. What was it that the people sitting at this table weren't getting? Fully flight ready or not, Ariel had already proved herself, and the ability for rapid deployment and reconnaissance might be something we would need.

Alice's gaze swept round the table. 'I think we have probably discussed this subject enough. We're in danger of going round in circles. I'm going to pull rank here and say my decision is final.'

I forced myself to bite my tongue. But as far as I was concerned this matter was far from over.

'Let's move things on to debriefing Lucy.' Alice turned her head towards the speaker mounted on the post. 'Are you there, Lucy?'

'Of course,' her voice replied from the speaker.

A huge pop-up window easily the size of a house appeared just over the projected mountain range across the cavern. Within it was a live video feed from the Cage where Lucy was sitting on a reclining chair sipping a large cup of tea.

'I assume you want to ask me what happened after we split up following the arrival of the fleet of Astras?' she asked.

'Absolutely,' Alice replied.

'Well, as you know, I tried to draw them away but unfortunately one of them locked on to the Tic Tac. The second, as you know, pursued Ariel. And the third locked on to me.'

'The thing I really don't understand is how they tracked you with that sensor of theirs,' I said. 'I thought you were basically invisible to everything if you chose to be.'

'It was a surprise to me too,' Lucy said. 'They have obviously developed some interesting tech that will neutralise our advantage over them, and we need to investigate that.'

Jodie leant forward in her seat. 'Did you manage to get any readings for it, Lucy?'

'Yes, and it wasn't like anything I'd encountered before. It mainly seemed to consist of a powerful light in the UV spectrum – plus a spike across the microwave frequency as they locked on to me.'

'A weapon designed to literally cook your systems?' Jack asked.

'No, the microwave wasn't in any way powerful enough to do that, besides my systems are heavily shielded against all electromagnetic forms of attack. No, by using that beam of energy they were able to stick to me like glue once they'd locked on. However, I was far more nimble than any Astra and able to dodge their rail-gun shots.'

Alice stared at Lucy's image on the large pop-up window over the mountain range. 'Wait, they fired at you?'

'Is that really any surprise? The Overseers almost certainly gave their flight crews standing orders to shoot down any alien craft.'

'That does make sense, but if so why didn't they fire on Ariel?' I asked. 'They had plenty of chances to do exactly that.'

Jack rubbed his neck. 'That doesn't sound like the Overseers I know. Shoot first, ask questions later is more their speed.'

'Maybe they had a weapons malfunction,' Jodie said.

'I did notice an unpainted panel in the ship,' I said. 'Maybe it had recently been repaired?'

'If so, thank goodness for that,' Alice said. 'But you can guarantee that next time we won't be so lucky and that they'll being firing at us too. Jodie, could we look at adding some sort of armour system similar to that used on the Armadillo?'

'To be honest I'm not sure even its rolled-steel armour could stop a rail-gun round,' Jodie replied.

Ruby nodded. 'Those rounds travelling at hypersonic speed can punch a hole through pretty much anything.'

'There might be something we can do about that, but let me think about it,' Jodie said. 'And this new microwave device of theirs is an obvious concern. We really need more data on it so we can come up with a way to counter it.'

'Would it be useful if I shared all my data from my encounter with the TR-3B with you?' Lucy asked.

'Yes, it would,' Jody replied without looking up at Lucy's image.

It seemed her professional attitude towards the AI only stretched so far.

'So if this sensor of theirs was so good, how did you manage to escape your pursuer, Lucy?' Jack asked.

'In the end it came down to sheer speed. Their Astra design might be fast, but I'm faster still. Although I had to increase my speed to Mach 10 before I managed to shake them.'

For the first time Jodie looked up at Lucy. 'Holy cow, I had no idea you could go that fast. Any chance you could share the technology that enables you to do that with us?'

'As always, I wish I could. Unfortunately, as you know, I'm prohibited by my core code from handing over that technology.'

I sighed. 'The good old *Star Trek* prime directive once again.'

'Exactly, Lauren. But apart from that I'll assist you in any way I can to improve your existing technology.'

'I'd really appreciate your input,' Jodie replied, her tone thawing a fraction.

'Well, at least you were able to outrun them. It's just as well you did, Lucy,' Alice said. 'I'm not sure I'll ever be able to thank you enough for coming to our rescue.'

Lucy shrugged. 'Oh, that was nothing.'

'It might be to you, but it wasn't to us,' I said.

'Actually, I do have a question about that,' Ruby asked. 'Why didn't you launch the escape pod when the REV drive failed?'

Alice dragged her teeth over her lip, her expression tensing.

We hadn't told anyone about how Alice had zoned out. But I

could tell by the way she set her jaw that Alice was about to reveal the truth.

I jumped in before she could. 'Actually, we were having some problems with Delphi when the systems started glitching out. I suggest that, rather than voice control that only the pilot can initiate, you should design the equivalent of a big red button that anyone can use.'

Ruby screwed up her eyes at me as if she knew I was deflecting the question.

But Jodie was nodding. 'That's a very good idea, Lauren, especially if the pilot is injured and can't issue the command.'

'Exactly,' I replied without meeting Alice's gaze, although I did catch the grateful look she cast my way in the corner of my eye.

Alice cleared her throat. 'OK, I think that concludes business for now. I for one need my bed.'

'After the day I had I need a stiff cocktail – or three,' I said.

'Then they are all on me,' Jack said. 'Plus it's pizza night down at the Rock Garden. I know my way to a woman's heart.'

More than you will ever know, I thought.

I caught Alice looking at me. Her eyebrow barely rose a fraction, but it was enough to make heat flash through my cheeks.

'Come on then, I'm starving,' I said, trying to get out of there as fast as humanly possible. I hoped Alice would be as good at keeping my secrets as I was with hers.

Beads of sweat had popped all over the chef's face as he shovelled pizza in and out of the stone oven with his paddle. There was a good-sized crowd in the Rock Garden – as there always was on a Thursday night. Leroy insisted on playing only Bob Marley on pizza night, and everyone seemed to appreciate it. But why Leroy felt there was a connection between the Jamaican musician and the classic Italian food was beyond me.

Jack raised his beer to my cocktail glass as we sat at a corner table. 'Here's to you and Alice getting back here in one piece.'

'I'll drink to that,' I said, raising my margarita glass to his and clinking it.

Jack took a sip of his beer and his smile faded as he peered at me over the top of his glass. He put the glass down and pulled at a thread in the sleeve of his shirt.

I could instantly tell something was up. 'Go on, out with it, Jack.'

'How do you know that I want to say something?'

'Look, I've had way too may close calls with death alongside you to know when you have something on your mind.'

'Yes, you probably have...' He breathed through his nose as his eyes met mine. 'Lauren, you do know that I was worried sick about you when you took off in Ariel with Alice like that?'

'Hey, you should know by now I'm a big girl. I can look after myself.'

'Oh, I more than know that, but it didn't stop me worrying. I kept imagining the worst – like you crashing straight into the side of a mountain.' He hung his head. 'Lauren, I don't know what I'd do if I lost you.'

This wasn't the Jack I knew. The guy sitting opposite me looked as if he was on the verge of tears.

'Hey, big guy, it's OK. That didn't happen and here I am, all safe and sound.'

'The thing is, it could have ended that way, Lauren, and that's my point.'

'But our lives have been on the line more times than I like to count on our missions. This was just the same.'

'No it wasn't. Usually I'm right by your side – and we can watch each other's backs.' He took a long hit of his beer.

I had a sense that we were circling round what he really wanted to say. Then the blindingly obvious struck me. When I thought I'd been about to die, my own instinct had been to leave Jack a last message to tell him how I really felt. Was it the same for Jack too? And then he answered the question for me.

'Look, I realise you have me in the friend zone. But even if I'm just your buddy, I can still be worried sick about you.'

Me putting him in the friend zone? I took a bite of pizza, as I tried to gather my thoughts, but it suddenly tasted like cardboard. At that moment my Sky Wire phone buzzed in my pocket. I took it out, playing for time so I could come up with a half-coherent response.

The screen showed a message from Lucy. *Just tell him how you really feel already.*

I quickly blanked the screen and put it back in my pocket.

'Everything OK?'

'Yeah, just Lucy keeping me in the loop about the data she captured from the TR-3B Astra's sensor device.'

'Oh, I thought she was sending that straight to Jodie.'

'She was just copying me in,' I replied, almost amazed at my ability to come up with a convincing lie in such an emergency situation.

Jack drummed his fingers on the sides of his glass. 'Getting back to what we were just discussing, can we at least agree from now on not to do any dangerous missions apart from each other? I can't cope with stress of it to be totally honest.'

I was taken aback by the unexpected tenderness in his eyes. I really did mean a lot to him then, but could it really be as much as he did to me?

My phone buzzed again and I took it out to see another message from Lucy. *Look, if you don't tell him, I will.*

Making sure I kept the screen angled away from Jack as he gave me a questioning look, I quickly typed a reply. *Don't you bloody dare or I'll come up to the landing bay and take a sledge-hammer to your micro minds.*

Touchy!!! came straight back from her.

I pressed the power button and shoved the phone back in my pocket, meeting Jack's eyes with a shrug. 'Lucy really wants to talk to me about that data. Anyway, back to what we were talking about, I completely agree, Jack. I would have felt exactly the same if you had been away on a dangerous mission and I didn't know what was happening to you.'

He gave me puppy-dog eyes. 'You get it then?'

'Yes, I really do...' There was so much more that I wanted to say, but I couldn't.

'No Woman No Cry' suddenly cut out from the speakers and I heard the unmistakable sound of Lucy clearing her throat.

My blood iced. She wouldn't dare...would she?

'Lauren and Jack, there's been a...development. Please get back down here for a briefing straight away.'

All eyes in the Rock Garden turned towards us.

'Why, what's happened?' Jack asked as we stood.

My watch buzzed and Lucy's face appeared on its screen. 'And now I have your attention again, you should know that a report has just come in that a Tic Tac craft, almost certainly the same as the one we encountered, has crash-landed outside a small town in Illinois.'

I stared at Jack. 'We're on our way,' I replied to Lucy. We both burst into a run as we headed towards a lift.

CHAPTER NINE

WE WERE deep in the bowels of Eden, inside an incident room I'd never seen before. My attention was on a large screen showing a satellite image of a rural area of Illinois, as Niki had just explained. The whole of our team had gathered round a large oval table of polished wood. Even Lucy had a virtual place in the form of a small monitor to one side of the main screen.

Niki pressed the button on a remote in his hand and a blinking green box appeared near the middle of the image. 'This is the region that Delphi's internet searches have narrowed in on.'

The view magnified to show a small town to one side with a large lake to the right of it, bounded by forest. A number of buildings clustered round its northern banks.

'Where's that?' Jack asked, peering at the screen.

'Lake Crest near the Shawnwee National Forest,' Niki replied. 'It lies to the north of the Mississippi and Ohio rivers, in the US state of Illinois. Delphi picked up dozens of reports of a strange glowing pill-shaped craft. It sped low over the lake before people lost sight of it. There were also reports of a flash of light on the southern horizon, suggesting it came down somewhere in that forest. Security agencies have been busy trying to suppress these stories, or, when they haven't been able to, attempting to discredit them, giving these sightings extra credibility.'

Mike leant forward in his chair. 'Assuming this is a genuine incident, you can bet the Overseers will be all over this like a rash.'

'We believe they may already be on the ground,' Nike said. 'There's already reports of cattle mutilations in surrounding farms – the Overseers' usual modus operandi.'

'But surely that only adds credence to this being a genuine event?' I said.

Nicky shrugged. 'That's all part of the Overseers' playbook. It's a classic Cold War strategy: seeding fear among those who might be inclined to believe, who then see that same possible alien visitor as a threat. Generate fear like that and you've already won half the battle.'

Jodie shook her head. 'When did the world get so complicated?'

Mike met her gaze and nodded. There was even a small smile exchanged between them. Was this a hint of thawing in their relationship? I spotted Niki looking between them and shaking his head, then Lucy actually scowling. I mentally sighed to myself. I had no idea what was going on with Niki, and maybe I didn't want to, but I really needed to have a woman-to-woman chat with Lucy about the Mike thing.

'Has there been any information about the Overseers managing to retrieve this Tic Tac?' Ruby asked.

'We have no idea about that yet,' Alice replied. 'Delphi has been unable to dig up any further information.'

'I've tried to look into it, but the same for me too,' Lucy said from her monitor. 'I checked the chatter on the military satellites, but there's been nothing to suggest they have found it yet. In fact, quite the opposite. The military are about to claim a military transport carrying some experimental highly toxic biological warfare chemicals came down. Within a matter of hours they're going to declare an exclusion zone for a fifty-mile area south of Lake Crest.'

'I call bull to that,' Jack said. 'You can guarantee it's a cover story for an active search and recovery mission.'

My pulse quickened. 'In that case we have a window of opportunity. Get our team on the ground and fast. Maybe we can find the Tic Tac before the military do. And if anyone inside survived, maybe we can form a potential alliance with them against the Kimprak.'

'Absolutely,' Lucy said. 'If we do make first contact, we could also discover why there's been such a dramatic increase in Tic Tac activity in recent months.'

'Holy crap,' Jack said. 'You mean we could have our very own Roswell incident on our hands here?'

'We won't know unless we try,' I replied.

Ruby nodded, her eyes shining with enthusiasm. 'We could get an Armadillo ready and have a team in there before the exclusion zone kicks in.'

'Then we need to launch immediately,' I said. 'But we don't have to go in high profile. We could start off in the nearby towns to get an idea of where the Tic Tac came down. Then we use the Armadillo to track it down before the US military and their Overseers handlers get to it.'

Alice remained mute, although the colour had drained from her face as she stared at her hands resting on the table.

In contrast, Niki was holding up his hand like a teacher trying to hold back the runaway enthusiasm of his class. 'Look, do I need to point out the obvious? This will be absolutely crawling with both soldiers and Overseer units. Even undercover you'd have a hard time keeping a low profile.'

'Oh, come on, this is a rare opportunity,' I said. 'Just think of the upside. Our world needs friends. And that's the last thing those aliens on-board that craft will be thinking humans are right now, after being shot down by a TR-3B. We have an opportunity here to show them what the other side of our humanity looks like – and that we're really worth helping as a species.'

'As noble as that sentiment is, I'm afraid it simply can't happen,' Alice said, breaking her silence.

'But why?' I asked.

Jack nodded. 'What are you thinking here, Alice?'

'We simply can't afford to lose anyone on what would be a highly speculative mission chasing an unknown outcome. Our priority has to be locating the next waking micro mind.'

'With all due respect, Alice, I think you're missing the point here,' Lucy said. 'Yes, of course, it's essential we recover the next fragment of my AI matrix. But it also makes an awful lot of sense to cultivate potential alliances where we can, despite the calculated risks.'

Alice drummed her fingers on the arm of her wheelchair, avoiding eye contact with anyone. 'Calculated risks is just a euphemism for throwing people's lives away. And as much as I value your opinions, this is still my decision. I'm not prepared to take the risk.'

I traded frowns with the others round the table, with the notable exception of Niki, who still had his professional mask in place. Instinct told me this had little to do with the risk profile of this mission – not when it had so many upsides. No, this was about Alice's scare in Ariel when she'd frozen. That experience was now clouding her decision-making. Which meant that I needed to tackle this situation with a considerable amount of tact and sensitivity.

I leant towards her. 'Look, Alice, I know you mean well, but, as the saying goes, you can't make an omelette without cracking a few eggs.'

Jack nodded. 'We have headed into previous missions knowing just how potentially dangerous they've been, but that didn't stop us from doing them anyway.'

'I agree – and I'm not exactly hero material,' Mike said. 'But even I can see that we wouldn't be where we are now if we hadn't all been prepared to face the risks when necessary.'

The smile that Jodie flashed him was even wider this time.

Alice folded her arms across her chest. 'And I'm the one responsible for your lives. I'm afraid I've mentally run the numbers and I'm telling you that this mission simply isn't worth it.'

Jodie spread her hands wide. 'But, Alice, you must see—'

Alice slammed her palm down on the table. 'Oh, for god's sake! I've made my decision. Will you all stop trying to undermine me?' Alice reversed her chair away and disappeared through the door in a matter of seconds as we all traded stunned looks.

Jack whistled when the door closed. 'What the hell was that about?'

Ruby chewed her gum and shrugged. 'She certainly seemed stressed about something.'

Every set of eyes turned to me, but I wasn't going to reveal Alice's secrets.

I crossed my arms. 'Hey, why are you all looking at me? I don't know anything.'

Niki rotated his coffee cup between his fingers. 'That was quite an overreaction on Alice's part.'

'Surely you can see the sense of sending a team in, Niki?' Jack asked.

He nodded. 'I can. As has already been said, this is a rare opportunity to gain a powerful ally in the defence of Earth. But Alice is right too – there is a risk element we can't ignore either.'

'But, Captain, it couldn't hurt to put feet on the ground with the strict understanding not to engage,' Ruby said.

Niki sighed. 'You haven't been deployed with these guys on a mission yet, have you?'

'No, sir, I haven't. And?'

'I can tell you now that following orders isn't exactly their strongest suit, and I'm sure they wouldn't disagree.'

'Hey, we simply adapt according to the circumstances,' I said.

Jack nodded. 'Niki, you're ex-military, right?'

'Yes, I've seen my fair share of action in the past. Why?'

'So you know you have to be flexible when you're on the ground. That is and has always been the reality of the best military strategies. They tend to go to pieces on a first encounter with a real enemy. If Tom were here, I am certain he would say the same.'

'Maybe so, but I can also guarantee,' he said, making air quotes with his fingers, 'that *flexibility* in interpreting orders will only make Alice less inclined to send you in to investigate.'

'OK, so if you can't trust us, then put together a security team and send them instead,' I said.

'Do you really think Alice would even agree to that right now?'

I sighed. 'No, she probably wouldn't. But are you saying you're at least a little bit on-board with a team going there?'

Niki narrowed his eyes on me. 'Maybe.'

'Then pretty please with icing and sprinkles on top,' Lucy said from her screen.

He held up his hands. 'OK, OK, leave it with me. I'll see what I can do.'

Although I nodded with everyone else, I wasn't sure Niki would get anywhere with Alice either. As a plan B, I was already plotting how to best tackle her in private. Her personal issues were getting in the way of a real opportunity to make a difference in saving our world. And there was absolutely no way I could stand by and let that happen.

CHAPTER TEN

I STRETCHED out in my small room, trying to let the calming blue ambient lighting wind me down a bit from my latest run-in with Alice. I'd also selected the most soothing screensaver I could find in Delphi's databanks and a gentle lapping sea was displayed on the video screen that filled the whole end wall of my room. I lobbed a crisp – or chip as Jack kept telling me to call them – from the huge supersized bag I'd helped myself to from one of the food stores – comfort food always helped me to destress. It landed as intended, right in front of the small robotic vacuum cleaner that'd just appeared from a rectangular slot in the wall. Without a complaint it spun towards the crisp and hoovered it up, leaving no trace.

I tipped my head back, resting it against the wall, and worked my neck muscles with my fingers, trying to untangle the tense knots.

I should have been out there trying to track that crashed UFO down, not sitting on my bum here. This was so bloody frustrating. I raised my face towards the speaker unit built into the ceiling. 'Delphi, retrieve latest images from Tic Tac crash site area.'

'Commencing retrieval,' Delphi replied.

The whole end wall changed from the beach scene to a series of images. They flashed up one on top of the other so fast that I couldn't make any of them out. Despite refining the search criteria regarding information about the Tic Tac, Delphi still managed to trawl up thousands of pictures every day. As I had done for several days now, I would have to wade through them manually.

A knock came from my door.

'Hey, Lauren, it's Jack.'

I swung my legs off my bed and sat up, hiding the crisp packet under my pillow. 'It's not locked.'

The door swung open and Jack stood there, hovering on the threshold. His gaze was immediately drawn to the images flashing on the screen wall. 'Still looking for a way to change Alice's mind?'

'I have to, Jack. Whether she realises it or not, she's so made the wrong call on this.'

'I know she has, but I'd tread carefully with her.'

'What's that meant to mean?'

Jack gestured to the walls of my room. 'Well, you sitting in here is evidence of just how well your previous attempts to tackle her have worked out.'

He wasn't wrong. I'd tried every tactic, from counselling Alice in private about her past crash trauma to cajoling her in front of everyone. I had discussed the subject of the downed Tic Tac at every opportunity. Today, two whole days after the crash, I'd pushed my luck too far.

I'd been trying to guilt Alice into letting us go, but her expression had only grown ever harder. That was the straw that had finally broken the camel's back. Way too calmly, she'd announced that she'd like us all to move out of her house and into the staff accommodation wing. She'd said she needed to concentrate uninterrupted on her own work. The truth was, and we all knew it, she'd just had enough of me being in her face and couldn't take any more.

As Jack gazed at me, waiting for an answer, I resisted the urge to grab the chocolate bar that was hidden in my drawer.

I sighed. 'I know, I know, but investigating that downed Tic Tac is important, Jack.'

'Yes, I know it is, but you do realise it's probably already too late. The Overseers will almost certainly have had the wreckage moved by now.'

'Maybe they have, or maybe they haven't,' I said. 'The strange thing is, there's still a military cordon in place. Why would they do that if they've already recovered it?'

'I see your point. But good luck in changing Alice's mind.'

I made a *humphing* sound. 'Talk about someone digging in their heels.'

'Says you, Miss Stubborn. Although I'd always had Alice pegged as someone who listened to people around her. But on this she's beyond paranoid. If anyone could make her see sense, it would be Tom.' He drummed his fingers on the frame. 'I just wish I knew what had got into her. Alice hasn't come as far as she has in life without taking a few risks.'

I had to bite my tongue once again, as I'd done constantly since we'd got back from the test flight. The trauma of our near crash had obviously badly shaken Alice and the reason for her current attitude was rooted in her original crash in *Suzie Q*. That was still a private matter, despite my annoyance with Alice. The only person I could talk to about it was Lucy.

Almost on cue, her voice came out of the speaker. 'I didn't want to interrupt, but I could try talking to Alice if you like,'

Lucy said. 'After all, I can hack my way into any system in Eden, so it would be hard for her to ignore me.'

'Hey, have you been listening to our conversation all this time?' Jack asked.

'What do you think?'

'I hope you give us some privacy most of the time at least,' I said.

'I don't tend to listen in whilst you're on the loo, if that's what you mean?'

'Thanks for that small mercy,' Jack said. 'But as I just said to Lauren, I would leave Alice well alone for now. Anyway, Alice may be *our* boss, but she certainly isn't yours. There's no reason why you couldn't take a quick jaunt over to Illinois to see if you can discover anything.'

I widened my eyes. I been so caught up in *us* going, I hadn't thought seriously about alternatives.

'That's genius, Jack,' I said, instantly warming to the idea. 'That could so work, Lucy, as long as you steer clear of any TR-3Bs hanging around.'

Lucy let out a dry laugh. 'I would if I could, but it turns out that the president of Sky Dreamer Corp. is as cunning as she's paranoid. Alice obviously anticipated that sort of move on my part. She issued an order to Delphi to keep all launch bay doors locked. They are only to be opened under her direct authorisation.'

'You mean your micro mind ship is trapped in the landing bay?' I asked.

'Absolutely. It's a complete pain in the bum.'

'Whoa there,' Jack said. 'We're talking about the all-knowing omnipotent super-being called Lucy. Surely you could just hack Delphi's systems and open the launch bay doors yourself?'

'I could, but that doesn't mean that I should, Jack. If I took that step it would be a direct challenge to Alice's authority. I thought we were in the business of building up a relationship based on mutual trust here?'

'Yes, of course we are,' I replied, although in my current mood I was tempted to say to hell with the consequences.

'Maybe she'll come round eventually, especially when she's had time to think it through,' Jack said.

'Well, it's already been two days and she doesn't seem to be budging even the slightest,' I said. 'Quite the opposite, in fact.'

'I agree,' Lucy said. 'If anything, she's hardened her position on the matter. And at some point the Overseers will recover the Tic Tac and any alien alive or dead on-board. There is some news there. I'm afraid I believe they may be close to finding what they're looking for.'

'How could you know that?' Jack asked.

'Because...'

The images flashing on the wall screen started to slow down. I began to pick out soldiers and military vehicles as the photos skimmed past, many from social media feeds such as Instagram and Facebook.

'I've been keeping an eye on the searches you've had Delphi running, Lauren. As you can see, many of these photos were snapped by locals. And they've showed increased military activity in the area, not less. That suggests something has been found out in those woods – or they're close to doing so. If they get their hands on a downed Tic Tac, you can guarantee it won't stay there for long. We can't have much time to get to the crash site before they whisk it away.'

'Damn, this is so frustrating,' I said. 'We bloody well need to do something now.'

'Well, I've got another bit of information that may help. Delphi's search has just turned up something that might be enough to change Alice's mind.'

A fluttery feeling filled my stomach. 'Seriously? What is it?'

'This...' Lucy replied.

An Instagram image of a dark wood filled the screen. It took me a moment to spot a pale shape in the gloom as it disappeared behind a tree. It was a human-like figure with a large head and dark almond-shaped eyes.

I put my hands over my mouth. 'Oh my god,' I said through my fingers.

'Is that an alien?' Jack asked, his forehead ridging as he peered at the image.

I turned to him, my eyes wide. 'Abso-bloody-lutely. That's a Grey alien, the same species that's rumoured to have been on-board the crashed UFO at Roswell.'

'You've got to be kidding me?'

'Nope. That image fits every description there's ever been of them. But are you sure this isn't a fake, Lucy?'

'Checking that now...' Lots of tiny squares appeared over the image, flicking round like a swarm of flies. 'No, I'm not seeing any composite artefacts that would indicate this has been faked.'

'So not Photoshopped in other words?' Jack asked.

'Basically yes. Although this could, of course, be an elaborate piece of disinformation deliberately put out there by the Overseers. Perhaps a child dressed in a bodysuit. However, it's highly unlikely they would want this level of publicity. This photo will attract every UFO hunter in the whole world – the very last thing the Overseers will want at such a sensitive time.'

'Where and when was this taken?' Jack asked.

'Last night in an area called Egyptian Hills just to the south of Lake Crest.'

A buzzing sense of anticipation grew inside me. 'Have you got any more evidence we can put in front of Alice to try to change her mind?'

'Nothing yet, but I'll continue to keep an eye on Delphi's searches.'

'Then this will have do,' I said. 'Let's call a meeting with the team and show this to Alice. Maybe a united front from us will make her rethink her decision.'

'A genuine Grey sighting has to tip the balance,' Jack said. 'And if we managed to find the Tic Tac before the Overseers, it could change everything. Even Alice has to see that.'

I beamed at him. 'I've got a good feeling about this.'

'Yeah, me too.'

Together we headed for the door.

'Absolutely not!' Alice said as she sat at the head of the meeting-room table, once again staring me down.

'But how can you say no to this?' I said. 'We have what looks like a genuine sighting of a Grey – who presumably escaped the crashed Tic Tac. And you can bet the Overseers will be on its tail. We need to get in there and rescue it before they find it, or you can guarantee they'll disappear it away to whatever facility it is they use for studying these things.'

Mike nodded. 'And with so many people swarming into the area because of this sighting, we'd be a lot less conspicuous now.'

Niki placed the tips of his fingers together. 'Certainly from a mission-profile perspective this helps to reduce the risk.'

'But not completely,' Alice said. 'And with the exception of Ruby, Lauren's team will all be on the Overseers' watch list.'

'Maybe so, but they'll be expecting them to turn up at the micro mind site, not chasing an alien sighting,' Jodie said.

Alice nodded. 'Exactly.'

I gave her a puzzled look. 'I'm not sure I follow.'

'They won't be expecting you there because it's not your team's priority, whereas locating the next micro mind is. That's my point.'

'OK then, how about this,' Jack said. 'Rather than us, Niki could send another security team in to recover the alien, as we've discussed before.'

But Niki was already shaking his head. 'We're already fully stretched with our intelligence-gathering missions as we try to locate the next micro mind.'

I nodded. 'Then it'll have to be us.'

Alice crossed her arms. 'So what would you have me do? Give up on trying to find the next micro mind, so you can go alien hunting? Or do I have my priorities the wrong way round here? You tell me.'

I glowered at her. 'You're making this an either/or decision. But it doesn't have to be like that. You could even just send one person.'

'It's got to be worth a shot,' Ruby said.

'No, this conversation is already over,' Alice replied. 'We need to keep focused on the bigger priorities. The chances of you successfully finding this Grey are minimal, especially as the Overseers already have the whole area crawling with military. Never mind the other UFO hunters looking for it out there.'

I felt my face growing cold as a simmering feeling of fury started to take hold of me again. 'You don't know that, Alice. Besides, we have Lucy on our side. She has to tip the odds in our favour of us finding that Grey before anyone else.'

Alice gave me a hard stare. 'And what it Lucy gets shot down? As so nearly happened in the encounter with the Astra fleet? Do you really want to chase a whim and endanger this entire world's future?'

The chill turned to heat in my blood as I stood up and leant my hands on the table. 'You know full bloody well this has nothing to do with a whim. I'm sorry, but you're letting your personal feelings get in the way of your decision-making process.'

The colour drained from Alice's face as she stared at me.

Everyone's eyes flicked between us as if we were two tennis players on a court smashing the ball at each other.

A ruby blush began to spread up Alice's throat towards her ears. She gave me the barest headshake, turned her wheelchair round and disappeared out through the door. This had so become a thing of hers – to leave a room when she was in the middle of an argument.

But as I watched her go, a bubble of guilt rose up through me, despite my anger. I knew I shouldn't have mentioned her personal feelings, but I couldn't help myself. Now there'd be no hope of getting Alice to reverse her decision.

'Can someone tell me what just happened?' Niki asked, peering at me.

'You'd better take it up with Alice,' I replied, trying to avoid his searchlight gaze.

'I see...then if you'll excuse me, I'm going to see what I can do in terms of damage limitation.' Niki got up and walked after Alice.

'Well, that went well,' Lucy said from her monitor screen.

'But we can't just sit by and let that Grey be captured,' Mike said.

'Then we do something,' Lucy said.

'How exactly?' Jack asked. 'It's not as if we can get out of here.'

'I know Ariel is out of commission, but what if we borrowed another craft?' Mike asked.

'As speed is of the essence, we would be better off in an X101 rather than an Armadillo. Just saying,' Ruby said, a slow smile filling her face.

'That would be great apart from the fact Alice has all the landing bay doors locked down,' Jack said.

'A well-placed C4 charge could sort that out,' Mike said.

'Hey, respect, buddy,' Ruby said as she fist-bumped him.

'No one is bloody blowing anything up around here,' I said.

'Tsk, tsk, will everyone please calm down?' Lucy said. 'Look, the locked bay doors won't be a problem if we really are going to do this.'

My eyes snapped to her. 'But what about everything you said about building trust?'

'Oh, Lauren, I'll burn that bridge if I have to – if you are determined to do this. And with all due respect to my AI sister, Delphi, I can easily hack round her security protocols. I can also give you full access to any craft you want to take for this little day trip.'

'You *can*, but do you really think that you *should*, Lucy?' Mike asked.

'Well, gorgeous, of course I do. But this decision has to be everybody's.'

I looked at us all gathered round the table. 'What do you say, guys? Let's see a show of hands if you think we should do it...'

Hand after hand went up, including Lucy's, until we finally got to Ruby.

She chewed her gum. 'You realise I'm not exactly thrilled to be disobeying Alice, or Niki, who is effectively my commanding officer?'

'I don't think I heard anyone issue you a direct order, Niki included,' Jodie said, smiling.

'Hey, good point.' A grin filled Ruby's face and she stuck her hand up. 'Let's do this, *amigos*.'

CHAPTER ELEVEN

WE HEADED along the red-painted corridor that indicated this was a restricted area, with Ruby and Mike taking the lead and Jack and me at the rear. Jodie had gone off, saying she had something we should take on the mission with us.

I felt certain that my supposedly relaxed expression was actually shouting, *Hey, look at us, we're about to steal an X101!* But apart from the odd nod and smile from a couple of technicians we ran into, no one tried to grab any of us in an attempt at a citizen's arrest.

We'd already stopped off at the weapons locker and suitably equipped ourselves. Mike had insisted on bringing a dart gun, nothing lethal as he had a strong moral aversion to killing anyone, to which Ruby had raised her eyebrows. I had my trusty Mossad .22 LRS pistol for whatever we might run into. Ruby had given me a look of respect. She'd helped herself to a sniper rifle that broke down into parts and was now stowed in her rucksack. According to her, with it she could shoot the ''nads off a gnat at eight hundred yards'. That probably wasn't an idle boast, coming from her, our very own weapon expert.

I immediately tensed as I spotted a surveillance camera pointing straight at us when we reached a junction in the corridor.

'Lucy, please tell me you've got that camera sorted?' I said into a discreet mic clipped on the collar of my jacket.

'Yes, all over it like a bad case of nappy rash,' she replied through the earbud I was wearing. The small electronic device was placed so deep into my ear canal, no one else would notice it with a casual look.

'How so exactly?' Jack asked. He and the others were wearing matching earbuds, set to a private channel to avoid anyone eaves-dropping.

'Right now anyone from Niki's team who happens to be looking at that camera's feed will see nothing but an empty corri-dor,' Lucy replied. There was a pause. 'Ah...'

'Don't *ah* us! What is it?' I asked.

'You're about to get company. Two guards are heading straight towards the junction you're nearing from the left-hand side.'

Ruby glanced back at me. 'Will you guys please look more chilled? Otherwise they'll know something is off right away. What did the hurricane say to the coconut tree?'

'Huh?' Jack said.

'You heard me. What did the hurricane say to the coconut tree?'

We all gave Ruby a blank look.

She grinned at us. 'Hold on to your nuts – this ain't no ordi-nary blow job.'

Mike and Jack laughed hard as the two security guards rounded the corner. The taller of the two stuck his hand up to stop us as they approached our group.

'Hey, you shouldn't be down here unless you've had security clearance.'

Still grinning, Ruby turned back towards him. 'Hey, Alex, my man. It's all cool. I'm doing some X101 training with the newbies here.' She hitched her thumb back over her shoulder at the rest of us.

Role playing or not, I had to suppress a spike of irritation. I'd give her *newbies*.

'Don't tell me, you haven't bothered to fill in the paperwork?' the shorter guy said.

I recognised him as one of Ruby's drinking buddies from the Rock Garden.

'Nope, sorry, Craig. But I promise I'll do it immediately afterwards.'

'I'll still need to see some sort of authorisation, or you know Niki will give me hell.'

'I'm on it,' Lucy whispered into our ears. 'Get him to check on his radio for a security clearance.'

Ruby gave the guards a straight look. 'Just call it in and you'll see we've got clearance.'

Craig nodded and unclipped his radio. 'Hey, I have Ruby and three others from her team in Launch Bay Twelve. Have they got authorisation to be down here?'

'That's affirmative,' Niki's voice replied. 'All part of a training exercise.'

Jack traded a discreet wide-eyed glance with me.

'OK, understood,' Craig said.

Ruby crossed her arms. 'Told you.'

'Yeah, you did. So go and knock yourself out with an X101. What were you all laughing about just now?'

'Oh, that old joke about coconut trees and blow jobs.'

Both security guards laughed. 'Same old Ruby.'

'Yep, that's me,' she replied, grinning. She snapped a mock salute as we headed past them.

Despite the smile I managed to give both men I only felt

myself relaxing when we rounded the corner and were out of their view.

'Lucy, that was one hell of a good impression of Niki,' Mike said into his lapel mic.

'Yep, I am so multitalented I should be on the stage,' Lucy replied.

'Maybe you should,' Mike said, shaking his head at us.

At the end of the red corridor was a heavy-duty circular blast-style door with the number twenty-three stencilled across it in white. Next to it was an electronic security pad. We hadn't even reached it when the numbers on the pad started lighting up by themselves.

'Let me deal with the door for you,' Lucy said.

A moment later clonking came from the lock and the door rolled sideways, disappearing into the wall.

'Nicely done, Lucy,' I said.

'No problem at all, my little sunflower.'

Ruby snorted.

I glowered at the back of Ruby's neck as we stepped through the doorway into a circular launch bay. The door rolled back into place and the locking mechanism clunked.

On the landing pads at the bottom of the launch shaft before us stood two X101s, the high-speed reconnaissance electric-powered aircraft of Sky Dreamer Corp. The nearest one had its cargo doors already open. There was a third craft on a landing pad too: an Armadillo, a heavily armoured and larger variant.

'I would say take an Armadillo,' Ruby said, 'but as speed really is of the essence we'd better go for an X101,' Ruby said. She gestured towards a large closed metal door to the side of the launch bay. 'That's the store containing kit needed for field missions. Lucy, any chance you can deal with its lock too?'

'Do you really need to ask?' Lucy replied.

There was a clanking sound and the heavy metal door swung open.

'Now, if you'll excuse me, I need to set to work on opening that launch bay door,' Lucy said.

'Great, I'll get the X101 ready for take-off whilst you guys go and grab what you need,' Ruby replied.

Jack leant towards me. 'Just remind me who is in charge of this mission?'

'Don't worry, I can so handle her,' I replied, but I knew I might have an issue on my hands. Ruby was exactly the sort of person to take over given half the chance. But, as I'd learnt from the Machu Picchu mission, I needed to find a balance between listening and telling people what to do. Leaning too far one way or the other would piss people off.

I turned to Jack and Mike. 'Let's get loaded up. We need to be ready for anything.'

They both nodded as we walked into the store. Much to my delight, inside were racks of equipment filled with every type of clothing imaginable, from body armour to wetsuits and everything in between. There were also racks of field rations and extensive medical kits. At the back of the store, behind a very solid steel door, were boxes of extra ammo and heavy steel containers full of grenades.

'This place is a prepper's dream,' Jack said, gesturing at everything around us.

'Isn't that the truth?' Mike's eyes widened as he spotted a rack of Zero motorbikes. 'We've got to take those with us.'

'Any excuse to be back on two wheels again, hey?' Jack asked.

Mike grinned. 'Pretty much.'

'Well, you won't get any arguments from me,' I said. 'The Zeros more than proved their worth on our last mission.'

We loaded four of the bikes on to the X101, along with the accompanying high-tech HUD helmets. We rummaged around the store further, and I had to do my best not to pack enough for a six-month expedition.

Jack gave me a look when I picked up a cooking stove. 'Lauren, seriously. This isn't a camping trip. Or were you planning to make the alien a cup of your famous British tea when we meet him?'

'There is no situation that a cup of tea isn't perfect for,' I said as I put the stove back. Instead, I settled for grabbing a box of energy bars and a crate of water bottles.

I also discovered Tom's disguise kits and loaded up with enough for all of us.

By now, the rear loading bay of the X101 was almost groaning with kit. I was seriously starting to wonder if our craft would even be able to take off.

Ruby appeared and stared at the mountain of stuff we'd managed to cram in. She shook her head.

'Hey, it's always good to be prepared,' I said, reading her disapproving expression.

'For you guys maybe, but all I need is a good sniper rifle and a ghillie suit and I'm gold.'

'A ghillie what?' Mike asked.

'Basically it's a camo suit that makes the person wearing it look like a walking bush,' Jack explained.

'Hey, buddy, don't knock it,' Ruby said. 'With it on I'm almost impossible to spot.'

I raised my eyebrows. 'We'll take your word for it.'

'You should because your lives will probably depend on it at some point,' Ruby said. She turned on her heel and headed for the cockpit.

'Is it just me or is she really starting to give you some serious attitude, Lauren?' Mike asked.

'No, not just you,' I replied with a sigh.

'Like I said before, I wouldn't stress about it,' Jack said. 'She'll come round soon enough. Ruby's the sort of soldier you need to win the respect of, that's all.'

'I just hope that's actually humanly possible for anyone.'

'Hey, we believe in you, and so will Ruby.'

'Thanks for the vote of confidence.'

Jack smiled at me. 'Any time—' His gaze snapped past me to a door opening.

I spun round, expecting to see a team of security guards heading towards us. Much to my relief it was just Jodie carrying a small case.

She walked over and handed it to me. 'Can you make sure Ruby gets this?'

'Yes, no problem.'

'Thanks.' She turned to Mike. 'Hey, can we have a quick word?'

'Of course...'

He unclipped his mic before following her over to the store. He obviously didn't want Lucy to listen into their conversation. Soon he and Jodie were out of earshot of us, facing each other, locked into what looked like an intense discussion.

'What's that's about?' Jack asked.

'What do you think?' I replied.

I saw Mike drop his head, his shoulders sagging. But Jodie reached out and squeezed his arm, then give him a quick peck on the cheek.

'Oh, thank god for that, it looks as if they've made peace at last,' Jack said.

'Hmmm,' Lucy said over our earbuds.

'Please just keep your nose out,' I said to the AI.

'Maybe I will, or maybe I won't. We'll just have to see.'

Jack shook his head at me.

'Oh hell, here we go,' Lucy said.

An instant sense of foreboding filled me. 'What's wrong this time, Lucy?'

'Niki, along with those two security guards you ran into, are heading this way. They must have reported back to Niki and he's realised what we're doing.'

'Then get that bloody launch door open already, Lucy.'

'Sorry, Delphi is putting up quite a stiff fight and it's taking longer than I expected to get past the door's lockdown controls. But I should crack them any second now. The better news is that I've already managed to infiltrate the X101 systems and it's ready for take-off.'

Mike must have heard the exchange via his earbud and was already running back over towards the X101.

A thumping sound came from the door and I looked to see Niki glaring at us through its round glass window. I shook my head at him and leapt with the others into the X101's cabin. Next Ruby was hitting a button and the cabin door hissed closed behind us.

The virtual cockpit was already up and running as we locked ourselves into our harnesses.

I looked at the view of the launch bay projected on to the walls, past Jodie, who had her hand raised in farewell, and towards the door leading out to the corridor.

'Delphi, get ready for immediate launch,' Ruby said.

'I can't comply. Launch bay door is closed.'

'Hurry up with that, Lucy – we're running out of time,' I said.

'Nagging won't help, but I'm nearly there...'

On the virtual cockpit I saw a flicker of flame burst through the door.

'Goddammit, Niki had the foresight to bring a cutting torch with him,' Ruby muttered.

I drummed my foot on the floor as the flame, flickering

molten metal, reached the top of the door and started to move sideways.

'Lucy?' I said.

'I know, I know.'

The red line of melted metal reached the next corner and started downwards.

'At this rate we'll be caught on the ground before we've even had a chance to take off,' Jack said.

'Really not helping,' Lucy said.

The red line turned the final corner and sped back towards its starting point. I tapped my foot faster as the section of door toppled forward and crashed on to the hangar floor with a huge clang.

Gloved hands appeared and the door was rolled away. Niki and the two guards came charging into the launch bay. Jodie headed straight towards them, waving her arms to try to stop them reaching our craft. But Niki pushed her aside, running now towards our X101.

'Lucy, seriously!' Mike said.

'And I've cracked it, gorgeous,' she replied.

Above us the launch door started to slide open.

'Prepare for an emergency launch, Delphi,' Ruby said.

'Launch procedure initiated,' the X101's inbuilt AI system replied.

With a whir of electric motors the stubby wings pivoted to a vertical position.

Niki had already reached our craft and was pounding on the door. 'Don't do this!' his muffled voice shouted.

'Cleared to launch,' Ruby said without so much as blinking.

'Launching now,' Delphi replied.

The electric motors whined and with a shudder our craft began to rise.

On the cabin's screens I saw Niki stumble back as the

shrouded prop wind wash began to buffet him. One of the guards raised a pistol, but Niki slapped it down whilst shouting something. Niki pointed to the Armadillo on the launch pad and he and his guards raced to it just as our X101 rose quickly up the shaft towards the now open exit.

Adrenaline tanged my mouth as Niki and the guards jumped into the other plane. Even as we cleared the exit and started to rise above the jungle, the Armadillo had already begun to lift into the air.

'Jesus, they're going to catch us,' Mike said, staring at the pursuing craft as it rose fast beneath us.

But then suddenly the other craft stopped and began to descend.

'What, they've given up?' Jack asked.

'Actually, that will be down to me,' Lucy said in a smug tone over the cabin's speaker system. 'I just overrode the Delphi AI controlling their ship – and for good measure...'

The landing bay door started to slide closed beneath us, shutting off the view of the launch bay. Over the jungle Lucy's glowing micro mind craft appeared from another silo half a mile to the right, rising quickly into the sky.

'I've completely hacked Delphi's systems. Nobody will be able to open those bay doors for days,' Lucy said.

'Has anyone ever told you that you're an utter superstar?' I said.

'Nothing like enough, but it's good to hear even occasionally,' she replied as her micro mind craft glided up alongside us. 'Oh, and get ready for a head rush. I'm going to extend my antigravity field and give you a lift. That way we can get you there in about twenty minutes.'

'You mean we could have stolen the Armadillo after all?' Ruby said.

'Whoops, sorry, my bad. Anyway, I thought this was meant to be a stealth mission...'

'It is,' I replied, giving Ruby a straight look before checking over my LRS pistol. But you could never be too prepared, especially when we were talking about one of our missions.

CHAPTER TWELVE

A SILVERY LAKE was just coming into view ahead of us on the horizon. Jack, Mike, Ruby and I were strapped into our seats as Lucy controlled our craft to avoid Delphi attempting a mutiny. Her micro mind ship was flying alongside us, both craft having been fully cloaked since we'd fled Eden, including a fully operational chameleon cloak for the X101. For the first time I was able to fully appreciate the cloak's abilities.

'Lucy, are you absolutely sure there's no sign of pursuit?' I asked.

Her face appeared in a window overlaid on the display of the landscape close to me.

'For the hundredth time I'm still not detecting even a hint of anyone coming after us.'

Ruby looked up from her Glock as she cleaned it with a barrel brush. 'Even if they do manage to somehow launch a pursuit vehicle, we've got a major head start thanks to Lucy giving us a tow. They won't catch us any time soon unless they decide to use Ariel, and we all know that's not going to happen.'

Mike nodded. 'And don't forget our last present to them. Quite a genius move on your part, Lucy.'

This time her video window popped up on the wall next to Mike's head. She beamed at him. 'It's going to take considerable time for them to get past the code I implemented to keep those launch bay doors locked.' She finished by actually fluttering her eyelashes at him.

Jack exchanged a knowing look with me. Lucy hadn't stopped flirting with Mike from the moment we'd boarded the X101.

Ruby blew down the length of her Glock's barrel to clear it after her work with a cleaning brush. 'Don't forget that even if they do manage to launch anything, we've disabled our location beacon. We're running dark for the duration of this mission.'

Jack frowned. 'They may not know where we are exactly, but they'll have a damned good idea of the general area we're heading towards.'

'Maybe, but by the time they catch up with us we'll hopefully have already rescued the Grey, which makes the rest academic,' I said.

Mike, who had finally mastered his airsickness from the magic carpet view, peered over at me. 'I don't want to sound pessimistic, but you really think we have a chance of pulling that off?'

'We have more than a fighting chance with Lucy with us.'

Lucy's video window popped up next to me again. 'Thank you for your vote of confidence, Lauren. Just remember that the next time I manage to upset you about something.'

'I'll do my best to keep it in mind.'

I gazed out at the mountain ranges of cloud skimming past below us, blindingly white in the sunshine. An intense azure-blue sky surrounded us. It was eerily silent as Lucy had shut down our electric motors as she gave us a tow. They were pointless whilst we were enveloped in Lucy's gravity field.

Opposite me, Jack cracked open an eye. He'd been sleeping for most of the trip so far. 'So what's the plan when we arrive, Lauren?'

'My instinct is to head to the Buck Ridge Campground near where the Grey was spotted,' I replied.

'But won't that area be swarming with UFO hunters and the military by now?'

'Probably, but that will hopefully mean no one will pay us too much attention. However, just in case we do run into an Overseer agent...' I dragged out my bag from beneath my seat.

Jack's eyes immediately narrowed on it. 'That's a disguise kit, isn't it?'

'Yes. As Niki said, if there are Overseers there already, we can't risk being recognised.'

'Makes sense to me,' Ruby said. It sounded dangerously like a compliment. 'So what look have you got in mind for me, boss?'

I opened the bag and tossed her a spiky blonde wig. 'I thought you might go for a sort of grunge-rock look. There's a nose ring too if you want it.'

That actually raised a smile from her. 'No way. It'll be the first thing an enemy would grab hold of and yank out. The hair will do just fine.'

'Dare I ask what you were thinking for me?' Jack asked. 'Please tell me it doesn't involve a ponytail!'

I traded a grin with Lucy who was watching from her video window. She'd surreptitiously helped me work out everyone's disguises during the flight, showing me mock ups on my Sky Wire. I'd had to bite back a laugh several times about the more hilarious ideas that she'd come up with.

'Oh, Lucy and I thought you'd really rock a wild-man-of-the-woods look. It comes complete with a bushy beard and straggly hair.' I tossed Jack the hairpieces and he caught them.

He gave me and then Lucy a suspicious look. 'Why do I get the feeling that you two are having fun at my expense?'

'That's pure paranoia,' Lucy said, giving me a theatrical wink.

Mike grimaced. 'And what about me, or don't I want to know?'

'Oh, don't you worry, handsome,' Lucy said. 'Your look is all down to me. I know it's going to suit you as I ran several thousand combinations in a simulation so I would choose the right disguise.'

I shrugged at Mike as I passed him a neat beard and slicked-back brown wig.

'A hipster look, seriously?' he said, examining them.

'Oh, that is so you, buddy,' Jack said, trying to suppress a smirk.

'I'm not sure that's a compliment,' Mike replied.

'Ignore him, he's only jealous,' Lucy said.

Ruby shook her head as she slipped her Glock back into her shoulder holster. 'You guys are a regular riot.'

'So people keep telling me,' I said, raising an eyebrow at her.

I returned my attention to the view on the wall screens. Through breaks in the cloud far below, Lake Crest was now visible, clearly labelled by a useful overlay. The tag next to it indicated we were less than ten nautical miles away.

'OK, as we're not that far out now, time to get your disguises on,' I said.

The others nodded and we started to get ready. I raised my head towards Lucy's pop-up window. 'Have you managed to locate a landing site yet?'

'Yes, I've been scouting suitable locations towards the southern end of the lake, near the campsite where the Grey was spotted. However, I'm picking up a lot of heat signatures from people crowding the immediate area, so we'll have to land a couple of miles away in an isolated creek. Once we land, I'll keep the X101 prepped so you can make a rapid escape if needed.'

'Good. We should also have a backup plan in place in the event of anyone getting captured.'

'We won't if I have anything to do with it,' Ruby said as she pulled on her spiky wig.

'Without taking anything away from your skills, Ruby, we still need to cover every eventuality,' I replied. 'Lucy, if anything happens to us, you're to head straight back to Eden. Ultimately, we're expendable, but you absolutely aren't. You need to keep yourself hidden and look after the X101. We don't want you falling into the wrong hands.'

'I don't entirely agree with you, but I'll play ball. I'll patch in a secure channel on your Sky Wire phones, so if you need backup you can just whistle for me. I'll also keep an eye out in case Alice somehow manages to send anyone after us.'

Jack winced. 'You do know there's going to be hell to pay when we do get back?'

'Yes, I know, but that's just the cost of an essential mission – even if Alice doesn't realise it.'

Mike sucked the air through his teeth. 'Maybe it is, but I do worry she'll take us all off active missions after this.'

'Don't be so sure about that,' Lucy said. 'You're all absolutely essential to helping me recover the rest of micro minds. Besides, if Alice is foolish enough to act out on this then I'll simply go on strike until she sees sense.'

'And if she calls your bluff?' Ruby asked.

'Who says I'm bluffing?'

'Got it. Respect.' Ruby made an OK symbol with her thumb and finger.

We started to slow as the lake slid below us. A slight shudder passed through the craft as the wings rotated and we began to descend towards it.

I could just about see that the lake was bounded by a small hamlet of houses towards its northern end. The southern tip was surrounded by woodland, meaning lots of cover for an alien to hide out. A number of small boats were out on the water. Pop-up windows appeared over each of them with a magnified view of the people in the boats. But none of the occupants even glanced towards the sky as we flew directly over them. Our chameleon camouflage was obviously doing a very effective job.

'OK, guys, five minutes to touchdown,' Lucy said.

'Then let's finish getting these disguises on,' I said. 'We'll make this mission such a success that Alice will question why she ever doubted us.'

'Amen to that, boss,' Ruby said as she checked the ammo for her Glock in a spare clip. She slid it into a pocket in her hunting-style khaki trousers and looked through the rucksack containing her sniper rifle.

We picked our way through a pine wood, ascending the slope. I was pretty happy with my disguise – I could have got used to my blonde hippie look. However, I was finding it hard not to laugh every time I caught sight of Jack in his wild man beard and checked shirt. I'd was sorely tempted to sing Monty Python's 'The Lumberjack Song', but I suspected it might go right over his head, as it did for most people my age. I owed my cultural enlightenment to Steve – my old boss at Jodrell Bank. He'd been the one who'd first introduced me to the delights of Monty Python during our movie nights. Not for the first time I wondered what Steve would think if he could see me now.

The scent of pine needles filled my nose and small flies buzzed in the woodland's languid heat. Every so often the rattle of a woodpecker drumming on a tree echoed through the woods. There was a sense of stillness but also anticipation, or maybe that was just me projecting my own mood on to the forest.

We were following the GPS marker for the Buck Ridge Campground on my Sky Wire phone, which Lucy had helpfully placed on it. The X101 had landed at the end of a small creek, and Ruby had left the craft fully stealthed. With the chameleon mode running you could only see a slight refraction in the air. I just hoped a bird didn't decide to perch on the basically invisible aircraft and blow its cover.

Voices drifted between the trees from the top of the ridge ahead of us.

I glanced at the map and raised a fist in the air to halt the group, as trained by Niki. 'The campsite is up there. That whole area is crawling with people, according to Lucy's thermal cameras as we came into land.'

'The question is whether they're military, and in cahoots with the Overseers, or UFO hunters,' Jack said.

'To play it safe, let me scout ahead and find out?' Ruby asked. 'I'll radio back if there's anything to be worried about.'

'Good idea – go ahead and we'll follow.' I appreciated the fact that for once she'd asked rather than just told me what she was doing.

Ruby nodded, adjusted the straps on her rucksack and jogged away up the slope on the balls of her feet, almost completely silent.

We started forward again. I peered at every shadow under the pine trees in case in there was a set of alien eyes watching us. But what if we did find the Grey? We hadn't really discussed what we'd do. Was an *ignore the rest of humanity, we come in peace* speech really going to cut it with an intelligent being that would probably be scared witless?

Men's voices came from somewhere in the woods just ahead,

much closer than before. I held up a fist signal, and everyone stopped behind me.

'I have eyes on two hunters closing in on your position,' Ruby said through my earbud.

'Understood,' I replied.

'It might be worth finding out if they know anything about the sighting of the alien or even the crashed Tic Tac,' Mike said.

'We've certainly got nothing to lose,' I said as the voices grew steadily louder.

A moment later the two men appeared, traipsing through the woods down a slope almost directly towards us, rifles slung over their backs and both wearing baseball caps. Their body language said they were exhausted – heads down, shoulders hunched forward.

'Just so you know, I have eyes on them if they decide to get fresh with those hunting rifles,' Ruby said over the Sky Wire link.

'Good to know,' I replied. I stepped forward and raised my hand in greeting. 'Hi there, how's it going?' I said in my best attempt at a neutral American accent.

The eyes of the heavily built guy snapped towards me. He had a bushy beard big enough to rival Jack's false one. The skinny guy narrowed his eyes on us with a calculating look, as if measuring us up.

I lowered my hand close to my holster beneath my shirt. But when neither of the two guys went for their rifles, I let my hand fall away.

There was a long, uncomfortable pause before the guy with the impressive beard made a throat-clearing gurgle and spat something green on the ground. 'Yeah, we're good.' His brow wrinkled. 'Don't suppose you've seen it?'

'Seen what?' Mike asked with wide-eyed innocence and with something almost resembling a Brooklyn accent.

The men exchanged glances and chuckled. 'Yeah, right, buddy. As though you're not up here for the bounty.'

Now this was new information. 'Bounty?' I asked, stepping towards them.

'Oh, come on, why act all so innocent?'

'No really, what bounty?' Jack asked.

'But you're looking for that damned varmint too, right? You're just another one of those nutter UFO teams that have been crawling all over these woods?'

'If you mean are we interested in finding out anything about the alien, or even a downed UFO, then, yeah, that's exactly why we're here,' I replied. 'But we really don't know about any bounty.'

The guy with the bushy beard shrugged at his partner. 'Well, for your information, miss, some stranger has put up a ten-million-dollar reward for catching that alien critter, alive or dead. And the latter suits us just mighty fine.'

The thin guy nodded. 'The damned thing has it come coming, the little bastard. There've been three more cattle mutilations in the last twenty-four hours.'

The bearded guy nodded. 'Yeah, when we find it I'll use my rifle barrel on it as an anal probe.'

The two of them cackled.

I bristled, ready to square up to the guy and tell him exactly what I thought of his attitude towards a sentient being, but I felt a hand on my arm.

Jack subtly shook his head at me before turning towards the two hunters. 'Don't blame you. But I'm guessing you haven't seen it yet?'

'No, we've been searching all night for it, but not a thing. Here's a tip for you all. If you're headed up to the campground, I wouldn't bother. The whole place is already packed out with the RVs of UFO nutters like yourselves – and not one of them has seen a thing either. Reckon that Jerry has sent us all on a wild goose chase so he catch it himself.'

'Jerry?' Mike asked.

'He's the guy who snapped the photo,' the thin man said.

'You think he's been holding back?' Mike asked.

'Wouldn't you if there were ten million bucks sitting on the table that you could keep for yourself?' the thin guy said.

'Good point,' I replied. 'So where can we find this Jerry?' I asked.

'Down at Lake View, at Jerry's Smokey BBQ Shack. He owns the place. Worth going for the ribs alone – the best this side of Mississippi. Or are you UFO types all vegans?' The thin guy gave us a yellow-stained toothy grin.

'No, I love a good rack of short ribs,' Jack said. 'And thanks for the tip-off about the campsite.'

'Any time. If you do happen to see the critter, we'd be more than happy to split the bounty with you for a solid lead.' The thin guy took out a bit of paper, scribbled his phone number down and handed it to me. 'Call me if you've see anything...or if you fancy a drink.' The guy almost licked his lips at me.

I fought the urge to be sick in my mouth. 'Thanks, we will.'

'Then good luck with your alien hunting, miss,' the bearded guy said. With a tip of their baseball caps the two of them walked off down the slope.

Jack whispered to me as we watched them depart. 'I think your luck's in there, Lauren.'

I shuddered as I screwed up the piece of paper and tossed it away. 'Not in a million years – no make that a billion. Anyway, I don't know what you all think, but suddenly I'm in desperate need of a BBQ.'

CHAPTER THIRTEEN

I'd called Ruby back and we'd decided to return to the X101 for our electric Zero motorbikes, since the shack was a way off and our stomachs were rumbling audibly. We parked them up outside and headed towards Jerry's Smokey BBQ Shack. The bustling restaurant was already pulling me in by the nose thanks to the smell of cooking meat wafting from a vent on the side of the building. It was obviously doing great business – going by the number of cars and SUVs crowded into its car park and even along the approach road.

No one paid us much attention as we entered the packed-out restaurant. Three waitresses glided around the room with pots of fresh coffee. An order of burgers and racks of ribs came past us, instantly reminding me just how hungry I was. The energy bars I'd managed to eat before we'd taken off on our clandestine mission seemed like a lifetime ago now.

Right then a group of four guys with hunting rifles slung over their shoulders vacated a table.

A smiling blonde waitress wearing bright red lipstick

gestured towards it. 'Grab yourselves a seat. I'll be with you in a second.'

Mike's gaze scanned the restaurant. 'Well, this place is way more popular than you would expect from its TripAdvisor rating.'

'You're seriously telling me you checked out its online reviews?' Jack asked.

'As a vegetarian, I needed to check there was something on the menu I could actually eat.'

'And is there?' I asked.

'The usual barbecued sweetcorn and salad, plus some hickory smoked wedges I've got my eyes on.'

'I wonder about your priorities sometimes,' Jack said, shaking his head.

Ruby's gaze skated over the menu before fixing me with a hard stare. 'Guys, I hate to ask an obvious question, but do we really have time to eat? The clock is running – somewhere out there is a little alien dude needing us to get to it first.'

Once again I bristled as she questioned my judgement. 'Look, there's no point us blindly hunting through those woods if we have a chance of picking up some information here that could help to narrow the search area. That's especially true when the owner happens is the guy who sighted this alien in the first place. And if we get fed the same time, hey, I see that as an added bonus.'

Ruby just shook her head as she returned her attention to the menu.

A short while later the blonde waitress appeared at our table. 'Welcome to Jerry's Smokey BBQ Shack. I'm Olivia, your server for today. Are you ready for me to take your order?'

'Sure thing,' I replied in the American accent I'd was warming to.

But Olivia barely registered me, her attention squarely on Jack. 'Sir?'

Jack looked up from the menu, registering Olivia's presence for the first time. 'A full rack of dry ribs for me, plus a side of the cheese nachos. And just keep the coffee coming.'

'I like a man with a good appetite,' Olivia said, her eyes lingering on Jack's longer than was professionally polite, then she turned to the rest of us. She took Mike's order and then mine before getting to Ruby. 'And you, mam?'

'Just a glass of tap water,' Ruby replied without catching my eye, judging me without even a look.

'Is there anything else I can get you?' Olivia asked.

'Actually, we were wondering if the owner was around,' I said. 'We'd just like to have a quick word with Jerry about the alien he saw.'

'Oh, you and every other person in here. But Jerry's hardly here at the moment. He might pretend to everyone that he isn't, but he's been off searching for that alien along with everyone else.'

The slight clouding in her expression told me she was holding something back.

But Olivia's lipstick smile had already glided back into place. 'Anyway, I'm afraid it will be a good thirty minutes before your orders arrive. As you can see, we're a bit rushed off our feet – another reason Jerry why should be here and not off having a grand old time out in those woods.'

'So all of these people are looking for the alien too?' Mike asked as he gazed around at the clientele.

'Absolutely. We'd be less than half this busy during the week normally. But as Jerry says, this is good business. That and all the publicity.'

'Publicity?' I asked.

'Well, like your good selves, folk have been coming from all over to talk to him. Jerry has turned into something of a local celebrity.' Olivia pointed to a newspaper article pinned to a wall.

It was the front page of a local paper, the *Lake Crest Gazette*, showing a smiling photograph of man probably in his sixties. He was holding up the blurry image we'd seen plastered all over the internet. *Local Man Spots Alien*, the headline declared.

'That's Jerry then?' Ruby asked.

'The great man himself,' Olivia replied, raising her eyebrows a fraction. 'He's been lapping up all the attention. And with every new mutilated cow the press races to our door for a fresh comment from Jerry, as if he's some sort of goddamn alien expert now. If you pardon my language.'

'So you don't think he is then?' Mike asked.

'How can he be? He's just an ordinary guy who was in the right place at the right time. He's grabbed his five minutes of fame with both hands and isn't about to let go for anyone. Anyway, will you look at me gossiping to you when there's a room full of people to feed? I'll be back in a moment with a pot of coffee.'

'That would be much appreciated, mam,' Jack said, flashing his widest knee-weakening smile.

Olivia coiled her fingers through her hair. 'Coming right up, sir,' she said with a flirtatious smile.

'You and the ladies,' Mike said once she'd gone, shaking his head at Jack.

Jack tucked his chin in. 'Hey, what do you mean?'

'If you don't know, I'm not going to spell it out.'

Ruby traded a frown with me, but Mike had a point. I'd seen Jack around plenty of women at Eden. Some of them had been even less subtle than Olivia at how much they were attracted to him. It was partly his lack of ego that attracted me to him too.

An old guy sitting at the next table turned his chair towards us. 'I hope you don't mind, but I overheard what you were saying to Olivia. So you're after this Grey too?'

'Yes, we are,' I replied. 'And you?'

'Yep, guilty as charged. But then a ten-million-dollar reward is hard to ignore.'

'About that – any idea who has put up the money?' I asked.

'All I know is that three strangers turned up in here flashing a case full of cash to Jerry, telling him a bounty was up for grabs. There are posters up everywhere around town too, although Jerry refused to let them put up any on his walls. It's almost as if the guy wants to keep that money to himself.' The old man's eyebrows arched over his eyes.

I thought about what the hunters we'd run into had said and nodded. 'It's a lot of money. No wonder he's out looking too around the campsite.'

The old man scowled at me.

'Sorry, did I say something wrong?'

'No, it's just that's the part that doesn't stack up. You see, based on what Jerry's been telling everyone, we've all been pouring all over the campsite. And not a single person has seen a glimpse of the alien around there. No tracks, just a whole lot of nothing.'

Ruby peered at the guy. 'What are you getting at?'

'Just that ten million dollars is an awful lot of money, if you catch my drift.' He tapped the side of his nose and turned away to face his companion.

Mike sat back in his chair. 'Sounds as if everyone has their suspicions about Jerry,' he said in a hushed tone.

'So what are we talking about here – that he deliberately sent everyone off on a wild goose chase so he could keep the real location to himself?' Jack whispered.

'I can think of ten million reasons why he might do that,' I replied.

Ruby chewed her gum and nodded. 'Also, throw in the fact there hasn't been a lot of military swarming around, which suggests the crashed UFO isn't near here.'

'But let's not forget this Jerry guy may have simply pulled this stunt to generate a whole load of publicity for his business,' Jack said. 'What would be better than Lake Crest's very own Roswell event?'

'And what about the people turning up with a case full of cash?' Ruby asked.

'Could be part of his cover story.'

I sucked my cheeks in. 'That doesn't add up based on what Olivia just said. He wouldn't bother to go off hunting for it too if it is all just make-believe.'

'Fair point, but where does that leave us?' Mike asked.

'With a lot of questions,' I replied.

My earbud buzzed. 'I don't want to interrupt, but I was just listening into your conversation,' Lucy said. 'I took it upon myself to do a bit of snooping, using your Sky Wire to hack into the Wi-Fi system in here through to a computer linked to it.'

'And I'm guessing you found something?' I asked.

'Oh, I most certainly did. Footage from the security camera here. Take your Sky Wire out and I'll play it for you now.'

I grabbed my phone and laid it on the table for the others to see. A video started to play – a view of the restaurant we were sitting in, but with hardly any people inside. I glanced over my shoulder and spotted the small security camera over the bar that must have taken the footage. I returned my attention to the Sky Wire. The time stamp showed the video had been recorded two days previously.

'I don't see any significance?' Ruby said.

'You will – keep watching,' Lucy replied through our earbuds.

On the footage, three burly guys entered the restaurant, all wearing black combat fatigues. But it was the one wearing sunglasses at the front who immediately caught my attention.

'That's Colonel Alvarez,' Mike whispered.

I nodded as we watched the colonel take a seat at a table. Meanwhile, the two heavies with him stood guard at the door. A moment later a man that I recognised as Jerry from his photo on the newspaper front page appeared and joined the colonel at a table.

'OK, the mere fact that Alvarez bothered to come here in person has just given this Jerry guy's story a lot more credibility,' I said.

'Exactly,' Lucy's voice said into our earbuds. 'And this next bit is the clincher.'

Alvarez beckoned to one of his men. He carried a silver brief-case over to the table and opened it, presenting it Jerry. It was filled with neatly stacked piles of hundred-dollar bills.

'So that confirms the reward is real and this isn't just an elaborate hoax,' I said.

'It also tells us something else,' Ruby said. 'Alvarez and the Overseers can't have located the Grey either. They must be desperate if they're throwing money around so publicly like this.'

'But surely Jerry would have just revealed the actual whereabouts of the Grey to them and claimed the reward?' I said.

'Not if he had a bigger game plan,' Lucy said in my ear.

'Why, what are you thinking?'

'That Jerry might think that if he managed to capture this Grey himself, he might be able to get a lot more than ten million dollars from Alvarez.'

'If the guy thinks he can put the squeeze on Alvarez, he has no idea just how ruthless the man is. Even if Jerry does manage to track the Grey down again and capture it, I can guarantee it won't be long before he's in a body bag.'

Ruby nodded. 'If I know anything about the Overseers' playbook, they'll then spread a rumour that Jerry was abducted or some similar crap.'

Mike sighed. 'Then it sounds as if we have to save this guy from his own greed.'

'Great in theory, especially if it also leads us to the Grey, but how are we going to do that when we don't where Jerry is?' I replied.

'Actually, I might have an idea about that too,' Lucy said. 'I was nosing through that computer and it turns out it has Jerry's calendar on it. I checked the day he was meant to have spotted the Grey, and it turns out he wasn't anywhere near the camping area.'

'So where was he then?' I asked.

'At his cabin up in the woods – near a place called Timpson Lake.'

'You mean that's where he was the night he saw the Grey?'

'I'm guessing so. I've already grabbed the address from his contacts and updated the Sky Wires with the GPS coordinates. It's about a twenty-minute drive away on your Zeros, faster if we fly there.'

'Has anyone told you that you're completely brilliant?' Mike said.

Lucy chuckled. 'Nothing like enough, gorgeous.'

I pocketed my Sky Wire. I had a good feeling about this. If Jerry really had held back, there was a real chance we could get to the Grey before Alvarez did. A tangible sense of relief started to fill me. Our decision to break out of Eden might be about to be fully justified – if we pulled this off.

'OK, we need to get those food orders cancelled,' I said.

Jack cast an eye towards the kitchen. 'Do you suppose they would make us up an order to go?'

I rolled my eyes at him as I beckoned Olivia over.

CHAPTER FOURTEEN

WE RODE our Zero motorbikes in a procession along a dirt track through the woods. The early-evening sunlight had taken on an orange hue that was tingeing the tops of the trees golden, shafts of light catching the dance of small flies in the air around us.

I peered at the HUD map being projected on to my helmet's visor. 'According to Lucy's marker, Jerry's log cabin is just a few hundred metres round the next bend.'

'Then I think we should dismount here and approach on foot,' Ruby said over the helmets' intercom system.

'Why, what are you thinking?' Jack asked over the open channel.

'For all we know Alvarez may have also realised that Jerry was holding back on the real location of the Grey. They may already be here to get the truth out of him.'

'That's a good point,' I said. 'In which case, maybe you should scout ahead, Ruby, and let us know if the cost is clear?'

She chuckled. 'I was about to suggest the same thing, boss.'

We pulled up and parked our motorbikes a short way off the

track among some bushes. Ruby took a rucksack from one of the Zero's panniers and slipped it over her shoulders.

'What have you got there?' Jack asked.

'An Accuracy International sniper rifle with a Nikon Monarch 5 scope. It's a great weapon. I mean, I'd prefer to bring my trusty Barrett M82 for stopping power, accuracy and range, but that cannon is massive to lug around, and might raise a bit too much attention for a group who are meant to be UFO hunters.'

'Yeah, but the Accuracy International is a fantastic alternative when you're not trying to stop a tank,' Jack said.

'It is indeed,' Ruby replied, winking at him.

'Oh, great, Jack,' I said. 'Now you have a weapon buddy you can go all weak at the knees with over *Guns Monthly* magazine.'

'Says the woman who is almost married to her LRS,' Jack retorted, which made Ruby snort.

Mike just eye-rolled the rest of us as he checked the ammo for his dart gun.

Ruby hoisted the backpack on to her shoulders and headed out into the woods. 'I'm going to circle round the target. Just wait for my all-clear before you try approaching.'

'Understood,' I replied, realising that yet again she was the one issuing the orders. But maybe in this situation that was actually the right call.

I checked the time on my smart watch: 8.45 p.m. According to its display, sunset was in about thirty-five minutes. We needed to get a move on.

Jack slipped his Glock into his shoulder holster and I did the same with my LRS, although I hoped I wouldn't have any reason to use it. Yes, I'd had to kill people during missions, but I would never want to unless absolutely necessary. It was the one way I was able to navigate myself through such an emotional minefield.

I pressed my fingertip to my earbud. 'Lucy, are you still reading us?'

'Loud and clear, my little sunflower.'

I grimaced as Mike and Jack grinned at me. 'Just how quickly can you get here if we need backup?'

'A minute tops if I travel over Mach 5.'

'Good to know. Be on standby in case we need you in a hurry.'

'And there was me thinking of doing my nails.'

I shook my head at the others.

'Just how dangerous do you think this is going to be, Lauren?' Mike asked.

'I didn't think it would be at all – until Ruby put the idea of Alvarez already being up here into my head.'

'It certainly doesn't hurt to be careful,' Jack said. 'But it would be nice if we managed to complete a mission without one of us getting shot for a change.'

'Amen to that,' Mike said.

Right on cue the old wound in my left arm ached. I'd received that little memento courtesy of one of Alvarez's bullets. Its presence was a reminder of just how high the stakes could run in an operation like this. And I'd seen too many good people killed to take any unnecessary chances.

'How are you getting on out there, Ruby?' I asked.

'I'm in position now – I can see the cabin,' Ruby's voice said over the earbud link. 'There doesn't seem to be anyone inside. But, just to make sure, I'm going to launch Hawk and do a quick sweep of the area using its thermal-vision camera.'

'Hawk?' I asked.

'It's a micro-drone – the thing Jodie gave you to give to me. She's had the labs working on it for a while. The US Marines have something similar called a Black Hornet, but Hawk has three times the range at six clicks. It also has a hover mode, which means it can sustain surveillance for up to three hours. Very useful when you're a sniper and need an extra pair of eyes in the sky.'

'We could have done with that little toy back in Peru,' Mike said.

'Well, we have it now,' Ruby replied. 'So let's see how good it actually is.'

I heard a faint whining not much louder than a wasp coming from the woods on the hillside above us. It faded away and I caught a glimpse of a small dark shape darting up into the sky and circling back.

'OK, I'm just doing a circuit of the surrounding area,' Ruby said. 'Yep, no sign of anyone apart from you guys. But if Jerry is inside the cabin, the thermal camera on the Hawk isn't sensitive enough to pick him up through thick log walls.'

'Then I think we need to take the risk and head in,' I said over the radio.

'Roger that,' Ruby replied.

Using the trees as cover, we made our way up the gentle rising slope. We crested the top and a squat wooden cabin with a veranda came into view. Moss grew over most of the roof together with a few missing shingles. It looked as if it needed some serious TLC. A large Ford F40 pickup truck was parked next to the cabin. What was on its back immediately caught my attention: a large metal cage. It was exactly the sort of thing that someone might transport an animal in...or an alien.

Mike gestured towards the vehicle. 'If that truck belongs to Jerry, it seems highly likely he's been hunting for the Grey around here somewhere.'

'And going by the fact that the cage is still empty, he can't have had any luck yet,' I said.

'If you hold up one of your Sky Wires to the truck, I can check the registration plate,' Lucy said through my earpiece. 'Then I'll be able to confirm whether it belongs to Jerry or not.'

'You can do that?' Ruby asked over the comm channel.

'Let's just say that Eden's systems have opened up all sorts of useful databases for me. I assimilated them into my memory banks.'

'Nice move,' Mike said.

'Oh, I have the best moves,' Lucy replied.

I could almost hear her grinning at the other end of the line.

I held up my Sky Wire, pointing the rear-facing camera towards the vehicle. A moment later a cropped-in view of the truck's number plate had appeared on the phone's screen.

'Right, I've just checked the database and that truck definitely belongs to Jerry,' Lucy said.

'OK then – let's find out if he's inside.' As I stepped up on to the veranda my boot caught something and pinged it away. I glanced to see a bullet casing just ahead of my toe. Then my eyes took in all the other shiny brass casings scattered over the veranda.

'Bloody hell, it looks as if there's been some sort of firefight here,' I said.

Jack squatted down and picked up one. 'Nought point four, four rounds by the look of it – I'm guessing from a hunting rifle. But these are cold, so this wasn't recent.' He stood up and ran his hands over the walls of the cabin. 'OK, I'm not even sure it was a firefight – I'd expect to see a few incoming rounds that would have impacted the walls.'

A trickle of ice ran down my spine. 'So what was he shooting at here?'

Our eyes travelled to the empty cage.

I walked to the door and rapped my knuckles on it. 'Jerry, are you in there?'

There was no reply.

'He could just be asleep?' Jack said as he joined me, although his expression told me he thought nothing of the sort.

I withdrew my LRS and put my hand to the door handle. Jack unholstered his Glock and took a position to the side of the door, ready for the room-clearing technique we'd been taught. We knew to never just stand there and open the door, as that would present an easy target.

'Guys, do you really think that's necessary?' Mike asked as he hopped up on to the tailgate of the truck to examine the cage.

'I really hope not,' I replied. I turned the handle and it started to swing open. 'It's unlocked.'

'Not unusual for a cabin in the back end of nowhere,' Jack said.

'Look, before you go storming in there, let me first check it out with Hawk from the perimeter where I've taken up a sniper position,' Ruby's voice said over the comm link.

I licked my lips that had suddenly become very dry. 'That sounds like a plan.'

Soft whining came from the sky and a small drone half the size of my Sky Wire phone descended rapidly towards us. The grey craft had two propellers mounted on stubby wings either side of a teardrop-shaped body. The wings pivoted into an upright position, much like our X101s could for vertical landings and the tiny drone came to hover just a metre off the ground behind us. Then, like a dog following a trail, the drone tipped its nose and sped into the cabin. The three of us watched from outside as it rotated slowly on the spot in the hallway. A moment later it buzzed back out of the doorway, heading up into the sky.

'You're all clear,' Ruby's voice said over the link. 'No sign of anyone...nor a corpse, before you ask.'

My heart rate decelerated as I holstered my LRS and headed through the doorway with Jack.

Inside, a small unlit potbelly stove stood in one corner. Motes of dust swirled through the air. A distinct whiff of stale cigarette smoke caught in my nose. On a table in the middle sat a bag of fresh groceries. Next to it were several boxes of bullets, some open. A bed in the corner with rumpled bedding suggested that someone had recently slept in it. But it was what was on the walls that really drew my attention.

Photos of Grey aliens were everywhere, from sketches to blurry photos, most of which I'd seen on UFO sites. There was another copy of the newspaper article featuring Jerry on the wall. Beneath that was a large map, with several areas that had big Xs scrawled across them.

'That looks like a search grid to me,' Jack said.

'Looking for our alien friend?' I wondered.

'Could be. The question is whether or not Jerry found it – and if that has anything to do with all those bullets out there.'

'Oh, bloody hell, I hope not.'

'Hey, guys, you're going to want to come and see this,' Mike called out.

We headed back outside to see him crouched by the rear of the truck, examining the ground.

As we walked over to join him, I saw droplets of a black viscous substance on the ground.

'Oil?' I asked.

'I'm not sure, but there also several bullet holes in the tailgate.'

'You're saying he shot up his own vehicle?'

'Hang on, it doesn't look quite right for oil,' Jack said. He dipped his finger in it, sniffed it and cautiously tasted it with the tip of his tongue. He pulled a face and spat it out immediately. 'That's not oil. It has the metallic taste of blood. I guess it could be alien.'

'Oh, Jesus, you're saying Jerry winged the Grey?' Mike asked.

'It would fit with what we can see here, but if so, where's Jerry?' I said.

'Remember what those hunters told us,' Jack replied. 'The reward for the Grey was alive or dead.'

I wrinkled my nose at him. 'So you think that Jerry injured the Grey and then went after it?' I asked.

'Actually, I think I might have an idea,' Ruby said over the comm link. 'I just flew Hawk down the track that leads to the cabin. There's a muddy section with two sets of fresh tyre tracks in it. I think there's a good chance that Alvarez and his people caught up with Jerry.'

'So they took him and the alien?' I asked.

'I don't think so, because look at this,' Jack said. He was standing a short distance away, studying a bush at the edge of the clearing.

We joined him and I spotted more of the black blood on its leaves.

My gaze fell to the ground. There were footprints that appeared to be similar in size to a small child's, but with four toes.

I pointed them out to the others. 'If that's our Grey, then it's definitely been wounded.'

Jack examined them and nodded. 'Going by the scrape marks from the right foot, you can see it was dragging its leg slightly.'

I was about to reply when I felt static wash over my skin.

'Crap, I'm losing control of Hawk,' Ruby said. 'Some sort of —' Her voice was drowned out by a burst of noise.

A moment later a blue flash came from the horizon.

'What the hell was that?' Mike asked.

'There was some sort of magnetic pulse in the local area,' Lucy's voice said in our earbuds. 'Thankfully not strong, but still powerful enough to take out Hawk.'

'Any idea what caused it, Lucy?' I asked.

'Well, it does bear all the hallmarks of an antigravity drive system failing, so...'

Jack stared at Mike and me. 'The crashed Tic Tac – it has to be.'

My pulse quickened. 'Lucy, any idea where the pulse might have come from?'

'From triangulating my sensors and your Sky Wires' inbuilt compasses, which all went haywire, it seems whatever caused it is centred over another small lake five miles north-east of your current position.'

I pressed my finger to my earbud. 'Ruby, that's within range of your Hawk, isn't it?'

'No can do, boss,' Ruby said as she emerged from the forest. In her hand was the mangled remains of her drone. 'That pulse knocked out its flight control systems and it came down hard. Unfortunately, Jodie didn't give me a spare.'

'The magnetic disturbance is ongoing, so I could make a flypast if you need me to do a bit of reconnaissance?' Lucy said.

'That's too risky if the Overseers are investigating too,' I said. 'Better that we head over on our Zeros and scout out the situation from the ground.'

'So let me get this right. You're worried about Lucy running into the Overseers, but not us?' Mike asked.

'Relax, I'm not suggesting we engage them if it does turn out to be Alvarez. But this way we see for ourselves what's going on and we can form a strategy to deal with the situation. And that may include bringing Lucy in if we need her.'

'And what about our alien buddy, who might be out there somewhere?' Ruby asked.

Jack's gaze lifted from the tracks. 'Well, as the Grey seems to have been heading in the same direction as the magnetic pulse, it suggests that the alien is trying to get back to his ship.'

'All roads lead to Rome in other words,' Mike said.

I nodded. 'So let's head out and discover exactly what we're dealing with here.'

CHAPTER FIFTEEN

THE SUN HAD long set and a weather front had moved in, blotting out the stars. Mike was at the head of our convoy of Zeros as he was by far the most experienced on motorbikes out of all of us. We had our lights completely off to avoid drawing any attention to ourselves and were heading along an isolated back road through the forest. We were closing in on the lake being displayed on our HUD screens.

A light drizzle was falling, leaving ghostly silver streaks in my helmet's night-vision image-intensifier system.

Ever since we'd left the cabin, I'd kept trying to imagine how I would feel if I were in the Grey's situation. If it was still alive, it had to be terrified out of its wits. And how would it react to us if we managed to find it?

A flash of torchlight appeared about a mile dead ahead of us.

'OK, everyone, stop, I see something on the road up there,' Mike said over the comm link.

We all pulled up. Ruby took her Nikon sniper scope out of her backpack, flipped her visor up and peered through it. 'Yep, it's a roadblock. There are two Humvees and just to add to the fun they're mounted with fifty-calibre M2 machine guns. There are some heavily armed soldiers on the ground too.'

'Then it sounds as if we're on the right track,' Jack said.

I focused on my HUD screen. 'According to the map we're less than three miles away from the source of that magnetic pulse.'

'Well, we're obviously not going to reach it along this road,' Mike said. He gestured to a small animal track leading up a wood-covered ridge. 'What do you all say to a bit of dirt biking?'

'OK, but take it easy,' I said. 'The rest of us aren't as experienced as you are.'

Mike beamed at me through his visor. 'You've got it.' He turned his bike to the side and led the way along the track into the woods.

At low speed the electric motorbikes were so quiet I could actually hear the raindrops splashing on to my helmet as we made our way up the slope that glistened under the steady fall of rain. The cover of trees and the lack of any moon should have meant the scene was pitch-black to my eyes. But thankfully the high-quality Sky Dreamer tech built into our helmets was once again doing a great job, illuminating what would have otherwise been impenetrable darkness.

The rain was falling faster now and the Zeros were slipping more frequently on the wet stones poking up through the soil. To counter this, Mike began to lead us in a zigzagging pattern across the slope. Whilst Mike looked as if he was taking this in this stride, the rest of us had fallen quiet, all concentrating hard so as not to fall off and land on our bums.

At last the ground began to level out beneath my wheels and I breathed a sigh of relief as we reached the summit of the ridge.

'Let's take a moment, guys,' I said over the intercom.

As we all pulled up to catch our breath, both mental and physical, I took the chance to gaze back down the slope we'd just ridden up. The Humvee roadblock was visible far below us through a gap in the trees.

I consulted the map on my HUD. 'It looks as if we can follow the top of this ridge and should end up overlooking the lake. Hopefully that's where we'll find the Tic Tac, not to mention our alien friend. I think we need to assume the Overseers are going to have soldiers out patrolling these woods to keep the area secure.'

'Oh, you can count on it,' Ruby said. 'That's exactly what I would do if I was in charge of guarding that area.'

I cracked open my visor to help defog the Perspex. 'If these woods are crawling with Overseers soldiers, maybe we should proceed on foot from here?'

Ruby nodded. 'Absolutely, boss. As quiet as these bikes are, someone hiding in these woods will hear us approaching and could easily ambush us.'

'And I have idea to help us,' I said.

I toggled the comm channel with the eye control for my HUD. 'Lucy, are you there?'

'But of course, darling,' she replied. 'I've been listening to your progress like a radio play. It really could do with a backing track. Something like "Born to Be Wild" could work well.'

Jack chuckled. 'Nice choice.'

'Well, that aside,' I continued, 'maybe now's the time for you to find somewhere to hide yourself and the X101 closer to us. With you in range I'll be able to make use of the Empyrean Key's functions, which would be incredibly useful right now.'

'You're planning to use the twilight zone to sneak us past those soldiers, aren't you?' Jack said.

I smiled at him. 'Mind reader.'

Ruby looked between us with a puzzled expression. 'The what already?'

'Oh, you'll see for yourself when Lucy gets here, but get ready for a real head rush,' Mike said.

'Right...' Ruby replied with a frown.

We crept on foot in the shimmering altered world, along the edge of the ridge from a clearing where Lucy had landed – together with the X101. They were both fully cloaked and whilst they might have been invisible in our particle-based world, in the twilight zone both stood out as shining objects.

We headed away from them without our disguises, which we'd ditched in the X101 – since there was no need for them when we were invisible. The ground oscillated to our steps like ripples on a pond. The solid tree trunks around us wavered as if they'd been turned to rubber. But as always, it was us that had gone through the most disturbing transformation of all in this waveform version of our reality. The only constant was our eyes, round which our bodies blurred as if someone had grabbed hold of us and was shaking us at high speed. There was no need for our helmets' night-vision system either, so we'd left them back with the bikes. In this reality everything glowed, making it easy to navigate.

'This twilight zone of yours is crazy,' Ruby said, staggering slightly as she walked towards Lucy like a drunk leaving a pub at closing time.

'Maybe it is, but we'll be totally invisible to any soldiers we run into from now on,' I replied.

'Don't get me wrong, that's great and everything, but it's seriously messing with my head.'

'Oh, you'll get used to it eventually,' Mike told Ruby. 'We all went through what you did, but it almost feels normal to me now.'

'I certainly hope so. Right now I feel like barfing.' She gestured back towards Lucy's micro mind ship. 'Lauren, do you really think it was a good idea to bring her in so close to whatever is going on in the valley around that lake?'

Before I could reply, Lucy jumped in.

'Ahem, I'm more than capable of looking after myself,' she said through our earbuds. 'Besides, you gain a significant tactical advantage with having me in close proximity, of which you're already making good use.'

'That may be true, but I can't help feeling that we're heading into the lion's den,' Jack said.

'It's a calculated risk,' I replied. 'But I still think the odds are on our side, not least because we can sneak in right under their noses within the twilight zone.'

'Let's hope so, for all our sakes,' Mike said.

The small track we'd been following began to open out as we approached the end of the ridge. I started to catch glimpses of the valley beyond between the trees and anticipation began to strengthen inside me. Then, like the curtains on a stage being pulled back for a sudden reveal, the woodland opened out. Now we had a clear, uninterrupted view, aside from the falling curtains of rain. No one said anything for a moment, our attention locked on what was below us.

I held the Empyrean Key in my blurring hand to better take in what I was seeing and selected the particle icon, dropping us back into our reality. In a heartbeat the wavering mirage around us was replaced by a reassuringly solid world.

Ruby shot me a grateful look as she steadied herself on a now very solid tree trunk.

Below us, nestling in the crook of the valley, was a small lake. Its surface shone with diamond reflections thanks to the banks of stadium lights that had been mounted on tall poles on the far shore. The air caught in my chest as I spotted what they were illuminating.

A huge gouge had been ploughed through the trees in a path

of splintered destruction. My eyes tracked along it to a large house that had been partly demolished by a crashed Tic Tac, which still had steam venting from it, earth piled up around its nose where it had finally come to rest. Teams of people in hazmat suits around the ship were just visible, crawling over the downed UFO like tiny white ants.

'Oh my god, so those bastards did manage to shoot it down,' I said.

'And what do you think happened to the people in that house?' Mike said in a small voice.

'Nothing good if the Overseers are already down there – if they weren't killed outright by the impact.'

Mike drew his lips back and nodded.

'Is that the same UFO you encountered with Alice, Lauren?' Ruby asked.

'I can't be sure, but it certainly looks similar. Whatever, we need to rescue our alien friend, if it's still alive.'

'Talk about jumping from the frying pan into the bloody fire,' Mike said. 'But why would the little guy want to risk coming back here?'

'Maybe it's hoping that its alien buddies will launch a search and rescue mission?' Ruby said. 'It would make tactical sense – that's the first place I'd start looking if it were me.'

'If so, I imagine that's exactly what the Overseers are hoping for too,' Jack said. 'Using a fly to catch a spider.'

'Well, let's get down there and see if we can get to our little friend before they do,' I said.

I activated the carrier tone in my earbud and at once the icons appeared again around the Empyrean Key in my hand. I selected the wave icon for the twilight zone and Ruby shuddered as we dropped into the shimmering ghost world once more.

We slowly began to work our way down the slope towards the lake, the adrenaline buzzing through my system only growing. A minute soon turned into thirty. I was just starting to think I'd maybe been overly cautious to travel via the alternative world when Ruby nudged me and pointed ahead of us.

The glowing forms of three soldiers in full-body armour and carrying carbines were only fifty metres out to our left. Ruby already had her Glock in her hand, raised and ready to take a shot.

I shook my head. 'Ruby, don't forget they can't see or even hear us.'

'Oh yeah.' A blurry smile filled her face.

Despite that fact, by force of habit we all crept past them. I wasn't able to swallow until we were well clear.

'Wow, that was seriously unreal,' Ruby said after we'd put a good few hundred metres between us and the patrol.

'OK, I have to admit it was a good call after all to bring Lucy up to the front line,' Jack said.

'Lauren's far too modest to say so, but she did tell you so,' Lucy said over the comm channel.

I gave him my best freaky twilight-zone grin.

Jack snorted. 'Yep, maybe she did.'

We continued to make steady progress towards the lake, having to sidestep round two further patrols. Then at last we were approaching the edge of the lake, a kaleidoscope of dancing light in the twilight zone. Beyond it, the shocking destruction the Tic Tac had caused became truly obvious for the first time. The house itself had been chopped in half, like a giant knife had sliced through it. Internal rooms on the upper floor were now open to the lashing rain. The roof had partly collapsed in on itself and a bed hung over the edge of the buckled rooms. In front of the house two burned-out cars had been thrown aside like toys by the impact of the crash.

It was far too easy to picture the utter terror of the family living in that house as their world was torn apart by something beyond their imagination. After all, home was where you were meant to be safe.

We all just stood there, soaking in the devastation, no one saying a word.

'Hey, what's that?' Mike said, finally breaking the silence. He was pointing along the shoreline.

I spotted a number of bouncing torch beams as a group of soldiers ran directly towards us.

For an awful moment I thought we'd been spotted, despite being in the twilight zone. I was about to shout orders for everyone to fall back when I noticed what the soldiers were pursuing.

A small humanoid shape was dragging its right leg as it tried to evade the soldiers, continually glancing backwards at its pursuers. It was wearing a body-hugging two-tone suit, purple with a gold top half, almost like a *Star Trek* uniform. The alien itself had an oversized head compared to a human's and its large black eyes were almost shockingly big. Certainly everything about it screamed other-worldly as it splashed along the shoreline, its feet sending spray flying.

'Holy crap,' Jack said as we all stared at it.

The Grey looked straight at us and then specifically at me, even though we were very much still in the twilight zone.

The world seemed to freeze as a cascade of images appeared in my head... I saw the Grey back at the log cabin. A man I recognised as Jerry was pointing a hunting rifle directly at the alien. Then the view shifted to some sort of strange cockpit with a holographic viewing screen. On it the view of a house loomed into view as the Grey fought to control the Tic Tac craft. A split second before the impact, the image dissolved away. Now the view was from same cockpit, but at a very different time, showing Lucy's micro mind ship and our X101 hovering a short way off on the viewing screen.

The sound of gunfire and then shearing pain blotted everything out as something tore through my flesh. Suddenly I could barely breathe...

I gasped as the world came flooding back in and I saw black blood erupting from the Grey's chest. He toppled forward – somehow I knew it was a he now – and his head crashed into rock as he hit the ground hard.

The sting of knifelike pain was fading fast from my chest. Confusion whirled through my mind. It hadn't been me who'd been shot; it had been the Grey.

A soldier with a raised carbine was grinning until Alvarez slapped the man's weapon down and glared at him.

With a sense of overwhelming powerlessness I watched Alvarez reach the Grey and stoop down over him. He pulled his glove from his hand and pressed his finger to the Grey's neck as Alvarez's squad converged on his position.

'Those damned bastards,' Jack hissed under his breath.

Unaware of our close proximity, Alvarez sat back on his haunches and pulled out a radio. 'The subject has sustained serious injuries and we're bringing it to the medical tent right now. Be on standby.'

'Roger that,' a woman at the other end replied.

He stood and his eyes locked on to the soldier who'd taken the shot. 'When I say hold your damned fire, I fucking mean it!' He raised his own pistol and, without so much as blinking, shot the guy through the forehead. The back of the man's head exploded in an eruption of blood and brains and he slumped to the ground. The rest of the squad exchanged shocked looks, but no one said anything.

'We should try to grab the alien whilst we still can,' Mike whispered.

'But there are too many of them,' Ruby replied. 'We need to pick our moment.'

Alvarez nudged the Grey with his foot. The alien let out a catlike howl of pain.

A pulse of anger surged through me, snapping my mind back into pure, determined focus. I had to fight every instinct not to drop us back into our world and shoot Alvarez in the head too. But I was in charge of this mission and my team needed me to keep it together.

'OK, let's get out of here before I do something stupid,' I finally said.

The team nodded and we all retreated into the woods.

Mike clasped his hands round the back of his neck. 'We've bloody failed.'

'There was nothing we could do,' Ruby said. 'Probably time to head back to Eden and beg for Alice's forgiveness.'

'Bloody hell, no way,' I said. 'We're not going to abandon that Grey. He's not dead yet.' It wasn't just raw emotion speaking. I felt linked to the alien; I could feel he was still alive – as if the Grey had become an extension of me, or me him. I couldn't be quite sure.

'Well, it looked in a pretty bad way to me,' Jack said.

'He is, but he's still alive,' I told him.

'You sound as if you know that for a fact?'

'I do. I'm guessing that none of you saw any images in your minds when the Grey looked directly at us?'

They all shook their heads.

'But you obviously did?' Jack asked.

I nodded. 'A succession of sequences, including that Grey's run-in with Jerry, crashing the Tic Tac, even the encounter with Alice and me in Ariel – which confirms it was the same ship.'

'But how could you have seen that?' Ruby asked.

'Telepathy,' Lucy said over the comm link. 'The few records I can access about this species say that is meant to be one of their abilities. And for some reason that Grey chose you to communicate with, Lauren.'

'Is that why I still feel linked to it somehow?' I asked.

'Almost certainly.'

'OK then, this feeling is real. And whilst that Grey is alive, there is still a chance to save him.'

'But how are we going to spring an alien from the clutches of Alvarez?' Jack said.

I turned to him. 'I don't know, but we have to, Jack. Like Ruby said earlier, we just need to time our move.'

Ruby nodded with a look of approval on her face. 'Now you're thinking like a soldier, Lauren. So let's take the fight to them, but on our terms.'

'Oh great, Ruby, so you're as batshit crazy as Lauren is,' Jack said as another squad of soldiers appeared, carrying a stretcher between them.

CHAPTER SIXTEEN

ALVAREZ's tightly knit squad of soldiers clustered round the Grey, two of them carrying the alien on a stretcher. I directed the team to trail them a short distance behind, through the glimmering version of the rain in the twilight zone. In full-body armour and helmets, the soldiers moved along the shoreline, circling back towards the Tic Tac crash site. I stared at their backs, my mind whirling as I tried to come up with something resembling a coherent plan that wouldn't end up with us all getting killed. But how could we rescue an alien creature that had just been badly injured?

'Any ideas about what we do next?' I asked the team.

Ruby turned towards me. 'The obvious thing is to take them by surprise. Maybe shoot them whilst we're still invisible?'

Mike shook his head. 'It doesn't work that way, Ruby. Whilst we're in E8, everything in this waveform version of our reality, including your weapons and ammo, won't work in the particle world.'

'Huh, can you give me that in some version of English I can actually understand?'

'What Mike is trying to say is that in the twilight zone everything behaves like the ghost version of itself,' I explained. 'Our bullets would have no impact on anyone in our physical world unless we drop back into our particle-based reality.'

Ruby's mouth twisted. 'OK, I get that. But we would still have the element of surprise on our side. I could drop at least three of them in the time it takes you to flutter your eyelashes, boss.'

I cast a frown her way as a spike of irritation rose through me. So much for feeling that we'd actually been on the same page for a moment. 'What exactly is that meant to mean?'

'Just I'm highly trained for this. And, with all due respect, you're an amateur, although admittedly a highly experienced one.'

That was it. I'd had enough of her attitude. I needed to slap her down. 'Listen, you, I'm the one in charge of this mission. Trying to spring an ambush when we're so heavily outnumbered would almost certainly end up with us losing people. Not to mention that a stray round could finish off that Grey. It's too risky a strategy, so just drop it. Are you hearing me?'

'Oh, *touchy*,' Ruby replied, pursuing her lips at me.

Ruby didn't know that she was picking at a raw nerve. I'd often questioned my own ability for this role. But before I could really lay into her, Jack jumped in.

'Ruby, I know this is your first mission with us. But you need to trust Lauren. She is the real deal when it comes to working in the field.'

Ruby tipped her chin up as she chewed her gum. 'I'm not easily impressed, but we'll see. Anyway, I've got a suggestion – and a good leader listens to their team, am I right, boss?'

I tried to keep the uncertainty she was triggering out of my voice. 'OK, what?'

'If you're going to try to save the Grey, you really need to make the most of my skills as a sniper.' She gestured along the lake towards the Tic Tac as Alvarez and his soldiers headed towards it. 'I can scope out a few sniping spots that I can move between. And from there I'll have a clear line of sight to the crash site, which is obviously where they're taking the Grey. It's over three hundred yards across the lake, so they won't be able to spot the muzzle flash with a suppressor fitted. What with that and in my ghillie suit, they'll have a hard time locating me. And I have some armour-piercing 7.62 rounds to punch through the body armour those soldiers are wearing. It means I can give you some useful backup in the event of a firefight during the rescue.'

Ruby might have been annoying, but she was also making sense. This was exactly her area of expertise. And if we needed to make a fast exit, she could lay down suppressing fire if we needed it.

'OK, sounds good – do it,' I said. 'But only shoot on my orders, or if you absolutely have to. Also, once you get to anything over a hundred metres away from me, you'll be dropped out of the twilight zone and will become visible again.'

'Understood, boss.' Ruby veered away towards a tall group of conifers on the lake shore. As she moved rapidly away and drew out of range of the Empyrean Key, she shifted back into the particle world with a barely stifled gasp. Thankfully, the soldiers had their backs to her and no one noticed a woman just magically appearing before she disappeared away into the treeline.

'I have to say, I'm liking this new, more cautious version of Lauren who thinks before charging in,' Mike said.

'I've learnt from my mistakes,' I said without glancing at Jack. His lecture to me during our last mission in Peru about listening to others had left a lasting impression. I was determined to apply that lesson in situations like this. But I was also grateful for the blurring cover of the twilight zone so no one spotted my lack of confidence in myself, which would have been written all over my particle face in the real world.

Alvarez and his soldiers were now just a few hundred metres from the crash site. There, large clusters of soldiers were gathered, along with around twenty military vehicles.

The alien let out an awful keening sound. The distress was so raw and so fearful that it twisted my heart. Once again it felt as if I'd made the noise myself; the sense of pain and confusion radiated through me. Whatever the Grey had done to be able to communicate with me, there seemed to still be some sort of lingering mental connection between the two of us. Why he had chosen me was a question for another time. Despite his discomfort washing over me, the real question was whether he could hold out much longer. And if he died, what then? It would be hard for me not to seek some form of vengeance on Alvarez and his people.

'Jack, if we manage to pull this rescue attempt off, do you think you could operate on that Grey?' I asked.

'Lauren, I've honestly no idea. Its alien physiology could be completely different to our own.'

'Damn, I hadn't thought of that. We need more information about the Grey if we're going to have a chance of saving its life. Lucy, are you listening in?'

'Always.'

'Good. Have you got any information on the Grey's physiology in your databases that could help Jack?'

'Unfortunately not,' Lucy replied. 'I'm afraid it'd be down to Jack's ability to wing it. I could help in another way, though. If you brought the Grey over to E8, I could conjure up a state-of-the-art operating theatre for Jack to use – as we did when you were injured.'

'Even so, maybe we should let Alvarez's people operate on

the Grey first,' Jack said. 'It would be much better for us to try and snatch the Grey from them once it's stable.'

I nodded. 'That's a good point. But even if they do manage to save him, that alien's life will be a living hell – full of interrogation and torture if Alvarez has anything to do with it.'

'So you're saying that if it comes to it we should put a bullet in its head to save it from suffering?' Jack asked.

Mike looked between us. 'But we can't.'

'As much as it breaks my heart, we may have no choice,' I said. 'Could you really live with yourself if you let the alien suffer under Alvarez's hands?'

Mike groaned. 'No, no, I couldn't.'

I sighed. 'I don't think any of us could, so let's hope it doesn't come to that.'

Despite my words, I really wasn't sure I could cross that line if it came to it.

Alvarez's squad reached the open lawns that sloped down from the shattered house towards the lake.

The Grey's head lolled to one side and Alvarez immediately placed his finger on the alien's neck. 'It's lost consciousness. We need help now!'

A group in hazmat suits appeared out of a green field tent pushing a gurney and rushed towards Alvarez.

'Do whatever it takes to save that thing's life!' Alvarez shouted as the soldiers transferred the Grey on to the gurney.

'We'll do our best, Colonel, but we're going to need specialist equipment that's back at base,' a bald-headed doctor replied.

'In that case I'll call in Delta squadron to airlift the subject out. Do what you can to stabilise it and prep the alien for transport.'

'The *it* is a he, Colonel.'

'I have no idea how you can tell.'

'Experience,' said the doctor as he and his team headed away with the Grey.

Alvarez thinned his lips at the man's departing back as they wheeled the alien into the tent. 'If you say so.' He walked over towards the soldiers surrounding the downed Tic Tac.

'It doesn't sound as if we're going to have much of a window of opportunity here,' Jack said.

'That's what I'm worried about,' I replied.

Through the flickering rain I saw Alvarez arrive at the alien craft illuminated by the banks of floodlights. Dozens of military vehicles, including a crane and some Humvees with mounted machine guns, surrounded the craft. At least thirty soldiers stood guard. A group of people wearing green coveralls were connecting a large harness with thick steel cables round the crashed alien craft.

I turned to face the others. 'OK, now the clock is well and truly ticking. This Delta squadron could turn up at any minute. Do you guys have any suggestions?'

'Let's get into that tent and monitor how their surgical team is getting on,' Jack replied. 'Then we'll know exactly when to make our move.'

Mike's face pinched as he gazed at the tent. 'If we're going to do that, can I ask one favour first?'

'Go ahead,' I said.

'If we need to deal with the medical team, please let me use my dart gun. After all, we're not talking combat soldiers here.'

I traded a look with Jack. This was Mike all over, but his moral compass was something I needed to pay attention to at times like this. Previously, I'd found it maybe a little bit too easy to shoot first and think later about the consequences for my soul. This was a real chance to do things right.

'Agreed,' I finally said. 'Ruby, are you in position yet?'

'Absolutely, boss,' she replied through my earbud. 'I've got a clear line of sight from here. But I can't see you, since you're all still shifted.'

'Damn, I didn't think of that,' I said.

'Relax, boss, no one can think of everything. But if you need me to give you covering fire, just tell me where you are first so I don't shoot you by mistake.'

'You can't anyway, Ruby – your bullets won't affect anyone in the twilight zone,' Mike said.

'Oh yeah, good point!'

I could hear the smile in her voice. 'OK, Ruby, we'll be in contact when we need to.' I gazed back up towards the top of the ridge. 'Lucy, you'll need to be ready for a fast extraction. This could get messy as soon as we try to grab that Grey.'

'Just say the word and I'll be there for you,' Lucy replied.

'Great.' I turned to Mike and Jack. 'Right, guys, time to cross everything and hope another seat-of-my-pants plan works out.'

'I adore your seat-of-the-pants plans,' Jack said.

'At least someone does.' Mike caught my eye and held up his hands. 'And that was a joke, *boss*.'

I hitched an eyebrow at Mike that made him grin.

CHAPTER SEVENTEEN

MIKE, Jack and I set off across the lawn that had been chewed up into rain-filled ruts by the military vehicles, the puddles acting as hundreds of mirrors reflecting the blinding arc lights around the Tic Tac. As we passed the house, my gaze was drawn to it again.

Up close, the damage was even more shocking. The front had been ripped away, like a giant version of an opened doll's house, revealing its interior. What would have been a modern open-plan living room had partly been buried under the collapsed floor from above. Wires and twisted pipes poked out from the shattered walls and the smell of sewage filled the air with a sickly stench.

Next to the house was a large double garage that looked relatively unscathed apart from a few missing tiles and the doors, which had blown in and twisted off their hinges. Among all the destruction it was the sight of a basketball hoop that brought a lump to my throat.

In my mind's eye I could see the parents shooting hoops with their children, a girl and a boy. Then, just to really twist the knife, my imagination threw in a small dog circling round them and barking as if they were auditioning for The Famous Five. Real lives had been destroyed by what had happened here. I swallowed hard as we approached the tent and tried to push the image away.

A tannoy mounted on a pole that swayed in the strengthening wind burst into life with a woman's voice. 'All personnel, be aware that Delta squadron will be arriving in five minutes. Ready alien craft for immediate recovery.'

At once the activity around the Tic Tac became frantic as a team in coveralls raised a large ring on the crane. The driver swung it over the alien ship and other teams began to connect the top of the harness to the loop.

'We need to get a shake on before that squadron gets here,' I said.

The others nodded and we started running through the now hammering rain towards the tent. Two burly soldiers with carbines stood guard.

'We might be invisible, but we still can't walk through them,' Mike said.

'Then let's try to slip under the tent round the back,' I suggested.

We skirted past the guards and soon the three of us were squeezing under the canvas. In the twilight zone the material left a trickle of static on my skin as the fabric slightly merged into my body. It was the strangest feeling, the physical boundaries of my own body no longer quite there.

My gaze swept over the tent's interior. We were standing in a curtained-off area at one end. From the other side of the curtain came a soft murmur of voices. Silhouettes were thrown up on to the material – a shadow theatre of people in hazmat suits working round the Grey.

'Oh god,' Mike said.

I turned to see him and Jack looking at gurneys carrying body bags. The zipper of the nearest one hadn't been fully drawn up.

The face of Jerry, the guy who'd been hunting the Grey, was staring lifelessly out of it.

Mike breathed through his nose, shaking his head. 'I guess that's what getting greedy gets you.'

But I barely heard him as I took in the other four body bags. Two of them were much smaller than the others. It had to be the family I'd imagined. All that was missing was the small dog.

I squeezed my eyes shut, fighting back sudden tears. I felt a hand on my shoulder, my skin tingling as it merged with it. I opened my eyes to see Jack gazing at me. His eyes were like anchors in this upside-down world and I felt something inside me steady.

'They were probably killed outright by the impact,' he said.

I shook my head. 'But what if they weren't? We know that Alvarez is entirely capable of killing them to avoid any loose ends.'

Jack grimaced as we turned back towards the curtain.

'So how are we going to play this, Lauren?' Mike asked, doing his best to look anywhere but at the body bags.

'We see how they're getting on with the Grey, then come up with a plan.'

We slipped round the edge of the partition, feeling the same tickling sensation of canvas briefly fusing with my body, into what turned out to be a temporary operating theatre on the other side.

The doctors were still wearing hazmat suits as they worked on the Grey under a bank of intense lights. I recognised the bald guy we'd seen speaking to Alvarez outside. He was injecting some sort of transparent fluid into the bullet hole in the alien's chest. The wound had been cleaned of blood to reveal a large patch of darkened skin. At least the Grey wasn't in a body bag yet.

Next to the operating table was a large metal sarcophagus. A network of fine pipes encircled it and gas cylinders with pressure gauges had been mounted on its sides.

The bald-headed surgeon turned to a woman next to him. 'Is the barometric chamber ready for the patient?'

She nodded. 'It's ready to be pressurised the moment you transfer the patient into it.'

Mike turned to Jack and me. 'Barometric chamber...isn't that what they use for divers who get the bends?'

Jack nodded. 'Maybe the Grey's home world has a different atmosphere to our own?'

'But that doesn't make sense,' I said. 'We've seen that alien running around.'

'Maybe he can tolerate our atmosphere for a short period, but can't cope with prolonged exposure, especially when he's injured,' Jack suggested. 'Whatever the reason, these doctors will be putting him into it for a very good reason.'

'It sounds as if they've got him stabilised, which is great, but how the hell are we going to move him when he's in that thing? It looks as if it weighs a good ton at least.'

Mike pointed towards the base of the sarcophagus. 'The same way they're going to, Lauren.'

For the first time I noticed the same sort of circular anti-gravity plates that we'd seen the Overseers use back in Peru. The Overseers had used these to easily carry a micro mind that had weighed a good couple of tons, with little effort.

'OK, that's definitely going to make things easier.'

A hiss came from a robotic arm and our attention returned to the operation as it swung out over the Grey. With a flicker of red light a projected target appeared on the alien's forehead. A drill began to whir up to speed with a disconcerting dentist-like buzzing and descended towards the Grey. I couldn't help but wince as the drill connected and the sickening sound of metal chewing into bone began.

'Jesus, they're going to kill it,' Mike said, his face paling.

Jack shook his head. 'Actually, they're not. I'm pretty sure that this has everything to do with when he fell and cracked the side of his head on that rock. It may have passed out due to a brain swell. By trepanning into the skull like this the surgeons are attempting to relieve the cranial pressure from the brain bleed. That will reduce the chance of any permanent damage. It's exactly what I'd do with a patient who had experienced a cranial injury such as this.'

A spray of black blood suddenly erupted from the drill's tip. It whirred to a stop before the robotic arm withdrew.

'See, I told you,' Jack said. He dipped his chin towards the medical team working round the Grey. 'This is like a home from home for me.'

Mike nodded, the colour returning to his face. 'Well, if we succeed in getting the little guy out of here, you'll be up next to look after him.'

'I do still have serious reservations about that,' Jack said.

'All you can do is your best, but make no mistake that, whatever the outcome, this Grey will be better off under your care than the Overseers,' I said.

'Yes, you may have a point.'

A woman's voice boomed out again from the tannoy outside the tent. 'Three minutes until Delta squadron arrive.'

'Bloody hell, we haven't got long left to make our move,' Mike said.

'We can't do anything until they finish stabilising him, otherwise we'll blow whatever chance of survival that alien has,' Jack said.

We watched in silence as the medical team placed a transparent gel pad over the hole they'd drilled in the Grey's skull. They gently moved him into the sarcophagus and began hooking him up to its internal monitoring equipment. At last, with a hydraulic hiss, the barometric chamber's lid was lowered into place.

'Let's get the subject outside ready for air transport back to base,' the bald man said.

'Right, this is our moment,' I said as I unholstered my LRS, my fingers merging with the stock, the pistol quite literally becoming an extension of me.

Mike's tranquilliser pistol was in his hand. 'Just remember our agreement outside and let me deal with the medical team.'

'OK, but do it as quickly as you can,' I said. I held the Empyrean Key up in my left hand, my LRS ready in the other. 'On my mark – three, two, one...' I selected the particle icon and rotated the orb forward. The world of shimmering energy steadied around us and grew solid again.

A medical nurse carrying a tray of instruments saw us as we materialised out of thin air and her tray crashed to the ground.

As everyone began to turn, Mike aimed his tranquilliser gun without hesitating and fired it straight at her. The nurse crumpled as Jack and I aimed our pistols at the others gathered round the sarcophagus.

I gestured towards the bald man. 'This is going to end one of two ways. The first and our preferred option is that my friend here shoots you all with his tranquilliser gun and you have a nice long sleep. The alternative –' I waved my LRS at them – 'will not be pleasant.'

'And please, don't do anything stupid like trying to raise the alarm, as that will force our hand,' Jack added.

Everyone stared at us, but they were all nodding. If they knew how my insides were doing a reasonable impression of jelly they might not have been so intimidated. In some ways this was worse than dealing with soldiers – this was a medical team trying to make a difference. And despite our noble motives, it was hard not to feel like the bad guys right now.

That feeling only increased as Mike began shooting them one by one. With small gasps they each fell to the ground like the nurse. Finally Mike turned his attention to the bald guy as he reloaded for the final shot.

The surgeon held up his hands higher. 'Please, you don't know what you're doing. We're trying to save that alien's life.'

'That's as maybe, but it's what your bosses will do next that worries me,' I replied. I nodded to Mike and he fired the last dart into the man's arm. A moment later he too lay motionless alongside the others.

'Delta squadron will arrive in one minute,' the amplified voice called from outside.

'Right, time to make ourselves scarce,' I said.

We headed to the sarcophagus. The Grey's face was visible through the glass hatch, his eyes closed. Mike bent down and pressed the button on the gravity ring attached to the chamber. At once it glowed blue.

'Guys, you're about to get company!' Ruby said over the earbud link. 'Alvarez and a group of soldiers are on their way to you right now.'

'Then we need covering fire immediately, starting with the two guards outside this tent!' I told her.

'I'm all over it, boss,' Ruby said.

Shouts and cries suddenly erupted from outside as we heard the hiss of sniper rounds. Soon the sound of return weapon fire started up.

'Shit, talk about stirring up a damned hornets' nest, I just missed Alvarez who is about to give you a house call,' Ruby muttered over the link.

'Thanks for the heads up,' I replied. I struck my tuning fork and the icons shimmered into existence. I selected the waveform icon, but just as I was about to activate it, Alvarez and six other soldiers charged in, throwing our plan into tatters.

His gaze instantly locked on to my face, his eyes widening in recognition. 'You!' His pistol was already pivoting towards me.

Someone grabbed hold of my shoulders as a spark of light came from the pistol's muzzle. I was shoved hard and spun away and someone cried out in pain. Jack yelled and sprayed bullets at Alvarez and his men. They retreated through the flap, returning fire as they went.

My heart leapt to my throat as I spun round and saw Mike clutching his leg and writhing on the ground.

CHAPTER EIGHTEEN

I barely registered the siren screaming outside the tent or the building wail of the storm.

Mike's eyes stared into mine. 'Sorry, it seems I just managed to break this mission's winning streak by getting myself shot.'

'Only by taking a bloody bullet meant for Lauren,' Jack said, his tone strained as he continued to fire rounds out through the canvas walls towards the shadowy shapes outside.

'You did what?' I said as I looked away to return fire too.

He managed a faint chuckle. 'I didn't really think it through. But, hey, those are the breaks.'

My heart wanted to burst. This man, my friend, had risked his life to save mine. 'I don't know whether to throttle or hug you.'

'I'll settle for a hug later.' He clenched his teeth as a spasm went through him. 'Oh hell, that hurts.' He pressed his hand over his leg and blood bubbled up between his fingers.

'Just hang in there, buddy; I've got you covered,' Jack said.

I emptied the clip in my LRS through the tent wall, trying to buy Jack time. Jack yanked out a medical pack from his rucksack, along with a length of rubber tubing, some glue and bandages. He tied the rubber tube round Mike's thigh and pulled it hard.

'Fuck, fuck, fuckity, fuck!' Mike squeezed out the words between his teeth as he clamped his jaw together.

I held his hand as Jack set to work, reloading my LRS with my free hand. 'How bad is it, Jack?' I asked, as more incoming rounds peppered the canvas and we took cover behind racks of medical equipment that sparked as they were hit.

'It looks as if the bullet has shattered Mike's knee. I'll do my best to slow the blood loss, but there's no exit wound. I need to get him to the operating theatre in E8 as quickly as possible to remove the bullet, otherwise...' Jack raised his eyebrows at me as he squirted the glue into Mike's wound and clamped the broken flesh together with his fingers.

Every muscle in Mike's face stood out as he jammed his jaw together even harder.

'That's it – I'm done for now, but we need to get him over to E8.'

'Lucy, prep the operating theatre, Mike's been injured,' I said.

'I heard. Hang in there, Mike.'

'I'm doing my best,' he replied as Jack worked as quickly as he could to wrap the wound with a bandage.

'I'll take off and get as close as I can...' Lucy said. 'Oh, damn it! Three TR-3Bs have just turned up and are directly over your position. There's no way for me to get close enough to be able to transfer you over to E8.'

'That is not what I wanted to hear,' Jack said, throwing me a tense look that I knew was matched by my own.

The gunfire from outside suddenly went eerily quiet.

Then we heard Alvarez's voice. 'Lauren and team, you may as well make things easy on yourselves and give up now.'

My mind raced. Mike needed treatment and he needed it

now. 'Lucy, we need to come to you if you can't get to us. I can still get us into the twilight zone. They can't touch us there.'

'OK, if you can get within a few hundred metres of me, I can whisk you all over to E8.'

'Understood.' A plan was starting to form in my head. 'Ruby, how many soldiers are outside the medical tent with Alvarez right now?'

'About twelve. It was twenty, but I thinned them out a bit for you. The rest are hunkered down in ditches and I can't take them out from here. You should also know they appear to be preparing for a direct assault on your position, with another couple of squads being kept back for the moment. I'll be able to take a few out when they show their heads, but I won't be able to stop all of them.'

'Got it.' I turned to Jack. 'We haven't got long. In the twilight zone, invisible or not, we still can't actually walk through them, especially if we're going to be bringing our alien buddy with us.'

'Then we need to create a distraction long enough for us to get away,' Jack said. 'Check my bag.'

I opened it and peered in. There were six grenades inside. 'Oh, now you're talking.' I pulled out two of the flashbangs. 'Right, we need to fall back to the other side of the sarcophagus so we can use it as cover from the flashbang grenade blast. When they attack I'll use the grenades to stun them. Then I'll shift us into the twilight zone and we can get back to Lucy before they realise what we've done.'

'You can seriously think on your feet, Lauren,' Mike said through gritted teeth.

'It seems to be one of my skills,' I replied.

Jack gave Mike a shot of adrenaline as more incoming rounds ricocheted off the medical equipment. Keeping our heads down, we carefully manoeuvred him, his face twisting in agony, to the far side of the metal chamber.

'Guys, heads up, they're starting to make their move,' Ruby said. 'One of the soldiers has just run up to the entrance...damn, I missed the bastard!'

Jack grabbed one of the flashbangs. 'Get ready!'

With adrenaline thundering through my system, I grabbed a flashbang too, as well as Mike's dart gun, which I stuck into the waistband of my jeans.

At the same time something was thrown through the tent entrance and clanged the other side of the sarcophagus. An impossibly loud bang numbed my hearing to silence as a blaze of light erupted, turning my vision white.

'The second assault team is coming round the back,' Ruby's voice said, a faint echo in my ringing ears.

My head spun, nausea rising through me, but my vision had started to clear. I turned to see a black hunting-style knife slicing up through the canvas walls.

Jack swayed, steadying himself against the sarcophagus, and threw his flashbang through the slit.

But I knew we weren't out of the woods yet. The other team would be coming through the main entrance at any second. I pulled the pin of my own flashbang and lobbed the grenade back over the sarcophagus. Jack threw himself over me as two more balls of white light exploded.

The world spun faster as the nausea tightened its grip. I felt a prick in my arm and heat shot through me.

My eyes came back into focus to see Jack's face close to mine, blood streaming from his ears. 'I've just given you an adrenaline shot,' he said, his voice muffled. 'Alvarez had the same damned idea we did and lobbed a flashbang in here. Mike's out cold, but that's probably not a bad thing.'

The ringing in my ears began to subside as Jack peered cautiously over the sarcophagus and then stood up, holding a hand out for me.

I took it and let Jack haul me to my feet. The first thing I saw was Alvarez and three soldiers groaning as they lay outside the entrance to the tent. That scene was repeated through the slit in the canvas near us: another three soldiers were lying on the ground almost exactly where Jack's flashbang had gone off.

'Guys, great work,' Ruby said, 'but I hate to break it to you, those other squads are making their move and will be on top of you any moment.'

Jack bent down, hooked his arms under Mike and laid him on the closed sarcophagus. 'We can move faster like this,' he said, reading the questions in my eyes.

'Good thinking,' I said. 'Lucy, operate carrier tone now!'

'On it...'

A faint chiming sound came from my earbud as I grabbed the Empyrean Key, selected the waveform icon and activated it. The world blurred to the alternative ghostly version I was coming to know so well.

My hands sank halfway through the handle at the front of the sarcophagus as Jack placed himself at the rear. That was one of strange side effects of being in the twilight zone. The waveform version of the particles that made up our bodies still partly inter-acted with other objects. Thankfully that included the ground, which stopped us sinking through it to the core of the planet. But there was also an area of overlap where we partially merged with the world around us, like now.

Ignoring the tingle of energy in my fingertips where they had disappeared a few millimetres into the metal surface, and with the antigravity plate taking the strain, we lifted the sarcophagus easily, Mike balanced on top.

My head was still woozy from the blast and I stumbled, but we managed to carry the sarcophagus out through the cut slit in the tent's wall.

The scene that met our eyes outside was chaotic.

CHAPTER NINETEEN

STEEL-ROD RAIN SLAMMED down to the ground, forming vast puddles in the wheel tracks that criss-crossed the chewed-up lawn. Together with all the bodies strewn everywhere, it was almost like walking into a movie scene of the Battle of the Somme.

A line of soldiers had hunkered down on the shoreline and were shooting tracer fire across the lake into the woods where Ruby had hidden herself. Another squad was racing towards the medical tent as a hiss sliced through the air. The head of a soldier with a sub-machine gun exploded in a shower of brains and blood as a bullet hit his skull. He toppled backwards as the soldiers around him dived to the ground.

An animal instinct drew my eyes skywards. Three triangular craft, TR-3B Astras, were hovering about a hundred metres above us in perfect silence. Rain swirled round them, but rather than striking their metal surfaces the water formed the blurring outline of a bubble a metre or so out, like an invisible force field. It had to be something to do with their gravity-disruption drives. Their propulsion-engine ports glowed orange like demonic eyes peering down at us. I felt numb to my core, like prey frozen by their stare.

Jack followed my gaze and stared up at the craft. 'We could do without that.' Then he looked back to all the soldiers hunkered down between us and the lake. 'How are we going to get to Lucy?'

It was a good question. Although Alvarez's soldiers couldn't see or hurt us now, there were simply too many of them to slip between.

'We'll need to rendezvous with her somewhere else. This alien needs urgent attention and fast.'

Jack nodded. 'Lucy, any suggestions of which way to head?'

'There's a road leading away from the house that appears clear according to my sensors. There's a large open field about two nautical miles from your position. Get there and I can circle round to rendezvous with you. I should be able to keep you in range so you can stay in the twilight zone. Fortunately, that needs a lot less power than bringing you over to E8, which I have to do at much closer proximity.'

'Then we'll make our way to the rendezvous point now.' An awful thought slammed into my mind. 'Shit, what about you, Ruby?'

'Don't worry about me, boss. I can make my way out of here —' A crack of automatic fire hissed in the background. 'Fuck! That was way too close for comfort. Time for me to move again – they're zeroing in on my current position.'

'Try to keep them busy for another few minutes and then fall back to Lucy and the X101,' I said.

'Understood, boss,' she replied.

We began to tow the sarcophagus, Mike still unconscious on top of it, away from the firefight and in the direction of the main gate set into a low boundary wall ahead of us. Through the heavy curtains of swirling rain I began to make out the outlines of the two guards and a Humvee behind the gate.

Jack and I froze as a humming sound grew louder and one of the three TR-3Bs started to descend.

Jack cast me a wild look and for a terrible moment I thought we'd been spotted. I braced myself for the impossible firepower that the craft would unleash on us even if they couldn't actually hurt us in the twilight zone. But then its landing legs began to extend. As it drew lower, I noticed the single red-painted panel in the belly of the craft.

'I'm pretty certain that's the TR-3B that pursued Ariel,' I said.

'The one that didn't open fire on you?' Jack asked.

'The very same.'

We watched it eerily descending, its soft humming growing louder over the crackle of gunfire as it landed next to the crashed Tic Tac.

Then Jack pointed upwards. 'Hey, where are his two buddies going?'

I glanced up to see the other two craft peeling away as they flew silently to a floating position over the lake. Searchlight beams suddenly lanced out from both, the cones of light swinging back and forth over the forested slopes opposite Ruby's position.

'OK, I think those TR-3Bs are searching for me,' Ruby said over the comm link, her voice completely calm as if this happened every day. 'I'll hopefully keep them distracted long enough for you guys to get away.'

'But you need to get moving now too,' I told her.

'Don't you worry about me, boss. I'll be long gone before they finally work out where I am.'

'Make sure you bloody are.'

A whirring sound came from the landed Astra as a ramp lowered from its belly and two pilots in blue flight suits walked down it. They shook the hands of one of the men in coveralls waiting for them. Two more men moved beneath the TR-3B as small hatches opened in the craft allowing cables with hooks to be lowered. The men took hold of the cables and carried them towards the Tic Tac, trailing lines over the lawn.

'So that's how they're going to get the UFO out of here – an airlift,' Jack said.

'It certainly looks that way,' I replied.

Still hidden in the twilight zone, we manoeuvred the sarcophagus over the lawn towards the armed guards at the gate. It was all going so well when Lucy's voice spoke through my earbud again.

'Oh damn!' she said. 'Those bloody TR-3Bs looking for Ruby are almost on top of me.'

I spun round to stare back. The two TR-3Bs had floated up towards the top of the ridge. Both crafts' spotlights converged, locking on to the same spot.

'And now they've bloody found me!' Lucy said.

'Then get the hell out of there,' I shouted.

'But if I do that I'll be out of range and you'll be dropped out of the twilight zone.'

'Then here's the new plan. Take them on a wild goose chase and then make your way back towards the rendezvous site out on the main road.'

'But, Lauren—'

'Just do it already. Leave the X101 behind for Ruby and leave the rest to us.'

'Then good luck to all of you,' Lucy said, her voice far tenser than I'd ever heard it.

Under the twin spotlights the trees on the ridge suddenly swirled aside as Lucy took off. A split second later, both TR-3Bs were zooming towards the eastern horizon chasing Lucy who was glowing like a lit-up Christmas decoration in the twilight zone.

But even though she was invisible in the real world, those sensor beams of the TR-3Bs had obviously still been able to detect her and lock on.

My mind raced as I fought the feeling of panic spinning faster inside me. 'Ruby, have you got a line of sight on either of those guards at the gate we're closing in on?'

'I have on the guy standing to the right of the Humvee.'

'Then take the shot now.'

A slight hiss of air sped past and one of the two guards crumpled to the ground.

'I'm going to be out of range in three, two, one...' Lucy said. A slight crackle filled the comm link and her voice hissed to silence.

The world started to grow solid again as we shifted back. Immediately the remaining guard's gaze locked on to us. He dropped down to hunker behind the Humvee.

'This is bad, Lauren,' Jack whispered.

'We've been in worse.'

I slowed my breathing down, my LRS aimed. Hundreds of hours on the kinetic firing range was kicking in. I was poised, ready to strike.

The guy's helmeted head appeared first, then his carbine being levelled towards us. I breathed out and squeezed the LRS's trigger. A single bullet hole appeared in the guy's forehead, the impact spinning him round into the Humvee's bonnet. He slid down it, leaving a smear of blood.

I breathed out, shocked at how calm I felt. When had it become so easy to take a life?

A whistle came from my earbud. 'Wow, nice shooting, Lauren,' Ruby said. 'Talk about being cucumber cool under pressure.'

'That's our Lauren,' Jack said.

I glanced back to see at least ten soldiers heading into the medical tent where as far as they knew we were still hunkered down. 'OK, we need to get out of here as fast as possible,' I said.

'So let's steal that Humvee and get the hell out of Dodge,' Jack replied with what I'm sure was meant to be a cowboy drawl.

Before I could reply, a blaze of bullets kicked up the mud behind us. The soldiers had reappeared from the medical tent and were rushing towards us. Alvarez was limping behind them, barking orders.

A bullet pinged off the base of the sarcophagus and sparks flew out from the impact.

I glanced down to see a bullet hole in the antigravity pad. Its lights flickered and died. The sarcophagus, with Mike on it, suddenly became impossibly heavy and we had to drop it hard on to the ground.

'Shit, we have no way of moving the Grey now,' I said.

'We have to abandon him,' Jack said.

'Bloody hell, all this has been for nothing,' I said as I fired off several covering rounds as Jack dragged Mike from the top of the sarcophagus and hoisted him over his shoulder.

'We have no choice,' Jack said as I waded with him away from the Grey through the mud towards the Humvee.

Shouts and cries came from behind us as soldiers in the pursuing squad toppled to the ground, bullet rounds slamming into their bodies.

'Ruby!' I said into my mic.

'I know, I know, but I want to make sure you get away OK.'

'Thank you for being so damned brave,' I said.

'No more than you guys.'

Ruby continued to snipe from the other side of the lake. I fell back as Jack headed towards the Humvee so I could give him covering fire. Between Ruby and I, we caught the approaching soldiers in a crossfire, forcing them to drop flat into the dirt as

Jack reached the Humvee and hauled Mike into the passenger seat.

I spotted a soldier at the front of the squad pulling back something beneath his weapon's barrel.

Jack had seen him too as he raced round to the driver's seat. 'That guy's about to fire a grenade at you!'

With a hiss, the man sprawled dead to the ground.

'Or maybe not,' Ruby said. 'But, boss, I really don't think I can hold out much longer here. They're bringing round two Humvees with M2 Brownings to deal with me. I think I may have kept their attention a little too well.'

'Then, as I said before, get the hell out of there already! Head back to the X101. Then fly round to pick us up at the rendezvous point.'

'I will, Lauren,' Ruby replied.

Even in this crazy situation, part of my mind noted she'd dropped her sarcastic use of 'boss'.

'Kill those bastards!' Alvarez screamed at his soldiers.

A hailstorm of fully automatic rounds lit up the faces of the squad as they fired towards us and we dived for the ground. I knew Alvarez would be determined enough to take out the Humvee with another grenade if that stopped us escaping. I needed to do something at a truly batshit level of crazy if any of us were going to get out of here in one piece.

And then it got worse. I spotted the helmets of a second squad running along the far side of the wall, straight towards the Humvee. Alvarez was attempting to catch us in a pincer movement, and they would be on top of Jack and Mike before I could get there.

'Jack, take the Humvee and make for the rendezvous point,' I shouted as I emptied my LRS clip and reloaded.

His eyes snapped from the second squad he'd been firing at back to me. 'But what about you?'

'I'm going to give you covering fire instead, so you can get away. If someone doesn't stay behind, no one will make it out of here.'

'But you can't!'

'I bloody can; I'm the one giving the orders. Just leave me with any grenades you have left.'

Jack hesitated, but then lobbed me his bag. We stared at each other for a second, even though we were painfully aware of the soldiers closing in rapidly on his position. There was so much I wanted to say, but there simply wasn't time.

'Lauren, I...' Jack began before his words trailed away.

'Yes, I know and if we make it out of this, you and I are so having a heart-to-heart.'

Bullets sparked off the nose of the Humvee as Jack stared at me. His mouth opened and closed as if he wanted to say something.

'Jack, for Mike's sake if nothing else, go!'

He gave me a nod, threw a smoke grenade at the squad closing in on him and at last jumped into the cab.

My heart ached, but I ignored it and returned my attention to Alvarez.

A sustained barrage of automatic fire hissed past me and I dropped flat into the mud again. I hunted through Jack's bag as I heard the Humvee's engine roar into life. As soon as Alvarez realised what we were doing, he'd have the Humvee taken out for certain. I needed to do something before that happened. I found two smoke grenades and a flashbang in the bag. I pulled the pin on one of smoke grenades and lobbed it at the ground between me and the soldiers who were closing in.

As the grenade erupted with billowing smoke, I immediately shot wild rounds through the growing murk.

Return fire hissed overhead.

Think like a soldier, Lauren...

Once again I slowed my breathing. I needed to keep a laser-sharp focus. I threw the second smoke grenade only metres away from me.

Smoke billowed from it and swirled over me. Within seconds the world became a haze of smoke and whistling bullet rounds skimming over my head.

'Hold your fucking fire! You're going to hit the subject!' Alvarez bellowed.

The sound of bullets whistled to a silence.

Now to really sow confusion among him and his soldiers. I pulled the pin on the final flashbang and lobbed it towards Alvarez's voice.

A moment later a ball of white light pulsed in the bank of cascading smoke. Shouts and cries came from soldiers. I jumped to my feet, moving sideways, and fired a few rounds to add to the general chaos.

I glanced back at the Humvee as its squat shape disappeared down the road. Jack and Mike were going to make it. A wave of relief rushed through me as the other squad finally reached where they'd been only seconds before.

Now I needed to get out of here fast before Alvarez and his soldiers had a chance to regroup. With any luck they'd assume I'd got away in the Humvee too after I lobbed those grenades at them.

I ran my eyes over the hazy shape of the sarcophagus lying less that fifty metres away. Apart from the antigravity plate damage, miraculously it didn't look as if it had been hit. But that didn't help me. I was going to have to abandon the Grey. Abandon what our mission had been for. I just hoped I lived long enough for Alice to lecture me about it.

My head down, I ran sideways away from the sarcophagus as the smoke began to thin. Shapes loomed out of the fog and closed in on the Grey, weapons drawn. I dropped to the sodden ground, grateful for the curtains of rain that were helping to reduce visibility.

'They got away in a Humvee, Colonel, but they didn't take the subject. It's still alive,' a woman's voice called out.

'Then get after those fucking terrorists!' Alvarez screamed.

Good, so they didn't realise I was still here. That might give me an edge.

The bark of a heavy-calibre weapon rattled out. For an awful moment I thought I'd been spotted and I dropped flat again. But when no bullets tore through my body, I looked up to see tracer fire speeding across the lake, shredding the branches of the trees opposite to matchwood.

'Ruby, please tell me that you're OK?' I whispered.

No reply came back over my earbud.

'Ruby?'

Still nothing.

Cold dread filled my gut. If I'd listened to Alice, I wouldn't have dropped everyone into this awful situation. I was such a headstrong stupid idiot. Part of me clung to that anger at myself. If nothing else, it helped me to blot out thoughts about what had just happened to Ruby.

A stream of Humvees sped out through the gate, their gunners pointing their M2s forward down the road where Jack had just escaped with Mike. At least they could still get away. That was all that mattered now.

Alvarez, his ears streaming with blood, turned away from the sarcophagus and walked towards the landed Astra with six of his soldiers. But I was between him and his destination. In moments he'd be right on top of me. I looked for cover – somewhere, anywhere to hide.

A long triangular shadow from the landed TR-3B Astra, cast by the arc lights, was a few metres from where I lay pressed flat into the mud. I crawled into its cover on my elbows as Alvarez and three soldiers closed in rapidly. I heard voices behind me getting louder.

Beyond the TR-3B, I spotted two pilots rushing back towards their craft with a group of engineers who'd just finished connecting the cable from the TR-3B to the harness tied round the Tic Tac.

I couldn't be more stuck between a rock and a hard place. All it'd take was one set of eyes to see me skulking here in the shadows and that would be it.

I tore my gaze away to the ramp leading up into the TR-3B. The rational part of my brain must have glitched for a second as I found myself racing up the ramp into the belly of the craft I'd been hiding beneath.

CHAPTER TWENTY

I TRIED to slow down my ragged breath as I hid inside the locker I'd chosen for cover. It wasn't the best choice, but I'd had no time to assess anywhere else. I was crammed beside some blue flights suits and various bits of kit, having to press my body into a series of lumps and bumps. Why hadn't I tried to take my chances and found somewhere to hide out in the ruins of the house until I could slip away? I seriously needed to have a word with the part of my brain that came up with crazy spur-of-the-moment decisions like this. In what universe was running into the TR-3B ever going to be a good idea? But I was here now and needed to make the best of it. I had to find the first opportunity to get out of here before the Astra took off.

I checked the clip in my LRS. It was half empty, although I had another full one in my bag.

Through three horizontal slits in the locker door I had a limited view of the TR-3B's cockpit. The design was very different to Ariel's. Rather than being spherical, three seats faced inwards towards a bank of monitors. Numerous panels of controls surrounded each of the seats, resembling the flight deck of a space shuttle more than anything else. The design was bewil-deringly complex compared to the almost minimalist styling of the Ariel. It also crushed the other even more stupid idea I'd had about stealing this TR-3B and flying it out of here. I was no pilot. And, knowing my luck, I would end up crashing the craft even if I did manage to get it airborne. No, my best bet was to get off and find a much more sensible hiding place.

A movement on one of the screens, showing a live feed beneath the belly of the Astra, caught my eye as the two pilots came into view. They shook the hand of an engineer with them. Then Alvarez appeared with three of his soldiers, who were moving the sarcophagus. They must have given it a new anti-gravity plate. The pilots disappeared from view and a moment later I heard the clunk of feet on metal.

Shit, shit, shit!

I held my breath and tightened my grip on my LRS as the two pilots appeared in the cockpit. The first guy, taller than his colleague, looked almost like a movie cliché, he was that good-looking. With a sweep of dark hair he could have passed for a taller version of Maverick from the *Top Gun* films. The guy prob-ably had a kick-arse motorbike back at home to complete his movie-like persona. In stark contrast, the shorter man had a soft, round puppy face with kind eyes, framed by a mop of dark hair that looked as if it needed a seriously good comb.

Both men were wearing blue flight suits with a US Navy emblem on the arm. They dropped into two of the seats and a clanking sound echoed from somewhere beneath. There were more footsteps and a moment later Alvarez's head appeared at the top of the ramp, peering in at the flight crew.

'The Grey has been loaded into your cargo bay. His condition is currently stable, but our specialists say he may go critical at any time. As soon as you've secured the Tic Tac, you'll need to make it back to base as fast as possible.'

'Understood, sir,' the taller pilot said.

I noticed he didn't call Alvarez 'colonel'. Maybe the US military didn't recognise Alvarez's rank. Was there any significance in that?

The shorter guy turned to Alvarez. 'You're not catching a lift with us then, sir?'

Shit, so they were about to take off. What the hell was I going to do? If I tried to flee now the pilots would raise the alarm and I'd be captured in an instant.

Alvarez was shaking his head. 'No, I'm still hunting down those damned terrorists. They stole one of our Humvees, but can't have gone far.' Alvarez nodded to the flight crew and then disappeared away down the ramp.

Still... So Jack and Mike hadn't been caught yet. I sagged into myself as some of the tension I'd been carrying released. Please, god, make it stay that way.

The shorter guy toggled a switch on the control panel in front of him and there was a hiss of hydraulics. The slit of light from the ramp disappeared as it closed and soft blue lights turned on to illuminate the cabin.

Oh bloody hell, I'm trapped now! Instinctively I pushed myself back further into the shadows of the locker. I just hoped the pilots weren't going to need anything from it.

'I tell you that guy gives me the creeps, Don,' the shorter man said.

The taller guy nodded. 'Yeah, I've never warmed to him. Anyway, how's our passenger doing, Zack?'

Zack pressed one of the control panels and what looked to be a medical read-out appeared on his screen. 'Like the man said, his vitals are low, but stable for now,' he said.

'Then let's get a move on so he can have some proper medical attention. Although on second thoughts it might be better for him if he died during the flight.'

The worry about my own situation was suddenly tempered by concern for the Grey.

'Yeah, Alvarez and his kind might deny the rumours of what they get up in Wing Twelve. But if what people say are true, the experiments they run on these captured aliens are nothing short of torture.'

'That's what I don't get,' Don said. 'It's like our standing orders to shoot down any UFOs we encounter. As far as I know, aliens have never once showed any hostile intent during any encounter, but we still treat them as an enemy.'

'Unfortunately we're not the ones who hand out the orders,' Zack replied. 'At least no one has picked up on the fact we haven't hit a single one yet.'

Don grinned as he began to scan the instrumentation on his panel. 'Yeah, such a shame.'

If how these guys was talking was typical of the other crews, this was an interesting insight. These US Navy pilots might have been following orders, but it seemed they weren't happy about it. Maybe I could use this to my advantage, especially if they were sympathetic to the Grey. Once airborne I could hijack the craft and persuade them at gunpoint to help me? It would be an extreme gamble, but it might have a chance of working out if I explained the bigger picture to both of them.

I felt a sense of calmness taking hold. This might actually work. I just needed to wait for the right moment.

A voice came over a speaker in the cockpit. 'Archangel, the Tic Tac ship has been secured to you. You are cleared for immediate take-off.'

'Roger that,' Don said.

He took hold of a complicated-looking joystick device with his right hand and placed his left on a second.

A gentle hum came from beneath the cockpit and I felt a

subtle shift of gravity within the craft. They must have just brought their antigravity drive online.

Don rotated a thumbwheel on his joystick slightly forward. The view of the house on his screen began to slide down as the TR-3B ascended slowly into the sky. When we'd reached a hundred feet up according to his display, Don rotated the trackball until the craft came to hovering stop. Despite the storm howling around us, we sat absolutely stationary in the sky, as stable as a mountain.

Zack toggled a switch on his control panel. The view on his screen switched to a camera pointing directly at the ground, showing the slack cables connected to the Tic Tac's harness being blown sideways in the howling wind. Beneath us a team of workers had placed two large antigravity discs to either side of the crashed alien ship. They began glowing blue.

'Agie plates have been activated, Archangel,' the voice said over the speaker. 'You are free to commence lift procedure.'

'Roger that,' Don replied. 'Winding in the lifting cables now.'

Zack pressed an icon on his touchscreen and a gentle whining sound passed through the cabin as the slack in the cables was taken up. We didn't so much shudder as the Tic Tac began to rise, soil and debris dropping away from its buried nose as it freed itself from the ground. The alien craft swung in the wind as it rose, beginning to fill the monitor view.

'Deploying grapples,' Zack said.

Several loud thumps came from below and two large mechanical arms rose into view. They reached out like the mandibles of a giant insect towards each side of the Tic Tac. With a slight tremor they locked on to the alien ship and it stopped swinging.

'Big fish is secured,' Zack said, toggling a switch. The image switched back to the forward-view camera filled with a view of swirling curtains of rain.

'Let's get this alien bird back to base so the techs can start playing with their new toy,' Don said. He rolled the thumbwheel forward and the view blurred once again as we shot upwards, then he rolled the controller back and we came to a stop again.

We were hovering over a bank of storm clouds, a full moon kissing their peaks with silver light.

'Flight altitude at fifty thousand feet,' Zack called out.

Just like Ariel, flying a TR-3B had to be one of the most prized experiences for a pilot. There was certainly a gleam in Don's eye as there had been in Alice's – until she'd lost it at least.

Don pushed the right joystick forward and just like that we were speeding towards the horizon.

'Mach eight. ETA at base in twenty-one minutes,' Zack said.

'Thank Christ for that,' Don said. 'I don't know about you, my friend, but I need my bunk.'

'Absolutely, bro,' Zack replied. 'These endless patrols are starting to wear me down. Together with that guy Alvarez sticking his nose continually into what should be Navy business. He gave me the third degree about why we didn't manage to shoot that UFO down.'

'Yeah, but as I said to him, that ship was as slippery as an eel swimming in extra grease,' Don said.

'All I know is that whoever was piloting that baby had some major skills to outfly you, bro.'

Far from looking annoyed, Don grinned at his friend. 'Yeah, tell me about it.'

They had to be talking about Alice. What would she think if she could hear this conversation?

'You're lucky that Alvarez guy didn't arrange for you to be court-martialled,' Zack said. 'He was practically spitting bullets at Commander Jenson about that little episode.'

'Just as well our cover story about me never getting a line of sight held. And I trust Jenson to not throw us under the bus.

Although he's never come out and said it, you can tell he isn't comfortable with the whole shoot-first-and-ask-questions-later approach either.'

This had to be the same flight crew we'd encountered during Ariel's test flight. And it seemed that they really were sympathetic. My hijack attempt might go easier than I first thought. I slowed my breathing as I held my LRS, getting ready to burst out of the locker.

A sudden warbling alarm came from one of Zack's control consoles. 'Crap, the alien's vital are crashing,' he said.

'Jesus, but there's nothing we can do for him while he's down in the hold,' Don said. 'How far out are we?'

'Twelve minutes.'

'Too long. I need to redline the propulsion rockets.'

'But we'll be in danger of blowing our reactor.'

'Let's just hope it doesn't,' Don replied.

'OK. Heating our reactor up to Mexican-sun levels of hot.'

Don chuckled as I slumped back into the locker. Just like that everything had changed. If I tried to hijack this craft now, I'd almost certainly be signing the death warrant of the Grey. And even if I did successfully get control of the Astra, what then? There wasn't much of a chance of finding Jack and Mike now.

And then the blindingly obvious hit me.

I hadn't thought of the simplest option. I'd call Jack on my Sky Wire and if I couldn't get through, I'd contact Alice for backup. As quietly as I could, I pulled the satellite phone off my belt. Cupping my hand to hide the glow of the screen so it wouldn't show through the slits in the locker, I toggled its phone mode back on. But as I looked at the screen, the hope inside me evaporated. There were no reception bars. The cockpit was probably shielded. I had no chance of letting anyone know where I was.

Fresh despair lapped through me, as all I saw was dead ends.

There was only one thing left I could try. I'd wait until we'd landed so the Grey could be saved. Then once Don and Zack had departed the TR-3B, I'd sneak outside and get reception again. Then I'd contact Eden and see if they could extract me from the shit in which I'd managed to land myself. Shit, I realised, that was entirely my own fault.

Zack raised his head after examining one of his read-out screens. 'Reactor is redlining. This bird is ready for Mach 9 whenever you are, Don.'

'Then let's shoot a burner out of this Astra's ass and see exactly what it can do,' Don replied.

He pushed the right joystick forward hard, whilst rolling the thumbwheel over. The landscape of mountain cloudscapes blurred beneath us as the craft hurtled faster than a rocket through the night towards a slither of growing sunlight in the distance.

CHAPTER TWENTY-ONE

MULTIPLE ALARMS SCREAMED from the control screens as I remained hidden in the locker. The atmosphere in the cockpit grew significantly more taut. Only single-syllable words were now being uttered between the pilots. It was pretty clear to me they were fighting to keep the TR-3B Astra flying beyond its designed speed limit. They were putting their lives on the line in a mercy dash to try to save the Grey. We might have technically been on different sides of this fight, but my respect for this flight crew grew by the moment.

'Reversing thrusters now,' Don said, toggling a bank of buttons.

We dropped out of *Enterprise*-like warp speed and a wave of G-force pressed me hard into the locker wall, even with the reduced gravity. My side aching, I peered out through the slits in the door. Don's flight monitor showed a view from the downward-facing camera. Beyond the edges of the Tic Tac still slung to the Astra's belly, I could see a substantial airbase below us. Its buildings were tinged with the golden light of the sunrise and cast long, standing-stone-like shadows. There was something familiar about the twin airstrip layout. One of them was wider than the other and both were very long. Where had I seen this before?

Zack wiped a bead of sweat from his forehead. 'Home sweet home.' He toggled a few more switches. 'Reducing reactor to fifty per cent, but we're still on the verge of venting plasma here.'

Don nodded and pressed one of the buttons in his chair. 'Control, we're coming in hot. We'll need a reception committee to cool our hide down.'

'Understood, Archangel,' a woman's voice replied over the cabin speakers. 'Ground robotic hoses are being deployed.'

Don rotated the joystick thumbwheel backwards and the Astra raced down towards the ground. Another alarm joined the cacophony of the others as Zack began furiously pressing buttons on one of the touchscreens in front of him.

Despite my growing anxiety that we might turn into one giant fireball, I took in more details of the base as we sped downwards. There was what amounted to almost a small town of buildings to the left-hand side of the airstrips, several huge buildings that had to be hangars...and then I knew exactly where I'd seen this before. This was none other than the famed airbase of myth and legend. I'd seen it in plenty of satellite photos across UFO-conspiracy sites.

This was Area 51.

As we hurtled down at a breakneck speed, the tiny H of the landing pad grew from a speck faster than was comfortable for my liking. My stomach rose into my chest.

I made out three arching geysers of water spraying the landing pad, sending up clouds of billowing vapour.

I instinctively curled into a ball, but Don seemed perfectly chilled as the landing pad rushed up to meet us. My brain was screaming at me that we were about to smash straight into the ground like a meteorite with a death wish. But at what seemed the very last microsecond, Don spun the thumbwheel back to the neutral position. We came to a dead stop just twenty metres above the pad.

The spray from the surrounding hoses pivoted downwards to envelop the craft. It should have sounded like Niagara Falls running down the outside of the hull but there was just a soft gurgling. And then on Zack's screen I saw why. An invisible oval sphere was surrounding the Astra like a force field. The water was running over it and not touching the craft. Just like the rain had done back at the crash site.

'Adjusting gravity-disruption vortex field to allow emergency cooling,' Zack said. He pressed a button on his screen.

The invisible force field disappeared and the waterfall sound I'd been expecting now thundered on to the canopy of the TR-3B. Water streamed down in torrents over the camera views, steam rising from the exterior metalwork as creaks and groans came from the ship.

'How's it looking?' Don asked.

'Reactor is cooling at three hundred kelvin, two hundred, and...yes,' Zack said, thumping the air, 'we're back in the green zone.' He slumped into his seat as all the alarms fell silent.

Don toggled the button in his seat again. 'Thank you, Control. We needed that nice cold shower.'

The woman laughed. 'Any time, Archangel.' The fountains of water around the craft slowed until the water only dribbled from the spouts of the hoses. They pivoted upwards and slid back into the ground, hatches closing over them.

'Please proceed to Hangar A,' the woman's voice continued. 'The medical and tech teams are on standby.'

'Proceeding to Hangar A,' Don repeated. 'And, hey, Julie, are you free for quick drink before I hit my bunk?'

The woman laughed. 'With you, always.'

'Then it's a date.' Don hit the button in the chair again.

Zack chuckled.

'What?'

'I'm not saying a word.' Zack just smiled and returned his attention to his instruments.

It struck me then just how normal these guys were. In another life we'd probably be friends. Unfortunately, they were on the wrong side of this situation.

Don gently rolled the trackball a fraction forward and the craft started to float towards a massive squat concrete building, its enormous hangar doors beginning to roll back. But rather than being met by a fleet of TR-3Bs as I'd expected, all I could spot inside were fighter jets. There were a couple of Chinooks and a Learjet over to one side too, but that was it.

Two spotlights illuminated two large red circles on the floor ahead of us inside the hangar. Gathered round the first was a group in blue coveralls and on the far side a woman in a high-vis orange vest was holding two glowing batons that she gestured towards us.

Don adjusted the TR-3B's direction a fraction and we floated towards her. As our TR-3B crossed over the centre of the circle, the woman crossed her two batons. Don immediately centred the trackball and we came to a dead stop.

'OK, let's lower that Tic Tac,' Don said.

Zack nodded and pressed an icon on one of his screens. The view cut to the camera in the belly of the TR-3B that pointed down at the alien ship.

'Releasing clamps,' Zack said.

The robotic clamps that had been holding the Tic Tac steady opened and it swung free on the cables.

'Now be nice and careful with that baby,' Don said.

Zack nodded and, with the tip of his tongue pinched between his teeth, he toggled a switch downwards. With the gentlest vibration the Tic Tac began to lower towards the ground until it had settled.

'Our alien bird is down, releasing the cables now,' Zack said. He pressed another control and the two large hooks holding the Tic Tac released and began to reel back up into the belly of the Astra. The men and women in blue coveralls headed towards it.

Zack switched the camera on the main screen back to the forward view. The woman in the high-vis jacket had backed away to the second circle and was once again gesturing at us with her glowing sticks.

Don manoeuvred the Astra forward to hover above the middle of the next circle. 'Commencing landing procedure... lowering landing legs.' A whir of hydraulic actuators came from the TR-3B as it began descending towards the ground.

'Five metres...four...three...two...' Zack called out.

A slight shudder passed through the ship.

'Landing confirmed,' Don replied. 'Shut down the GR drive.'

'Shutting down now,' Zack replied.

A constant quiet hum in the background stopped and I felt a slight shift in gravity.

I'd almost been hypnotised by the choreographed landing sequence, but now my brain whirled back into action. This situation was about to get serious for me – and quickly. On the plus side, the hangar doors to the outside still stood open. Slip through them and I could hopefully use my Sky Wire to contact the others.

But there were a lot of people in the hangar to get past first. I just hoped their eyes would be on the recovered Tic Tac. In theory all I needed to do was wait for Don and Zack to go and then I could slip outside. And then my plan crumbled like a badly baked cake as a siren came from outside.

I tensed, flicking the safety on my LRS, ready for anything – or so I thought. As Don and Zack continued to shut down the flight systems of the TR-3B, the view of the hangar floor started to move upwards.

What the hell?

The hangar slid away, replaced by large riveted panels sliding past. Thanks to my time in Eden I knew exactly what I was looking at. The circle we'd landed on was actually a huge lift pad. It confirmed all the rumours I'd ever heard about Area 51.

I'd read numerous articles online about there being a huge subterranean base hidden beneath the surface. That was apparently where the real action at this not so top-secret location was meant to happen – according to testimonials from people who'd blown the whistle after working there. The reports included everything from recovered UFOs to actual aliens. And stowed in the hold of this Astra was another specimen that would shortly be added to the collection.

The steel panels continued to scroll past as Don and Zack gazed at the screens and readouts, making notes on electronic tablets.

With a burst of bright artificial light we cleared the exit of the lift shaft into a large arched cavern. It was vast, at least a mile long, with steel beams that curved overhead to meet in the middle. On the floor below was a squadron of TR-3Bs that stretched away along the length of the chamber. Many were at various stages of construction, some just an open latticework of metal. They were too many to count, but the nearest thirty or so sat on raised circular pads like the one on which our Astra was now descending.

Gantries criss-crossed the enormous space. Crane units trundled along them, one of which was now carrying a large green-metal case towards a TR-3B. Another of the Astras had its top section lifted up by one of the gantry cranes. A team of mechanics were working on the exposed guts of pipes and machinery round a plasma accelerator ring similar to Ariel's.

This place was beyond a conspiracist's wildest dreams. And it looked as if they were building enough craft down here to start a war. Did this have anything to do with the Overseers' preparation for the coming Kimprak invasion?

Don returned the camera to the belly view and the raised circular gantry we were being lowered towards. Waiting to one side was a team in medical scrubs and masks, no doubt ready to deal with our alien passenger. The lift platform came to a shuddering halt in line with the circular gantry that ringed it and the medics rushed forward.

'Opening the cargo bay door for the medics now...' Zack flicked a switch and a distant whirring sound hummed through the hull. 'Someone really needs to look at that lift motor – the vibration is getting worse,' Zack said, shaking his head.

'You can put it in your report,' Don replied.

'As though anyone will be interested, especially when they have a new alien craft to play with.'

'Yeah, tell me about it. Anyway, how are our patient's stats looking?' Don asked.

Zack cast an eye over his display. 'Crap. His BP has dropped through the floor, so he must be bleeding out.'

The team of medics that had disappeared from view beneath us reappeared a moment later pushing the sarcophagus down a ramp from the circular walkway towards an arched passageway in the wall at the end of the hangar.

Zack watched them go. 'I hope they're in time to save that Grey.'

I caught the face Don pulled at his friend. 'Maybe it's better if they don't,' he said. 'We've both heard the rumours of what they get up to with them down here. According to several guys I know, that Alvarez guy and his team have been effectively torturing the aliens with all sorts of crazy experiments.'

Zack sighed. 'I heard that too and I tell you it's not right.'

'I know, but there's not exactly a lot we can do about it. Above our pay grade.'

'Maybe it is, but it doesn't mean I have to like it.'

'Yeah, me too, bud. Anyway, let's get our debriefing out of the way. The sooner we do, the sooner I can have that drink with the ever lovely Julie, followed shortly by a much-needed kip.'

Yes, both of these men would have been my allies in a parallel world.

I watched them unbuckle their harnesses and then heard their footsteps fade as they headed away down the ramp that Don had lowered.

I was just about to push the locker door open when I heard the pilots through the open ramp talking to a woman.

'Just give her an oil change and wipe down the windshield please,' Don said.

Laughter. 'If only it were that easy keeping these birds in the sky,' the woman replied.

A moment later lighter footsteps came up the ramp and a woman in her thirties appeared in the cockpit. She was wearing oil-stained grey coveralls and her dark hair had been tied back with a scrunchie. She leant over the displays and began to note things down on a tablet she had with her.

I almost groaned out loud. I hadn't factored in any ground crew. I sat thinking, and soon realised it didn't change much. All I had to do was wait until she was gone and then sneak out of the TR-3B. Then, god knew how, but I'd make my way back to the surface. Oh so very easy.

But then that sketchiest of plans even by my standards was blown away as the woman walked straight towards the locker I was hiding in. I just had time to raise my LRS at her as she opened the locker door.

My heart thudded as we stared at each other for a full second. I wasn't quite sure who was more shocked, her or me. But then she whirled round and dived towards the pilot's chair. She stabbed her finger down on the button that Don had used to contact the control tower.

A rush of adrenaline surged through me as I stumbled out of the locker, my muscles screaming with cramp as I pointed my gun at her head. But even in that split second I felt something slump inside me. This woman wasn't a soldier and I knew there was no way I could shoot her.

'Control here, what is it, Archangel?' a woman's voice asked. 'You're not calling off our date, are you?'

I reversed my LRS and slammed its stock on the back of the engineer's head. With a soft moan she slumped down over the chair.

I held my breath.

'Archangel?' the woman's voice repeated over the radio.

The next few seconds seemed like an eternity as I waited for her to speak again.

A sigh finally came over the radio. 'Get a tech to check Archangel's ride. Seems as if the comm system is on the blink.'

I heard a click and the cabin speaker went quiet.

I let out my breath and stared down at the unconscious woman. It had definitely been the right call, but when she came round she would tell them exactly what had happened. I dug into my bag and unloaded one of tranquilliser darts from Mike's pistol and carefully pressed it into the woman's arms. That would buy me some more time, but not much. I set to work on pulling off her coveralls as quickly as I could.

CHAPTER TWENTY-TWO

WITH MY DARK hair tied back with the engineer's scrunchie and wearing her coveralls, I bore a passing resemblance to the woman, maybe even good enough to pull this off. I had her blue ID badge round my neck and her tablet tucked under my arm to complete my impromptu disguise. But what I wouldn't give to be able to shift into the twilight zone right now.

A number of hoses had been connected to the TR-3B, but thankfully no other ground crew were around as I emerged. I quickly saw that most of them had clustered round the Tic Tac on the adjacent pad in this vast underground hangar. Hopefully, thanks to that, it would take them a while to discover the woman I'd knocked out and tied up with duct tape back in the locker.

In the wide-open and well-lit hangar I felt very exposed. There were no shadows for me to hide in. I needed to do my best to brazen this out.

I headed past the Tic Tac, where the ground crew's attention was on a man with greying hair wearing a flight suit. He had epaulets on his shoulders, suggesting a senior military rank. As they listened to him, no one so much as cast a glance towards the woman in grey coveralls walking briskly across the hangar. Even so, my heart was thundering in my chest so fast I swore they were going to hear it.

I walked towards the corridor I'd seen the medics take the Grey, which had a fire-exit sign above the doorway. Thank god for health and safety, even in a workplace like this. I hoped if I followed those signs they would eventually lead me to a stairwell that would get me back to the surface. The rest I would just have to wing from there. There was nothing new about that.

My mouth grew drier by the minute as I strode into the corridor. It was then that my mind decided to make a flit back to the events at the crash site. How were the rest of the team doing? Had they even escaped? Had Jack managed to stabilise Mike in time? A hollow feeling filled my stomach. What if none of them had made it?

I swallowed down a knot of fear. I told myself that Jack and Ruby were both formidable. And I couldn't afford to second-guess the situation. I could only deal with absolutes right now and I *absolutely* had to get out of here as fast as possible.

The long corridor had doors on either side of it and what looked like a hundred internal windows. Just how many secrets were hidden down here behind those doors and windows?

My attention focused on a man wearing a white lab coat who'd emerged from a door just ahead of me, heading my way. No way was he not going to notice me.

I clenched my hand round my LRS hidden in a pocket of the coveralls. But the guy didn't so much as look up from his tablet as he walked past me towards the hangar.

I felt myself relax a fraction. Of course, just like Eden, there were probably thousands of people working down here, and they wouldn't all know or recognise each other. So for now, if I didn't mess this up, I was just another face in the crowd.

I headed along the corridor and my confidence began to grow

as more people passed me without so much as a second glance at me – even the numerous soldiers carrying pistols.

At last I spotted a fire-exit sign above a doorway to my right. I was about to step through when my attention was caught by a large window next to it.

Beyond the window, was a white room that looked like some sort of lab and in it was a dark-haired woman I recognised instantly. Cristina, the woman that Alvarez had abducted back in Peru, who had a similar synaesthesia gift to my own, which might have explained her presence here.

She was sitting in a chair wearing some sort of skullcap with wires trailing from it. Those wires were linked to a bank of machines that a guy in a lab coat was currently studying. And then I spotted something even more important. An unmistakable tetrahedron-shaped crystal stood on a plinth: a micro mind.

How in the hell had they secured an operational one?

The implications were huge and all bad.

The micro mind had been wired up to the bank of machines. Presumably they were running tests on it and Cristina. But this micro mind was emitting a dull red light, not the strong blue I was used to.

The technician turned round and his eyes caught mine as I stared openly at him. I quickly ducked through the adjacent door – the one with the fire-exit symbol and found myself in a concrete stairwell. This was it – I'd found my way out of this labyrinth. Yet I felt like groaning.

The moment I'd seen Cristina and the micro mind I'd realised my priorities would have to change. An opportunity had fallen right into my lap. Our highest priority that overrode every-thing else was finding Lucy's missing micro minds – and this one looked operational.

Then an astonishing, this-changes-everything thought struck

me. The micro mind was in the lab right next to the stairwell, so that should mean...

I took the Empyrean Key out of one of the larger pockets in my coveralls and found the tuning fork in a despatch riders bag I'd found in the locker. I mentally crossed everything I had as I struck the stone orb with it.

The note rang out and my heart leapt as two icons appeared in the air hovering over the ball – the self-repair and wave icons. I stifled the urge to whoop. This would so give me the edge I needed as I could shift into the twilight zone and become invisible.

I selected the wave icon, flicked my wrist forward and held my breath. Almost instantly the world shimmered and blurred around me.

Yes!

I turned round in the twilight zone and my hand partly merged with the door handle as I tried to grab it. But there was just enough resistance for me to turn the handle. I quickly stepped back out into the corridor and saw the guy in the lab clearly panicking and heading towards the door. He was almost certainly on his way to call security. I waited for him to press the door-release button and then grabbed my chance as he stepped out into the corridor. I ducked into the lab before the door swung closed behind him.

Cristina was gazing into empty space, as if she was in a trance. What had those bastards done to her? Probably some sort of serious sedative to keep her in a comatose state.

The last time I'd seen Cristina had been in less than ideal circumstances. I'd forced the car she was travelling in with Alvarez off the road, nearly killing her. I'd had no choice at the time. And I'd explain that to her now. I needed to tell her she could escape with us and be reunited with her husband, Ricardo, and their child back in Peru. This was my chance to make things right at last.

The lab shimmered around me as I approached her. I selected the dot icon to move into particle reality and activated it.

As I dropped back into the real world, Cristina's gaze snapped immediately to me. Then her eyes grew wider. 'You!' she shouted.

I held up my hands. 'It's OK, Cristina. I'm a friend. I'm going to get you out of here.'

'But you tried to murder me!'

'Look, you don't understand...'

Cristina leapt up from the chair. She tore the wired skullcap from her head and before I could stop her, she slammed her hand on a red button on the wall. At once an impossibly loud alarm shrieked out.

She spun back to stare at me, her eyes wild. 'You have everything that's coming to you, bitch!'

CHAPTER TWENTY-THREE

'WHAT THE HELL HAVE YOU DONE?' I shouted at Cristina over the shrill cry of the alarm.

She placed her hand on her hips, squaring up to me. 'Are you really surprised after you destroyed my life?'

I gawped at her, trying to process what she was telling me. 'What do you mean?' I glanced back out of the window and saw several guards in black uniforms already rushing down the corridor towards the lab. There was no time for me to argue some sense into the woman.

I struck my tuning fork against the stone orb and immediately selected the waveform icon.

Cristina stared defiantly at me as the world started to blur. 'That's it, run like the coward that you fucking are.'

I glowered back at her as the world shimmered into the twilight zone. Immediately, I turned and bolted for the door. Invisible or not, if those guards trapped me in here it would be over for me. My palm slid into the door-release button several times before I was finally able to make it move. The door swung open on its actuator and I burst out of the lab, the group of guards less than twenty metres away along the corridor.

Cristina raced out of the room behind me. 'She's invisible!'

The guard at the head of the group nodded, not at all surprised by this revelation, and grabbed a radio from his belt. 'Initiate an immediate lockdown in Corridor Twelve, Sections A through to C.'

A clunking sound came from the fire-exit door. Sure enough, when I tried the handle, the tingle of metal merging into my fingers, it was locked.

Another alarm, this one more like an air-raid siren, began to cry out in a long mournful rising and falling call. A loud grinding noise came from a massive blast door at least a metre thick began to slide down from the ceiling. A similar metallic grinding echoed from behind me. I spun round to see a second blast door nearer to me beginning to lower. A group of people beyond it in the corridor were scattering through doors.

I lowered my head and raced towards the closing door nearest me, arms pumping the air. The gap at the bottom was already less a metre deep. I sprinted, my hands clawing the air as I threw myself forward, sliding over the polished floor. In the mirage world of the twilight zone I felt the tingle of the steel door on my heels as I slipped beneath it just before it slammed shut behind me with a shuddering bang.

I sprang back to my feet and saw the next security door a hundred metres along the corridor closing. This one was too far to reach. That was it – I was trapped in this section. As soon as those guards worked out I'd managed to slip away from them, they'd search this area next. I needed somewhere to hide.

Ahead of me, two guys in scrubs were pushing a trolley full of equipment seemingly as fast as they could, heading towards a door being held open for them by a colleague in a lab coat. He frantically beckoned towards them.

I veered towards the group, intending to slip in behind them. A familiar feeling of pain and distress slammed into me, the emotions only strengthening as I neared the room. The Grey, it had to be.

What the hell was happening in there?

The two guys had already pushed the trolley into the room. I didn't have time to think as I stumbled towards the door and squeezed through it before it slammed shut with the sound of a bolt locking into place.

I gasped as the feelings of the Grey pressed into my skull.

With nausea spinning through me as I fought to keep standing, I crossed to the right-hand-side wall, the room rippling around me as I steadied myself against it. The group with the trolley had already disappeared through a gap in the racks of equipment that lined the room.

I took deep breaths, trying to fight the pain coursing through my body, and tried to focus on the room I'd found myself in.

In contrast to the bright corridor outside, it was dark and lit with blue light. Large glass cylinders lined the walls with some vague dark shapes inside, but I could barely focus on them with the fear that radiated through the air, almost as if I could taste it. I found myself shivering despite the warmth. With a growing feeling of dread I crossed to one of the glass cylinders and peered into it.

Through the thick glass the dark shape resolved itself into a small humanoid figure with a large head. A dead Grey. My eyes darted to the other cylinders and the forms within them. They were all Greys. I gagged when I realised I could see exposed skeletons and internal organs in. In one I could even see a brain, considerably larger than a human one, its stem floating in the liquid.

The fear ratcheted up even further as I struggled to push down the rising bile in my throat.

I turned towards the bank of equipment obscuring whatever was happening in the middle of the room with a very bad feeling. I steeled myself as best as I could as I headed towards the space between two large equipment racks.

In the middle of the room was the Grey from the crash, strapped to a gurney, the equipment trolley beside it. That was of course the source of all the emotions that had been hammering into me since I'd entered this room. Somehow we were still mentally connected.

The Grey blinked up at the masked surgeons hovering over him. Tubes with black blood ran from his arm into some sort of dialysis machine.

A fresh sense of horror swept over me when I saw that a section of his skull had been removed to expose a glistening grey brain. The bullet wound in his chest had been patched with some sort of transparent plastic through which I could see his heart beating.

A soft keening came from the Grey and once again a wave of dread crashed into me. I could feel his trauma like my own. But how and why had it chosen to link to me in this way?

'Get a move on! We need to extract the information from this thing before it dies,' said one of the surgeons – a man wearing round glasses.

I felt my hope crumble for the Grey, understanding exactly why it was so afraid.

One of the other surgeons manoeuvred a metal arm with two large electrodes on flexible metal rods to each side of the Grey's cranium.

The surgeon leant over the alien. 'Last chance. Tell us what we need to know. Why has there been a significant increase in Tic Tac activity in the past year? Is this a precursor to a full-blown invasion of our world?'

The Grey just looked up at the man, blinking his big dark eyes.

The surgeon stared down at the alien. 'If you're not going to answer me, then we'll just have to loosen your tongue.' He nodded to an older grey-haired woman with a pinched face standing next to the trolley. She flicked a switch on a control panel and a humming sound came from the device.

'Stand clear,' the woman called out.

The surgeons round the gurney took a step back, their hands raised, and she pressed a button. Flickers of electricity lanced out from the probes each side of the Grey's head into his skull. The alien spasmed, his features twisting as his heart beat faster, the voltage flooding his body. Excruciating pain roared through my own body and I had to grip the equipment rack to stop myself toppling to the floor.

The woman flicked the switch and the crackles of electricity faded away. I gasped in air, tears filling my eyes.

'Vitals?' the surgeon with the glasses asked a man standing next to him.

He scanned the screens next to him. 'BP is dropping fast. The subject won't last much longer.'

The doctor sighed and leant over the Grey. The alien was once again gazing up at him as pools of black blood dripped from his small nostrils and ran down over his cheeks.

'Tell us what we need to know and we will stop all your pain,' the surgeon said. 'Look, you're going to die anyway, so why extend your suffering?'

The alien just blinked again, utterly helpless. Out of nowhere a mental image came to my mind. I could clearly see the grey-haired flight officer who I'd spotted back in the hangar discussing the Tic Tac with the ground crew. As his image strengthened, I somehow knew I could trust this guy. The image vanished and my attention snapped back to the room as the surgeon spoke again.

'Make it five hundred volts this time,' he said.

'But that will kill the subject,' the woman operating the controls replied.

'Maybe we'll get lucky and it will loosen its tongue long enough for us to get something useful.'

The woman scowled as she adjusted a dial and the machine emitted a loud humming sound. Fresh crackles of energy erupted from the electrodes and poured straight into the alien's skull.

A new feeling began to radiate from the Grey, swamping my thoughts. There was anguish, yes, but also something else. I could feel that the Grey wasn't angry or even afraid. In fact, more than anything there was a sense of disappointment and even sadness transmitting from him. Then a new image appeared...of me shooting the Grey.

But I can't...

I heard a single word in a strange wavering voice that was not my own.

Please...

I just can't! I replied.

Then I'm so very sorry, the alien voice said in my head.

My hand started to raise the Empyrean Key by itself. I tried to fight it, but my wrist flicked forward and activated the particle icon. The shimmering lab became solid around me. I pocketed the Empyrean Key, still powerless to stop my actions, and took out my LRS.

I knew where this was going and I gritted my teeth, trying to force my hand to put the pistol back in its holster. But the alien was in charge of my body now, my hand not obeying me as it raised the pistol.

The Grey turned towards me as tears ran down my face. Thoughts of warmth and understanding, love even, flooded my mind. I knew in that instant that this alien, his whole species, cared deeply about all of humanity – despite what the people in this room were doing to him.

My tears almost blinding me, my hand raised the LRS at his skull.

A tingle ran down my spine at the sound of a pistol being cocked behind me.

I spun round, suddenly in control of my body again, to see Alvarez pointing a pistol straight at my head. Cristina was standing next to him, an orb similar to the Empyrean Key in her hand, but made from plastic not stone.

'Oh, two can play at your game, bitch,' she said.

I spun, my training reflex kicking in. I pivoted back on to my left foot and just managed to duck as Alvarez's bullet hissed over my head and I heard something metallic being struck behind me.

'One of the oxygen tanks has been hit,' someone shouted. 'Get the hell out of here!'

Everybody started racing for the door with shouts and cries, Alvarez dragging Cristina away as she snarled at me. I turned round to see the Grey still staring directly at me, his body continuing to jerk as electricity poured into his skull.

Once again I lost control of my own hand. The LRS aimed itself at the alien. And then I – no, *he* – fired. A bullet hole appeared in the Grey's forehead.

As his head dropped back on to the gurney, a single thought replaced the agony of a moment before... *Thank you, Lauren Stelleck.* And then the thought faded to silence as he died.

I stood there for a second, the pistol in my hand now hanging by my side. Gas was venting the bullet hole in the oxygen cylinder with a steady hiss. I tore my gaze away to the electrodes still sparking each side of the Grey's head.

My survival instinct kicked in and I dived back behind the equipment rack, striking the tuning fork against the Empyrean

Key as I landed. This time just a single icon flickered into display – the star-shaped one for E8.

I managed to flick my wrist forward as a whoosh came from the middle of the room and a bright fireball rushed out as the oxygen tank detonated. I felt the wash of heat over my skin as a rack toppled towards me. Then it and the room vanished as I was pulled out of the particle world into a higher level of reality.

CHAPTER TWENTY-FOUR

FOR A MOMENT I couldn't quite understand where I now found myself. Fortunately for me, it wasn't the cold vacuum of empty space in E8. I wouldn't have lasted there for long without any air to breathe. I would have been immediately forced to return to the lab and take my chances that the explosion blast wave had passed. I began to take in my surroundings – whatever this place was, it was like nothing like anything that Lucy had ever conjured up for us before in E8.

I was standing on a mountain and around me were a ring of dome-shaped summits. But I only had a split second to take the scene in before a wind screamed into me. I crouched behind the lee of a stone wall to shelter from the sudden howling storm.

Overhead, storm clouds materialised in what had been an inky blackness. They scudded and flickered with a strobing electrical storm without any rain, illuminating the darkness with spotlight bursts. Every so often a blinding zigzag of lightning crackled down from the sky to earth itself on one of the surrounding peaks.

OK, what was going on?

This specific location had obviously been conjured up by the captured micro mind. But why something like this and not a tropical paradise like Lucy sometimes favoured? If the feel of this place was anything to go by, the micro mind that had created it seriously needed some counselling. But I realised there was something distinctly familiar about the bulbous mountain ranges. When I glanced up the slope suddenly everything fell into place. The jagged shapes of the Inca site of Machu Picchu were silhouetted against the stormy sky above me.

This location had to be everything to do with Cristina. With me, Lucy had conjured up my aunt's old rooms at Christchurch College in Oxford, somewhere I felt immediately comfortable. But for Cristina the micro mind had created a version of somewhere familiar to her. The implications of that were huge – the Overseers had obviously finally realised what someone with an audible-based synaesthesia condition could do. And they must have put two and two together about the significance of the stone orb they'd previously seen me with. Maybe they'd 3D-printed the facsimile I'd seen Cristina carrying. It was obvious, just based on the fact that this place existed at all, that she'd learnt to control the micro mind just as I had. And the consequences of that could be bad – very bad.

I drew in a lungful of the hot and sticky air that was already making my coveralls cling to my body and I glanced down the mountain, but I couldn't see any sign of lights of the town below. Maybe this simulation didn't run that far? But the real question was what I going to do next? Wait for the fires back in the lab to die down, then return and take my chances?

A slight flicker of light drew my attention to one of the buildings above me. It was the Solar Observatory, the same building that Professor Evelyn Fischer had blown up back in the particle world to expose the hidden tunnel beneath it, which led down to the underground city of the dead. But here in this alternate reality the whole building looked very much restored. Was that significant?

The orange flicker of light in its window shone like a beacon in the darkness. Maybe I would find more answers up there? Certainly being inside the Solar Observatory was preferable to being stuck outside during a lightning storm in the mountains.

The wind howled across the slope as I leant into it and began my ascent. The gale screamed louder, turning small bits of gravel into projectiles that peppered my body with stinging pinpricks of pain.

With a blast of noise and thunder a lightning bolt lanced from the sky to strike the ground only a few hundred metres further down the slope, close enough to leave my ears ringing. But it was the second bolt that smashed into the mountain even closer that woke me up to what was happening here.

This wasn't a natural thunderstorm. It was as if this whole place had been built with some sort of intent and every sense told me that intent was to kill me. Cristina had to have everything to do with that.

I did my best to run up the slope into the battering wind as it did its best to sweep me back down the mountain. I drove myself forward, fighting for every step until I made it to a stone staircase at the edge of the site. I stumbled up them as another crack of lightning hit, this time splintering a rock. I glanced back and any doubts that I was the intended target were swept away when I saw the rubble from the bottom steps I'd only just climbed. They were being whipped away down the slope in a cloud of falling debris.

I raced to the top of the steps and dived left along a passageway between two buildings sheltered partly from the wind. The sky rumbled again and again, as the AI equivalent of Zeus launched almost continuous lightning bolts at me.

I weaved through the Inca site, my feet slipping on the rocks, drawing closer to the Solar Observatory and its glowing light. The wind was now a full no-messing hurricane. As I left the cover of the stone buildings to reach a plateau, it roared around me, making my grey coveralls vibrate like a flag in the wind. I raced across the open area and ducked down an avenue between buildings, the Solar Observatory only twenty metres ahead of me now.

I sprinted straight towards its door as the sky blazed with sheet lightning. I was certain the next strike would leave nothing of me behind but a pair of smouldering boots on the mountain. My heart slamming in my chest, I finally leapt through the doorway into the small stone building. The roar of the storm fell instantly silent.

Disorientation slammed into me. Rather than the stone interior of the Solar Observatory, I found myself standing in Cristina's apartment back in Aguas Calientes in Peru. But this wasn't a personalised version of her home, filled with happy memories, but a twisted, darker version. Furniture had been tipped over, papers thrown everywhere, the small kitchen wrecked. This looked like the last time I'd seen it – after Villca, the chief of police, and his sidekick had ransacked it. They'd been looking for Cristina's drawings about the symbol she'd seen with her own synaesthesia ability at the Solar Temple at Machu Pichu and had then abducted her.

But why had the AI in the micro mind recreated such an awful moment in Cristina's life? Maybe there was a clue here somewhere.

To one side of the room was a short corridor, and I could see a bathroom through a doorway. Straight ahead was a closed bedroom door. I moved towards it with a dark sense of foreboding building inside me, not helped by the strong stench of something decaying now pulling at my nose.

I opened the door and gasped as my eyes locked on to the two figures on the bed.

Gabriel, Cristina's husband, was curled round their baby boy, the skin of both grey with death. I didn't want to see the awful details, but my eyes wouldn't look away. Gabriel's back was riddled with bullet holes, with dried rivulets of blood running from them. The blood had soaked the sheet beneath to black. Flies skittered over the faces of Gabriel and the baby.

Nausea rushed up through me and I backed out of the room. I tore to the bathroom and vomited into the bowl of the toilet. Why, when I knew this awful nightmare had never actually happened?

I wiped the last of the sick from my mouth with some toilet paper and took a shuddering breath. It was then that I noticed a red light beginning to pulse behind me.

I turned slowly to see the glowing red micro mind I'd seen in the lab now floating in the corridor, a sense of malevolence radiating from it that electrified my senses. This thing certainly wasn't anything like the cheerful Lucy avatar who had welcomed me on my first visit to E8.

I desperately needed answers and raised my head to it. 'Why are you showing me this? This never happened.'

The micro mind just hung there, the ruby light pulsing slowly deep within it. Somehow its silence was even more terrifying than if it had actually spoken.

'OK, so you obviously made this for Cristina, but why?'

'As though you don't know,' Cristina's voice replied from the next room, her tone like brittle glass.

The tetrahedron dissolved into the air and disappeared.

I felt beads of sweat pop over my forehead as utter dread swept through me. I stepped forward and turned into the main room.

Cristina was sitting on the sofa waiting for me. She was

holding a pistol aimed at my chest and had the plastic version of the Empyrean Key in her lap. It was only then that I realised that everything I'd been carrying, including my LRS and stone orb, had vanished.

I raised my hands. 'What is this, Cristina?'

'You mean you don't recognise your own handiwork in my home, Stelleck?'

I tightened my gaze on her. 'What you mean?'

She shook her head at me. 'Don't play innocent with me. I brought you back to the scene of your crime.'

'I promise you that whatever you think you know is wrong.' I gestured towards the bedroom. 'And that never happened.'

Cristina glowered at me, her eyes thin slits. 'Even now you can't face the evil that lives in your own heart.'

I took a half-step towards her, but Cristina tightened her grip on the trigger.

I stopped dead again. 'I don't know what you've been shown, but this is a lie,' I whispered. 'Please think this through, Cristina. You were abducted by Villca. He was the one who ransacked your house looking for your drawings. You must remember that?'

'Yes, and maybe that part is true, but, as Colonel Alvarez told me, that action also saved my life from the terrorists who then turned up and murdered my family.'

I held up my hands. 'Whoa there, Cristina. That's not what happened. Can't you see that Alvarez has been lying to you?'

She let out a hollow laugh. 'Lying? I saw the photos of how you butchered Gabriel and my beautiful son. You even killed my cousin, Ricardo. And now I'm going to make you pay for every-thing you did.'

'But, Cristina, your husband and child are still alive. And it was Villca who murdered Ricardo.'

Cristina's eyes blazed and she clenched her jaw. 'Liar!' She raised her gun towards my head.

I knew in that second that this was only going one way. Electricity hummed through my nerves, preparing me for action. I took rapid breaths to fill my lungs with oxygen.

I took in the window beyond Cristina and once again all my endless combat training with Niki kicked in. Almost on autopilot I dropped to the floor, sweeping my foot out at Cristina's ankles to hook them away, toppling her sideways. Her pistol went off with a crack and punched a bullet hole through the ceiling. But Cristina twisted away from me on the ground, bringing her weapon back round for a second shot.

My eyes snapped to the window. Even though part of my brain registered that her apartment had been on the third floor, I still leapt towards it. It was my only chance.

A bullet ricocheted off the window frame as I brought my hands up to protect my head and crashed through the glass.

My mind stuttered when I found myself back outside the Solar Observatory, lying on the ground, not falling from the third-storey window. The thunderstorm still crackled overhead.

It was only a brief reprise as Cristina came bursting from the doorway, her pistol aimed towards me. I rolled sideways as a bullet ricocheted off the stone floor.

Pure survival instinct kicked in and I was back on my feet and sprinting away through a passageway between the buildings. There was another crack of a bullet and stone splinters flew out from the wall less than a metre from my head.

I glanced back to see Cristina running after me, her features contorted into absolute hatred for the woman she thought had murdered her family. There was no way I would be able to talk her down before she put a bullet in my head.

Cristina screamed at me, a cry of animal fury, and the storm seemed to answer her. Thunder roared all around us, lightning crackling down over the ancient Inca site. My stomach was a hard ball, my lungs burning, as I sprinted flat out towards the end of the passageway, opening up some distance between us as I turned a corner. I dived on to the steps covered with boulders and small stones from the earlier strike. Cristina would be on top of me in seconds.

I grabbed a rock the size of a tennis ball and drew my arm back. As Cristina rounded the corner, I swung it towards her head with full strength. Cristina tried to turn, but the rock smashed into her temple anyway, the impact sending a sickening jar up my arm. As she lurched into the opposite wall and slumped to the ground, her pistol skittered away.

Blood trickled down her face as Cristina turned, her eyes burning into mine. 'I don't care what it costs me – it's time to die, bitch!' She raised her arms in the air.

In the sky directly overhead a glow of brilliance started to flicker in the clouds, growing stronger fast. I could almost taste the static charge building in the air.

Cristina screamed, her body shaking like some mad Inca priestess summoning the sky gods. And then those gods answered her.

I just had time to leap away as a massive lightning bolt came streaking straight towards us. With a roar the buildings around us exploded. The world spun, white light blinding me, a concussion wave slamming into me like a giant's fist. Rocks pounded my body as I was thrown over a low wall. I crashed on the far side as a choking cloud of debris rained down on me.

My ears sang with a high-pitched whistle and I tasted something metallic in my mouth. I spat out the blood from where I'd bitten down on my tongue.

The dust began to settle and wooziness rolled through me as I staggered back to my feet, my brain throbbing inside my skull. All that remained of the blast area – where there had been buildings a moment ago – was a huge pile of rubble. Cristina was nowhere to be seen.

'Where are you?' I cried out as the wind roared past me, but no reply came. With every part of my body aching I hauled myself over the wall and staggered back to where Cristina had pulled the lightning down on top of us. I started to heave away the boulders, ignoring the stinging cuts in my hands and only dimly aware that the storm had flickered to silence at last.

Nails splitting, shredding the skin on my hands, I kept digging desperately at the dirt. Then with the tips of my fingers I felt something give beneath all that hardness.

I scraped the dirt away to reveal Cristina's hand clutching her plastic version of the Empyrean Key.

'Cristina!'

Working as fast as I could, I cleared more rubble away to expose her wrist and pressed my thumb to it. There was a pulse – faint but still there.

I somehow found impossible strength to lift the huge stones that had buried her face. I worked frantically, cleaning the rubble from her mouth. I could already see from her shallow breaths that she was barely breathing. She needed urgent medical attention. And I was the only one who could make that happen.

Despite the fact Cristina had just tried to kill me, I had to help her. I gently prised the Empyrean Key from her hand. In E8, like the twilight zone, I didn't need a carrier tone to see the icon controls. A single particle icon was already hovering over the key.

I wrapped my left hand round Cristina's wrist and activated the icon. At once Machu Picchu and the storm shimmered away around us.

The lab materialised and the smell of smoke flooded my nose. Figures appeared out of the gloom wearing respirators, their weapons levelled towards me. I was still holding on to Cristina's wrist, who lay curled up in a ball beside me.

One of the figures loomed over me and I looked up to see the Alvarez's scar through his mask as he stared at me.

'Help her!' I shouted at him.

As his gaze turned to Cristina, his eyes widened. 'What the fuck have you done to her?'

Before I could say anything, he yanked her away from me.

'Get the medics in here now!' he shouted.

The room filled with doctors, soon kneeling by Cristina.

Rough hands pulled me to my feet and dragged me to the door. And I knew in that awful moment that by saving her I'd just thrown everything away.

CHAPTER TWENTY-FIVE

THE BLAST DOORS in the corridor had been opened again. I stood next to Alvarez, cuffed and held by two military police. Firefighters were still dampening down the smouldering lab that was filled with smoke.

Alvarez's attention wasn't on me but Cristina, as he watched her being rushed away on a gurney along the corridor by the team of medics.

Only as she disappeared through a door did Alvarez turn to me, his face as hard as steel. 'What the fuck did you do to her?'

'Me?' I stared at him incredulously. 'Oh no, this is all on you, mate. You murdered her husband and child. Then the absolute icing on the cake is that you tried to put the blame on us. Thanks to that, Cristina was out of mind in her very own version of a personal hell. She was desperate to kill me. Unfortunately for her she managed to seriously injury herself instead.' I stared at him. 'I know how twisted your heart is, but even for you that's downright evil.'

Alvarez's mouth thinned. 'Cristina's a very special woman

who needed extra motivation to work with us. And what better motivation is there than revenge?'

Cold fury boiled through me. 'You bastard!' I strained against the police's vice-like grips as I struggled to get free. When that didn't work, I spat in the colonel's face. 'I should have put a bullet through your head when I had the bloody chance.'

'Yes, and I have to say I'm rather looking forward to interrogating you about that particular episode. I'm also very intrigued to discover how you've been able to evade us for all this time when we have such considerable resources.'

'As though I'd tell you that!'

Alvarez grabbed hold of my hair and yanked my head back. 'Oh, we'll see about that, Stelleck.' He trailed a finger down the side of my skull. 'All those secrets in that pretty head of yours are going to be mine shortly. And you'll be begging me to kill you by the end. But I'll keep you alive long enough for my people to dissect your brain. You see, our research team have been looking for a subject who can control the alien orb as we build our understanding about their technology. Cristina is far too precious an asset for us to risk, but you, on the other hand...' He slapped me hard across the face.

I struggled to kick out at him as the police yanked me backwards.

'Take Stelleck to an interrogation room. I'll be along shortly to deal with her personally.'

The two guys holding me nodded and hauled me away. But I wasn't going to make this easy for them. I let my legs fold beneath me, forcing them to lift me by the elbows as they carried me towards a lift that had just arrived. Its doors opened to reveal Don and Zack, the pilots of the Astra. They both cast questioning glances at the police holding me as they walked out, the doors closing behind them.

I stared at the pilots. 'Don, Zack, you've got to help me.'

'And who the heck are you?' Don asked as I was dragged past them towards the lift.

'My name is Lauren Stelleck. I stowed away on your TR-3B back at the Tic Tac crash site. That's how I got here.'

Zack gaped at me. 'You did what? You're kidding, right?'

'I promise you it's true,' I said.

One of the guys holding me pressed a button on the control panel by the lift.

'What are you, a spy?' Don asked.

'Nothing like that. Just someone trying to make a difference, like you did with that alien.'

Zack's jaw became set. 'Oh, don't tell me, a UFO conspiracist.'

I heard the lift door ping and the doors began to open. This wasn't so much a plan as a last Hail Mary thrown out into the cosmos.

'No, not like you think,' I said. 'But like you I was worried about what would happen to that Grey. And with good reason.'

I was nudged in the back with a truncheon. 'In there, you.' The military police guys started to push me forward into the lift.

'Hang on a minute there, soldier,' Don said, stepping towards me. 'What do you mean, with good reason?'

'I mean they killed that Grey in one of their damned torture labs.'

Don tucked his chin in. 'You witnessed that?'

One of my guards stepped in between us as the other tightened his grip on me. 'Sorry, Captain, but you're not authorised to talk to the prisoner.'

'He'll talk to who the hell he wants to,' Zack said as the lift doors started to close behind us.

I strained my head round to look at the pilots. 'You've got to help me. The fate of our whole world depends on it. Tell whoever you can trust!'

Don and Zack traded frowns as the door slid shut, cutting them off from view for me. That was my very last chance gone.

My handcuffs had been chained to a metal hoop on a pitted table. The moment the military police had left me I'd tried pulling my hands every which way to free myself. Useless, but it didn't stop me trying and I'd soon rubbed my skin raw beneath the steel manacles. At one point a woman in a lab coat had wheeled in a trolley of nasty-looking surgical tools, making a point of not looking at me. I'd redoubled my efforts to escape after that, but to no avail. Screaming hadn't helped either – the walls were heavily padded and clearly soundproofed. Alvarez would be able to do what he liked to me in here and no one would be any the wiser. My mind baulked at what he might get up to alone with me in this room. And there would be nothing I could do to stop him.

A solitary camera with a red light was mounted in one corner of the room and a mirror ran the length of the wall. Almost certainly it was two-way, so people in the adjacent room could watch what was going on...not that I thought Alvarez would want any witnesses when he set to work on me.

If I hadn't ignored Alice in the first place, I wouldn't have got myself in this stupid situation. But thanks to my own pig-headedness I was all alone and without any backup. No one from Eden even knew I was here. Worse still, they wouldn't ever find out about the existence of the micro mind down here. And, without that, Lucy wouldn't be able to complete her AI matrix, meaning the secret Angelus plan to save our world would fail.

Despite all that, I was no longer the woman I'd once been. I wouldn't give in to the despair lapping through me. Not now, not ever. What if there was an alternative scenario? Even Alvarez had to see just how dangerous the situation with the coming

Kimprak invasion would be. As much as I hated the guy, if our two sides worked together – and the Overseers actually helped us find the rest of the micro minds – there could still be a chance for our world.

Voices came from outside and I prepared myself for the speech of my life as the door swung open.

But instead of Alvarez, it was the grey-haired flight officer I'd last seen in the flight hangar who entered the room. Maybe more significantly, it was the same man the Grey had telepathically shown to me.

'I need some time alone with the prisoner,' the officer said in a deep southern drawl.

The guard who'd opened the door stiffened. 'But I'm under orders not to—'

The flight officer waved the man to be quiet. 'I'm not interested in what your orders are from those damned civilians. You are military and I outrank you, son. So get the hell out of my face before you find yourself in a cell too. Do we understand each other?'

The guard snapped him a salute. 'Understood, Commander.'

'That's better. Now see that we're not disturbed.'

The man nodded and closed the door, shutting the commander in with me.

A spark of hope flickered in my chest. It sounded as if the commander might have had more than a few issues with Alvarez and his people working at Area 51. If so, maybe I could persuade him what was really on the line here – the future of our whole world.

'Look, Commander, you've got to help me,' I said as he sat down opposite me. 'I doubt you even have any idea about what has been going on in the labs down here.'

'You don't think I know what's going on in my own henhouse?'

'I didn't mean to imply—'

He waved me quiet as he had done with the guard. 'Relax, I didn't say I liked what they're up to. Anyway, you can thank Don and Zack for telling me about you. If they hadn't, I wouldn't have even known that you managed to sneak in here.'

This wasn't the direction I'd expected the conversation to take. 'Hopefully you can pull rank over Alvarez. Anyway, that Grey...'

The commander once again waved a dismissive hand at me. 'Yes, Alvarez and the rest of the Overseers are prize bastards. And they have everything that's coming to them.'

'You don't agree with their tactics?'

'Of course I bloody don't!' The commander sighed. 'I don't know whether to be exasperated with you or give you a hug, Lauren.'

I stared at him. 'What? How do you know my name?'

'Four months of deep cover are about to blown. If I don't do something, you'll be dead before the day's out.' He opened his flight suit, took out my LRS and Empyrean Key from an inside pocket and placed them on the table.

'You'll be wanting these if –' his southern drawl faded and was replaced with a crisp familiar British accent – 'we're going to escape this bloody place.'

I gawped as my mind scrambled to make sense of this new reality. I peered at the older man's face. 'Tom, bloody hell, is that really you?'

He broke into a wide smile. 'I'll take that as a compliment on my disguise. Unfortunately for him he's currently being held captive by some contacts of mine.'

'But how? We thought...?'

Tom once again held up his hand to stop me. 'Look, Lauren, I know you've got a thousand questions, but we haven't got much time. We've got to get out of here and quickly.' He gestured towards the camera in the room.

I turned round to see the red light had gone out.

'As soon as they realise that security camera is offline, they'll be here to investigate,' he said. 'When the drugged guard comes round, they'll quickly realise it's me that's responsible for your jail break.'

'What drugged guard?'

Tom grinned and pulled back his flight suit further to reveal a holster containing a dart gun. 'Once I've dealt with the guy outside, we'll get back to the surface and escape.'

I raised my hands that were still chained to the desk. 'You'll need to pick the lock on these first.'

'Oh, I can do better than that.' Tom took out a set of keys. 'I borrowed these from the guard out there. I really must give you and the others some pickpocket training. It can come in very useful, particularly in situations such as this.'

As Tom released me from my cuffs, I leant across the table and hugged him. 'It's fantastic to see you.'

He returned my embrace with a slightly stiff hug, patting my back. 'You too, Lauren.'

I rubbed my aching wrists before picking up my LRS and the Empyrean Key.

'OK, first we need to deal with that guard and then we get out of here,' Tom said.

I grabbed his arm. 'Hang on, Tom. They have an operational micro mind down here. We can't leave it behind.'

'I know they do. Why do you think I'm here?'

I stared at him. 'You're telling me you're here to retrieve it?'

'Correct. At least, I *was*. But there's not much chance of that if I'm going to save you.'

I held out the Empyrean Key. 'But there is, Tom. Get me near enough to it and I can shift us both into the twilight zone now

Cristina is out of the picture. Then we can slip it away under their noses.'

Tom's gaze tightened on mine. 'You do know that's an insanely risky plan?'

I tipped my head to one side. 'Would you expect me to come up with anything else?'

He snorted and a wide smile filled his face. 'I've rather missed your sunny, always-can-do disposition. And even though I should know better, you've talked me into it.'

CHAPTER TWENTY-SIX

A TRICKLE of sweat tickled down my back as I walked along the corridor beside Tom. We were heading straight to the lab where I'd last seen the micro mind. Eden's chief of intelligence was carrying a case that he'd casually just signed out from a stores unit, which was essential to our improvised plan.

It felt like every set of eyes was on us as we made our way through the base, but no one gave us so much as a second glance.

'All my months of work infiltrating one of the most secure facilities on the planet and you basically manage to just swan in,' Tom said.

'I didn't exactly *swan* in. I flew in on an Astra,' I replied.

He quietly chuckled. 'You do know that makes what you've done even more extraordinary. You've proven you really are someone who can think on their feet – one of the most important skills a spy can have.'

'I'll take that as high praise coming from you.'

'You should.'

The smile that had been threatening on my lips faded as we neared the lab. This was getting all very real again. I prepared to grab my LRS from my concealed shoulder holster at the first sign of trouble. But as we neared and glanced through the window, the tension flowed away. There was no one inside.

'Well, at least that's one break,' I said.

'We're going to need an awful lot more than one if we're going to pull this off.'

I gave Tom a grim look and nodded as he punched a number into a security pad and we slipped into the lab.

I lowered the blinds on the window to the corridor then headed towards the micro mind. A red swirl of faint stars were spinning beneath its crystal surfaces. It was a pattern I'd never seen before with Lucy's other micro minds. What made this one so different?

'Have you any idea how the Overseers managed to get their hands on this?'

'It was dragged up in a net by a Chinese trawler off the coast of the province of Jiangsu. At first the authorities thought they'd captured another foreign spy UUV.'

'A UUV?'

'An unmanned underwater vehicle. Basically an American miniature drone sub. But when the Overseer agents who had infiltrated the Chinese government got wind, they realised what it really was. Alvarez was called in to retrieve it and bring it here to Area 51.'

'So do you know whether it was glowing red like this when they first found it?'

'No, it was dead when they first brought it here. Alvarez had Cristina working on it and, together with the techs here, she managed to coax it somehow back to life. From my contacts here I believe they then tried to drill into it to remove a sample core. That's when it turned red.'

'That doesn't sound good.'

'I know. Hopefully Lucy will have more of an idea what that

means and how to reverse it.' Tom opened the case he'd brought from the store. Inside was a small Agie plate, Tom explaining to me the name was a shortened version of antigravity. He attached it to the micro mind and with a push of a button the antigravity plate glowed blue. 'OK, it should be light enough for us to lift between us now. Lauren, time to pull your disappearing trick.'

'I'm on it.' I took out my Empyrean Key and unhooked the tuning fork. I struck it against the stone surface and the icons appeared. I looked for the self-repair function, but it wasn't there. The one for E8 I was so not going near again any time soon, but the twilight zone icon shone a steady green.

'Tom, stand close, and I'll activate the waveform function.'

He pushed back the blind he'd been peering round and walked towards me. 'So what's this twilight zone actually like?'

'There's no easy way to describe it. But it's very disorientating the first time you experience it.' I selected the waveform icon and activated it.

As the physical particle world shimmered away around us, Tom gasped. The only rock-solid thing was the micro mind.

Tom's legs shook as he hung on to a lab bench, his fingers merging into its surface. 'You could have warned me, Lauren. I wasn't quite expecting this!'

I patted his arm, my blurring fingers partly melding with his shimmering arm. 'I did try to, Tom, but there really isn't any easy way to prepare. Try to breathe normally and the vertigo you're probably experiencing will pass in a moment. It's amazing how quickly people adapt.'

'I'll have to take your word for it,' Tom said through a clenched jaw. 'Anyway, unless that device of yours has a way to freeze time too, we need to get out of here as quickly as possible before they realise we and the micro mind are missing.'

We took hold of the micro mind between us, Tom wincing as his hands partially disappeared into it, and carried it towards the door. I pressed the door release on the third attempt and the door swung open. We slipped out into a passageway that was nearly deserted aside from a woman pushing a cart with office supplies. I was just thinking that this was almost starting to feel too easy when an alarm shrieked out.

A voice came from a speaker over the door. 'Security breach detected in Cell Twelve. Lockdown initiated.' The sound of bolts sliding into place came from the door to the stairwell ahead of us. A blast door began to lower to shut off the hangar on the other side of it, a red light spinning above.

'They must have realised that you've escaped and are locking down all the exits,' Tom said.

'But you must have studied every conceivable way in and out of this base, lockdown or not?' I said, knowing Tom well.

'I have, but it's sealed tight. Not so much as a fly can get out of here.'

Just like that my misplaced confidence evaporated. Invisible or not, just like before I was about to be trapped inside this base.

But then I saw the woman with the cart had managed to get it jammed under the descending blast door, wedging it open.

'How about stealing a TR-3B?' I said.

Tom's shimmering mouth fell open. 'Bloody hell, Lauren. It's such an utterly insane plan that I have to say I actually rather like it.'

I grinned at him as we carried the micro mind towards the jammed-open blast door.

A lift door opened in the corridor and Alvarez and a team of Overseer soldiers appeared. I mentally held my breath, but they rushed past us towards in the direction of the cell we'd just come from.

'OK, we need to get a move on,' Tom said.

'What really?' I asked, unable to keep the sarcasm out of my voice.

We reached the blast door just as the woman who'd been frantically pulling at her jammed cart was joined by a guard. He tried to help her, but it didn't shift and he pulled a radio from his belt. 'This is Reece. Raise and then lower Section A doors. We have a jammed obstruction beneath one that needs clearing.'

'Affirmative,' a woman's voice replied over the radio.

With a grinding sound the blast door began to raise, freeing the cart. As the guard pulled it clear, Tom and I quickly carried the micro mind through. A moment later the heavy door slammed closed behind us with a loud, reverberating clang.

We ran across the empty hangar towards the nearest TR-3B as the wail of an alarm echoed throughout it. It seemed everyone working there had disappeared and then I spotted the last few people disappearing through a door, no doubt into a secure area for the lockdown.

'I'm assuming you know how to fly one of these things?' I said as we neared the Astra.

'Not exactly,' Tom replied. 'But I've been studying this ship's schematics. Although the theory is one thing – putting that knowledge into practice is entirely another matter.'

My brilliant plan didn't seem quite so clever now, but I did my best to inject utter confidence into my voice. 'You've got this, Tom. So how do we get this ship back to the surface?'

'Well, that guard will be out cold for another thirty minutes before he comes round to tell anyone I'm involved. Lockdown or not, I still have some clout here for now. I can issue an order to Control to give us clearance to fly out.' He pointed towards the blurring pips on his shoulders. 'Rank does have its privileges.'

We reached the craft and Tom pressed a button on its belly. A short while later, with our precious cargo stored in the hold, we headed up the ramp into the now familiar cockpit of a TR-3B.

With a flick of my wrist I dropped us back into particle reality, much to Tom's evident relief.

He settled himself into the pilot's seat and I sat beside him, in the seat Zack had used on the other ship. The screens before me were filled with what seemed like hundreds of readouts. It would have taken years of training to fully understand them. Unfortunately, that was a luxury we didn't have.

Tom stretched his fingers. 'OK, let's give this a whirl.' He pressed a button in his chair arm. 'Control, this is Commander Jenson,' he said with the southern drawl back in place. 'Immediate permission for departure with ship –' he glanced at one of his screens – 'zulu, delta, four, three, one, for an infiltration mission. Authorisation, Skybird.'

'Commander, I've no record of any mission in the flight log,' a man's voice replied.

'This mission is off-book, son,' Tom replied.

'But, Commander, we have a lockdown in place. You'll need to wait for the all-clear.'

Tom huffed. 'For god's sake, this mission is time-critical. We have an asset that is about to be captured by the enemy. Don't make me come down there and tear a strip off you. Or would you prefer to be thrown in the brig for ignoring the orders of a commanding officer?'

There was a long silence and I raised my eyebrows at Tom. He just shrugged.

A coughing sound came over the channel. 'Initiating platform-raising procedure now.'

'That's more like it, son. I'll put in a mention of your cool, level-headed thinking in an emergency. You're a credit to this base.'

'Thank you, sir,' the man said in a much happier tone, and Tom killed the channel.

'That was an absolute masterclass in how to bluff your way out of a tight corner,' I said.

Tom raised his chin towards me. 'Oh, I have years and years of experience in how to excel at exactly that.'

With a lurch, the view on the monitor screen of the outside hangar started to scroll downwards as our TR-3B was raised on its platform towards the entrance to the shaft in the ceiling above. We were travelling at a respectable ten miles per hour or so, but I was itching to accelerate our ascent. It felt like several lifetimes passing as we entered the shaft and the steel panels began to move past us as we moved up towards the surface. With every passing second I became increasingly convinced that our deception would be discovered and the platform would come to a shuddering stop.

Oblivious to my building paranoia, Tom busied himself with the flight controls, practising moving the joysticks through all orientations and spinning every button. When he at last seemed satisfied he turned to me.

'I'm going to have my hands full flying this bird, Lauren. So just in case I am going to need you to familiarise yourself with the weapon systems.'

I stared at the bank of controls. 'How the hell do I do that? This thing looks like the deck of the *Enterprise*.'

'Relax, it's not as complicated as it looks. The large middle touchscreen is the gunner's target control system. All you need to do is double-tap something you want to shoot down and a lock icon will appear if the target is in range. This ship's AI control system will then track it. You'll just need to take the shot by squeezing the button of the joystick on the right arm of your seat.'

I glanced down to see the controls exactly as he'd explained them and nodded. 'OK, that sounds straightforward enough. But let's hope we're long gone before there's any need to shoot anything down.'

'Here's hoping,' Tom replied as the surface hangar finally came into view.

As before there were jet fighters parked up, along with some helicopters. The hangar doors were already open revealing a clear blue sky...one that hopefully we'd shortly be flying through.

'You are authorised for immediate departure,' the man's voice said over the cockpit speaker.

'Thank you, Control,' Tom replied. He took a deep breath and gave me a sideways glance. 'Do you remember your first driving lesson, Lauren?'

'Of course. I scared my Aunt Lucy half to death. I managed to mix up the accelerator and the brake pedal. I nearly hit a lamp post in an empty car park.'

'Well, this feels about a thousand times more stressful than that.'

'I've every faith in you, Tom.' I made sure I didn't let my nerves come through in my voice, only injecting Tom with confidence.

'Let's just pray your belief is well placed then. Commencing pre-flight checks.'

He toggled several switches and I heard the familiar gentle hum of the drive buzzing into life as gravity relaxed its grip within the cabin.

Tom squeezed his eyes shut before snapping them open again. 'Close hatch and then raise legs...'

His verbalised checklist so didn't fill me with confidence.

Tom pressed a few more buttons and a hiss came from the hydraulic systems beneath the cockpit floor. The slit of light from the hangar vanished as the ramp closed. 'OK, we're floating free on the GR drive.' Tom gently twisted the right joystick round until the nose was pointing towards the open doors.

An alarm warbled out and the doors ahead of us began to close.

'Commander, you're instructed to shut down your systems and prepare to be boarded,' came the voice from Control.

'What do you mean?' Tom asked as he placed his left hand on the trackball.

'I've just had confirmation that no flights are to leave. The base security level has been raised to FPCON Delta. A terrorist is believed to be on the loose in the base.'

'Sorry, I'm having problems hearing...you...you're breaking up.' Tom made some pop and crackling sounds, before pressing a button to kill the comm link.

'Do you honestly think they'll buy that?'

'Not for a second, especially when I do this.' He pushed the right joystick forward and we sped towards the gap that was surely already less than the width of the ship.

I pressed myself back into my seat. 'Um, Tom...'

'Relax. Remember I studied all the manuals...twice.'

I couldn't help but notice the beads of sweat popping out over his forehead. I was absolutely certain Tom was about to slam our craft into the closing doors, and my stomach muscles instinctively clenched as I braced for the massive impact.

But then, at the last second, Tom tipped his left joystick to the right and the Astra veered over on to its side. With centimetres to spare, and thankfully no shower of sparks, we shot through the gap in the doors and into the outside world.

I whooped. 'Amazing flying, Tom. We've bloody well made it!'

Tom cast me a frown. 'Nothing like it, Lauren. Trust me, they'll already be scrambling an intercept squadron to chase us.'

My brief feeling of euphoria evaporated.

CHAPTER TWENTY-SEVEN

WE'D BEEN SPEEDING away from Area 51 at a steady Mach 7 for the last ten minutes. From my understanding of physics I knew that this was even faster than a bullet, which only travelled up to Mach 2.5. It was mesmerising watching the dusty barren hills covered in swathes of dark scrub, whipping past at an incredible speed.

Under Tom's directions, I'd managed to turn off our flight transponder, making it harder for anyone to locate us. Meanwhile, he'd settled into his role as pilot and had honed his skills as best as he could in the short time available. Testimony to that, the ride had been silky smooth so far. And of course there was no turbulence to worry about when you were flying in a ship that didn't rely on aerodynamic lift but sat in its own gravity bubble.

I had just begun to think that maybe this might be easy compared to what we'd just been through when an alarm shrieked out. I made a mental note to myself to never relax when out on a mission.

Tom glanced at one of his screens. 'I knew it was only a

matter of time. We have pursuing craft at six o'clock behind us. Keep an eye on them with your gunner's screen, Lauren.'

'How do I do that?'

'Just move the joystick in the direction the arrows indicate.'

So far I'd been using my gunner's screen targeting reticle to follow our progress towards the horizon. Now three arrows had appeared to its side. I tilted the control, following the direction indicated by the arrows, and immediately the screen view spun round until it was pointing backwards.

The arrows vanished and three small green boxes appeared, ascending fast into the sky. Next to them was an information tag that read: *TR-3Bs – 60.5 nautical miles.*

Goosebumps broke out across my back. 'Tom, what range do the weapons on this craft have?'

'According to the schematics, the rail gun should reach a hundred miles or so if fired in a parabolic arc.'

'Then I can take a shot.' I centred one of the tiny green boxes in my targeting reticle and began to tighten my finger on the firing trigger.

'Lauren, stop,' Tom said. 'Those Astras shouldn't be able to catch up with us and can only maintain a steady distance, so there's no need to shoot. Besides, they could dodge even a hyper-velocity round at that distance. A rail gun might be a great weapon for a static target at long range, like a naval gun on a battleship, but less so with a target that can manoeuvre fast enough to avoid it. You'll need to wait until they're almost on top of us to stand a chance of hitting them.'

'You're telling me they don't have guided missiles?'

'There's little point because they're far too slow to react at the speed that TR-3Bs fly. Skunkworks are researching antigravity-driven missiles for the Navy who operate that fleet of TR-3Bs out of Area 51. However, they aren't ready to be deployed yet.' He tapped his breast pocket. 'Saying that, I have the schematics for them on a USB memory stick, procured from Area 51. Jodie is going to have a field day when she sees it, especially with all the other secrets I managed to steal. On balance, my mission, though somewhat truncated by your appearance, has been a success.'

'God, I'm so sorry for blowing your cover, Tom. I had no idea you'd be there.'

'You weren't meant to. Nobody was. Anyway, we can discuss all that later when we get back to...' His words trailed away as a warning red arrow appeared at the side of my screen.

Enemy radar lock flashed up on my screen.

'I thought you said they weren't going to be a threat?'

Tom stared at one of his screens. 'It's not them. I'm seeing two other incoming aircraft flying at Mach 2. They're one hundred and forty miles out at our one o'clock position.'

'Oh, bloody hell!' I spun my gunner's screen round to see the targets for myself.

As the view shifted forward, the new arrows that had appeared were replaced by two red lock boxes with text-info tags alongside.

'Targets identified, Tom. They're US Airforce F-22 Raptors.'

'They must be flying flat out with their afterburners to achieve that speed.'

'But there's no way they can stop us, right?' I asked.

'As far as I know—'

The rest of his sentence was drowned out by an alarm. Two diamond boxes had appeared over the red lock boxes and were growing larger.

'Enemy missile lock,' a female computerised voice announced. *Thirty seconds till impact* flashed up on my screen.

'Good grief, they've just fired at us,' Tom said. 'You try to shoot those missiles down, Lauren, whilst I do my best to avoid them altogether.'

Adrenaline thrummed through my body as I pressed the

screen icon locked on to the left-hand missile. 'Target lock,' the computerised voice said.

I tightened my jaw as I pulled the trigger.

A rising tone hummed through the ship and a circular cloud of shockwave air appeared in front of our Astra as a dart shape sped away from us at an impossible speed. I counted to ten. A tiny fireball appeared beneath the left-hand missile lock box on my gunner's screen. I stared at it as the missile vanished in a cloud of tumbling debris. The rocket engine burst from it and cartwheeled towards the ground.

'Nice blooding shooting!' Tom said.

But I ignored him, focusing fully on the other lock box that was growing rapidly in size. I stabbed the gunner's screen, desperately trying to lock on to it, but the AIM missile was closing way too fast thanks to our crazy speed. It hurtled towards us, leaving a corkscrewing smoke trail behind it.

'Ten seconds until impact,' the computerised voice calmly announced

'Tom!' I shouted.

'On it!' He flicked his right joystick sideways.

Even with the gravity-reduction drive, I was shoved hard to the side of my seat as our Astra instantly switched direction and hurtled at a right angle to its original flight path.

The gunner's screen spun round automatically as it tracked the remaining missile as we sped away at an incredible speed. The missile's turn was almost slow motion in comparison to the manoeuvre we'd just pulled as it desperately tried to reacquire its lock.

But Tom was already centring the joystick and pushed it forward. I was slammed back into my seat as our TR-3B raced forward at Mach 7 again.

The view on the gunner's screen continued to track the missile as attempt to turn. But it was already falling away far behind us. Now I'd seen for myself exactly what Tom had meant when he'd said that conventional missiles were no match for this craft.

'OK, we're past those Raptors and are out of range of their weapons' range,' Tom said. 'We're lucky that our systems even picked them up. F-22s are incredibly stealthy and present an almost invisible radar profile. That's testimony to just how sophisticated the sensor suite is on these TR-3Bs.'

I let out a long puff of breath I hadn't realised I'd been holding. 'And thank god for that.' My heart only gradually beginning to decelerate, I spun the gunner's screen back towards the other pursuing squadron of Astras. As I read their info tags a trickle of electricity ran down my spine. The distance between us had closed to fifty miles. A moment ago I would have considered that a huge distance, but not after our encounter with the F-22s.

'Tom, those pursuing TR-3Bs are closing on us,' I said.

Tom stared at one of his screens. 'How the hell are they managing to do that?'

A chill blanketed me. 'I think I know. When I was stowed away on that other TR-3B, Zack redlined their engines for a mercy dash to Area 51 to get the Grey back quickly.'

Tom looked over his flight consoles and turned his gaze to me. 'I didn't know that was technically possible. Can you do the same for us?'

I stared at the array of screens and the maze of information and shook my head. 'Sorry, I haven't got a clue how to do that. But the good news is that they were only able to keep up that speed for about twenty minutes before their reactor started to overheat.'

'That helps, but they're going to catch up with us in the next ten.'

'Oh, bloody hell.' My eyes swept over the screens as I looked for an answer. Tom was right – they were nearing quickly. The distance was now down to forty-five miles as they continued to reel us in.

'So we're going to have to fight them after all?' I asked.

Tom's lips curled over his teeth. 'We can try, but those TR-3B pilots are the best of the best, the real top guns in every sense. Once they catch up with us, we'll be heavily outgunned and almost certainly outflown too.'

'Then maybe we're thinking about this back to front,' I said and peered at one of my screens that displayed a scrolling map.

'What are you thinking?'

'If we can't outrun them, we need to use cover to even our odds up a bit.'

'There's not exactly a lot of that up here, Lauren.'

'True.' I gestured at my navigation screen. 'But according to the map I'm looking at, we're not too far away from the Grand Canyon. How about hiding out down there where radar can't get a lock on us thanks to all that rock?'

'Flying a top-secret triangular craft at high speed close to the ground... You do know that you really are certifiably crazy, don't you?'

I grinned at him. 'So everyone keeps telling me.'

Tom chuckled as he pushed his left joystick forward. We curved down towards a bank of clouds and plunged into mist. On my screen I saw beads of water streaming over the invisible force field round the craft. With a rush of sunlight we punched through into clear air again.

'How far behind us are they now?' Tom asked.

'Thirty-five miles.'

Tom nodded. 'Let's see if we can bluff our way out of this.' He pushed the comm button. 'Pursuing craft, you are to stand down and return to base,' he said, his southern drawl back in place.

A pulsating spot appeared next to the lead ship with the ID tag *Skyscraper* next to it.

'I'm afraid we can't do that, Commander Jenson,' a man with a New York accent replied. 'We have orders to bring you in. So do us all a favour and turn that bird round right now.'

'As much as I'd like to comply, that's not an option, Skyscraper,' Tom replied. 'I'm on a clandestine mission that's time critical.'

'I'm sorry, Commander, but you have to abandon your mission. If you don't, you'll leave us with no choice but to engage you.'

'Sorry, but no can do, Skyscraper.'

A sigh came over the radio. 'Have it your way, Commander. I hate to have to do this, but you can't say you weren't warned.'

A warbling warning sound came from my gunner's screen. My heart leapt as a shockwave appeared in front of the Skyscraper craft. A line of silver shot out from it, streaking through the sky and eating up the miles between us in a shockingly small amount of time.

'Incoming hypervelocity projectile!' I shouted as I read the data info next to it.

Tom nodded and rolled the thumb control on his left joystick.

The seat's harness bit into my body as our Astra shot downwards, racing towards the scrubland far below. Ribbons of vapour flowed over the plummeting sphere of our gravity bubble, creating a shockwave at the leading edge of it.

My jaw tightened as the gunner's view automatically tracked the projectile. It was the barest blur through the air and the tracking system was doing an astonishing job of keeping it in frame. I instinctively winced as a whistling sound came from outside, speeding past us. The camera view spun round to show it streaking away towards the horizon. A moment later its sonic boom rattled our cockpit.

Tom breathed hard as he levelled out our flight path again.
'Hold your damned fire, Skyscraper!'

'Order are orders, Commander. You of all people should
know that.'

Tom stabbed his finger down on the comm button, killing the
link. 'I never liked that man. Played things too much by the book
rather than thinking for himself. Still, I don't want take their lives
if we can at all help it.'

'Me too. After all, they're US Navy pilots not Overseer
agents.'

'Agreed. With that in mind, there should be an option on
your screen that says Firing Solutions. Select that, Lauren.'

I hunted across the displays and spotted a grey box with that
wording in the bottom right of the gunner's screen. I pressed it
and two options appeared. The first one, Target Critical Systems,
was already selected. My gaze scanned down to the next item,
Target Non-Critical Systems. I selected it and the tension that I
hadn't even realised I'd been carrying in my jaw faded away. This
was a good call from Tom.

'OK, locked and loaded,' I said.

'Good, so our rail gun won't blast them out of the sky now as
it will only take out secondary systems, hopefully enough to slow
them down.'

'And how about them with us?'

'I'm afraid as far as they are concerned we're a legitimate
target.'

'I was afraid you were going to say that.'

Tom adjusted the flight controls and we sped towards a series
of valleys ahead of us, one of which was unmistakable. The
Grand Canyon was on my bucket list, but I'd never in a million
years thought I would see it in anything like these circumstances.
Slabs of golden rock towered either side of a deep valley, multi-
coloured rock strata visible throughout like stacks of stone

pancakes. Its size was breathtaking – it was an awesome spectacle of nature and maybe our only hope of staying alive.

It was then that I realised Tom didn't seem to be aiming for it, but flying towards one of the parallel canyons just to the left of it.

'We have a better chance of evading them in the smaller canyons,' Tom said, answering my unasked question.

A warbling alarm came from my display and three more blips appeared in the far distance behind the craft already chasing us. 'New targets detected,' the female computerised voice said far too calmly.

'Oh, this day just gets better and better,' I said.

'Someone really doesn't want us to get away,' Tom muttered as we tore towards the smaller canyon dead ahead of us.

CHAPTER TWENTY-EIGHT

WE DROPPED to what must have been less than a hundred metres above the ground, skimming over it at heart-stopping velocity. Tom's face was drenched in sweat, his eyes laser-focused on his flight screen. He pulled back on the throttle control as we raced towards the entrance of a wide valley. The landscape whipping past on my screen slowed from a nose-bleed blur to a still ridiculously fast six hundred miles per hour.

'Why are you slowing down?' I asked.

'I've no choice unless you want us to plough straight into a cliff face. Just keep an eye on the pursuing craft. We're well within effective target range now.'

The weapons' targeting joystick grew slick in my hand as I watched the distance indicator for the pursuing squadron tick down to five miles. Flying just above the ground, our gravity field bubble was large enough to throw up a spreading bow wave of orange dust in twin radiating swirls that spread out behind us, obscuring the view.

The square targeting reticles grew larger on my screen, the labels indicating they were only four miles away. Like three riders emerging from an apocalypse, they burst out of the dust stormed we'd created, three black triangles flying perpendicular to the ground and suddenly decelerating hard too.

The distance between us ticked down to three miles as we raced into the valley, rock walls skimming past. Tom jinked our craft, throwing the ship left and right within the confines of the canyon.

A warning alarm blared out from my display, red lights appearing across it.

Enemy lock flashed up on my screen.

My throat constricted as a shockwave appeared in front of the TR-3B on the left of the chasing squadron.

Tom twitched his joystick left. We rolled sideways and a black dart sped past us, the sonic boom only a split second behind it at this range. With a whump the hypersonic round slammed into the side of the valley. It was like an instant earthquake had taken hold of the cliff and shattered it. With a roar of splintering stone the whole rock face exploded into a shower of boulders. Rattles and bangs came from outside as rocks slammed into the ground, throwing up huge plumes of red dust ahead of us.

His teeth bared, Tom yanked his left joystick back, using the vectoring rockets to adjust our flight path. We hurtled through the top of the expanding cloud before diving back into the valley. The TR-3B hummed and creaked around us, the antigravity drive reducing some but not all the stresses on the airframe.

Even with our reduced speed, all this happened in less than three seconds and then we were past and it was receding into the distance.

'Return fire!' Tom shouted.

My heart surged as I centred on the TR-3B that had fired on us. The green reticle round it turned green as it locked on.

I squeezed the trigger on the joystick. Our ship vibrated as a harmonic sound came from the Astra. With a whoosh our own thread of death sped straight towards the pursuing craft.

In all the chaos a sense of calm filled me as I thought of the hunter about to bring down their prey. But at the last second the chasing craft bobbed upwards and my shot sped uselessly beneath it, cutting out a huge furrow in the canyon's base, trailing dust and debris.

Tom grimaced. 'I told you these guys were all bloody top guns.'

Two more shockwaves appeared as shots blurred away from them towards us.

A hissing sound came from the multiple vectoring rockets round the circumference of our ship as Tom desperately pulled the TR-3B round a bend in the canyon.

The air felt as if it were being sucked out of my lungs by the intensity of the manoeuvre as I was pressed into my seat. A split second later, like the bellow of a giant being felled, the rocky bluff behind us exploded in a shower of rock splinters, right where we'd been just a second before.

We curved away, spinning as we went, the canyon walls speeding past at a nausea-inducing rate. Tom was entirely dripping with sweat now, his jaw muscles prominent. He threw us round a series of increasingly dangerous switchback bends in the now winding canyon.

My hands clawed my seat arms as he just managed a sharp turn to the right. A shudder passed through the ship, the gravity bubble doing its best to cushion us from the rock face just metres from our fuselage.

The canyon opened up again into a straight and we raced along it.

We couldn't last much longer at this rate. I needed to increase our odds of survival.

In all the chaos I somehow found the mental space to take a

centring breath. Once again a sense of serenity took hold of me and I aimed my rail gun's reticle towards the exit of the bend we'd just taken. A bead of sweat tickled down my nose, but I didn't allow anything to break my focus as my finger trembled on the trigger.

Three reticle squares appeared. No time for using the automated weapon systems. I adjusted my aim by a millimetre and took the shot as the three TR-3Bs banked the corner.

There was no chance for the pilot to do anything as my rail-gun round smashed into the lead ship. I blinked, barely able to believe I'd actually hit it as their Astra spiralled towards the ground. For a moment I was the pilot in that ship, imagining it was us crashing. My stomach lurched in sympathy when it smashed into the rocky floor in a cloud of smoke and fire.

I found myself shaking. Those were US Navy pilots I'd just shot down.

Tom grabbed a split second to throw me a sideways look. 'You did what you had to do, Lauren,' he said, reading my mind.

I swallowed hard. But then I caught sight of a round pod on a parachute slowly drifting down to earth. 'It looks as if they had time to eject!'

Tom nodded as he got us round the next bend.

It was only then that I realised just one of two remaining TR-3Bs had appeared from the expanding dust cloud. Had the other been taken out by flying debris?

That hope died inside me as another warbling alarm shrilled out. 'Enemy lock,' the female AI announced.

A flashing arrow appeared at the top of my display. I yanked the rail gun's joystick back. My gunner's screen pivoted upwards towards it in a blur of movement. I spotted the missing TR-3B diving straight for us as a shockwave appeared in front of the ship.

Tom was already yanking the joystick hard over, flipping us

sideways. The incoming rail gun round smashed into the canyon base just beneath us with a detonation so loud it seemed as if the whole world was screaming.

On my screen I saw the TR-3B still coming for us, a hawk plummeting from the sky towards its prey. As Tom punched the accelerator and tried to race us away, a stillness filled me once again. I saw the craft starting to pull out of the dive as though my response rate had sped up a thousand times, almost bringing its manoeuvre into slow motion. I centred it in my sights and squeezed the trigger.

At close range the impact of our hypersonic round was shocking. The rail-gun projectile ripped straight through the tip of the triangular craft. The panels vaporised into a cloud of molten metal as the nose of the craft was sliced off as if cut by a surgeon. The Astra yawed sideways towards the canyon wall as its pilot lost control.

I gritted my teeth for the inevitable impact. At the last moment a circular hatch opened in the roof and a large metal sphere shot out into the sky. The Astra ploughed into the rock face in a huge explosion.

'Enemy lock,' the computerised voice calmly announced.

Something streaked past us and a massive bang followed by a rumble like a rushing tsunami came from above. The last pursuing Astra!

I pivoted my screen to see half a cliff starting to collapse right on top of us from the hypersonic round that had just been fired into it.

It was like watching an avalanche rolling down towards us, but made from stone and dust, not snow and ice. Tom had run out of sky and, with nowhere left to go, we plunged headlong into it.

Jarring impacts came from all around the ship as if we'd run into a hailstorm of ball bearings. The scent of my own sweat filled my nose and my mouth went bone dry as our gravity field became overwhelmed and our whole ship shook. Would this be how we died?

But Tom was screaming, 'Come on!' His hand muscles cabled as he pulled his left joystick hard back, pushing the other joystick forward.

A whining sound came from the ship's gravity-reduction drive and we started to rise back through the avalanche as it tumbled past us into the bottom of the canyon. We were faced with a shock of blue sky as we rose out into clear air.

But I knew that the other ship had to be somewhere behind us still.

I spun my sight back down towards the expanding cloud of dirt. And then, like a whale breaking the surface of the sea, the chasing craft burst out too.

Tom was already reacting, speeding us down into an adjacent valley, spinning the craft as we descended. Another projectile blurred past us as Tom jinked us sideways just in time.

A fresh alarm warbled in the cockpit.

I stared at the warning display, tears threatening my eyes as I absorbed the information. This was so bloody unfair. 'Tom, that second squadron is almost in range of us now, just five miles out.'

He managed a vague nod as he manoeuvred us hard round another bend. And then another alarm sounded.

'Fuck, make that two!' I screamed as I saw new contacts light up on my gunner's screen. 'The craft travelling towards us at Mach 6 will be on top of us in two minutes.'

Tom weaved from one side of the canyon to the other, like a hare tracked by hounds, as he desperately tried to escape. But the last ship from the first squadron matched Tom's increasingly frantic manoeuvres move for move. The skin tightened across my forehead as I blazed round after round at the pursuing TR-3B, but kept missing. How the hell was I going to hit that thing...? Then the answer burst into my mind. Of course!

I swung my gunsight to the top of the canyon wall above. I'd use the same tactic on them that they'd already tried on us. I tried to keep the cliff centred, but it kept spinning out of view as Tom threw us fiercely around.

'Tom, I need you to keep the ship level for a second so I can take a shot.'

'But a second is all that other ship needs.'

'We'll be dead anyway soon if you don't. Just trust me.'

He gave me a sharp nod. There was no time to argue. No time for anything apart from cheating death.

The gyration of our craft slowed and the canyon wall steadied on my gunner's screen. I breathed out and fired.

The hypersonic round slammed almost instantly into the cliff wall behind us. What had been solid a moment before rose up in an expanding cloud of shattered stone before tumbling back to earth.

'Enemy target lock,' the computerised voice said.

Tom spun the accelerator wheel forward and we hurtled straight up into the sky. But not fast enough. A massive bang came from our craft and it shuddered as red lights lit up the gunner's screen.

'Weapon systems are offline,' the ship's AI announced.

Fear roared through me. I braced for the next shot that would take us out as the other craft began to rise up from the valley towards us. But the cliff was still slipping down towards it. An avalanche of boulders, some easily the size of houses, smashed straight into the rising craft. With a pulse of blinding light, the TR-3B grounded itself in the surrounding canyon. It shook violently as more rocks slammed into it with sledgehammer blows. Great panels of metal were sheared away like a tin can being opened. The Astra's momentum crawled to a stop. And then it began to fall back, carried down into the boiling maelstrom of destruction.

I didn't have time to catch a breath as a fresh alarm came from my console and a new target arrow flashed at the top of my gunner's screen.

'Out of the bloody frying pan and into the fire,' Tom muttered as he gazed at one of his information panels.

I was emotionally and physically wrecked; I had nothing left. We had no way to defend ourselves any more. We would never escape this. But I followed the targeting arrows anyway and spun my gunner's screen up towards the sky.

A new TR-3B squadron of three ships streaked into view. Like avenging angels they came to a hovering stop directly overhead. A second target arrow appeared on my screen, pointing off to the right edge. That had to be the Mach 6 craft about to arrive too late to the party.

Tom didn't say a word as he pitched our ship back towards the ground and accelerated hard.

Two shockwaves came from the ships on the left and right of the squadron. It was as if inside me a switch had been thrown and I was filled with a state of absolute calm. We'd thrown everything into this, but we'd lost and were about to die – and with that we'd probably sealed the fate of our world.

But Tom wasn't giving up yet. Not by a long shot. He rolled us away in a fast corkscrew that made the view on my screen spin like a fairground ride gone mad.

The whole world seemed to shake as a huge bang came from our craft and it shook like a coin in a tumble dryer. The smell of electrical burning filled my nose as wisps of smoke slipped between the gaps in the floor. Gravity, no longer dampened, smashed me into the edge of my seat and my body screamed in agony from the violent impact.

'We're hit and we're going down!' Tom shouted as he fought

the controls whilst the Astra shuddered and moaned, tumbling towards the ground end over end.

I breathed through my nose and what felt like several tons pressed directly into my sternum. There was no way we'd survive a second shot.

Our comm channel crackled into life. 'You've got to eject now!'

That was Don's voice!

'Preparing to take those fucking bastards down!' another man said over the channel.

'Hold your fucking fire, Hell Demon!' Don screamed.

Tom yanked at the handle in the floor next to him, but nothing happened. 'Oh, for Christ's sake, the escape pod has been taken out too.'

Calm filled me as Tom released the joystick. The ship groaned around us, the dying cries of a hunter shot down. I closed my eyes, ready for the end.

And then the world stopped whirling.

'How the hell did you do that?' Don's voice said over the radio.

I opened my eyes to see a now static view of the canyon and the three TR-3Bs hovering above us.

Somehow Tom had managed to get our drive back online. I turned to see him staring at his screens.

'How did you do that?'

Tom shook his head. 'That wasn't me.'

The view on my gunner's screen shimmered. For a moment I thought it was another glitch. But then a saucer-shaped craft rippled into view. 'That will be thanks to Ruby distorting our gravitational field and extending it round your craft,' Alice said over the comm channel. 'It's a tip we picked up from Lucy.'

I stared with utter disbelief at Ariel hovering before us on my screen, the most beautiful sight I'd ever seen in my life. I thumped the air and let out a whoop.

'You're pleased to see us then?' Ruby's voice asked.

'That might be the understatement of the century,' Tom replied.

A warbling alarm came from my weapon systems.

'Like I said before, stand down, Hell Demon and Cat Fight,' Don said over the comm link.

'No can do, Archangel. We have our orders,' a woman's voice replied.

Two craft hurtled towards us in a swooping dive away from the central Astra now labelled as Archangel in my display, lining up to take the shot. Ariel might have come to save us, but she had no way of protecting either of us from that.

Despite the grief I felt that my friends were about to throw away their lives too, the stillness deepened inside me, growing into a lake of tranquillity in which I floated.

My mind snapped back as a clattering noise came from outside. It took a moment for me to realise that the sound wasn't our craft being ripped apart, which was remaining rock steady within Ariel's extended gravity field. It was coming over the comm link.

I focused back on my gunner's screen to see a twin storm of tracer fire lancing out from two small domes on top of Ariel's cockpit, straight into the two diving TR-3Bs. The projectiles tore through both ships, sparks erupting as they punched holes in the craft. Panels of metal exploded, billowing smoke as they were shredded away.

A large sphere shot out from the ship on the left – the pilot's pod ejecting. But I saw no such thing from the one on the right, which slammed into the ground with an awful life-ending impact.

'Surprise, surprise, you bastards,' Ruby's voice said over the comm link.

Don's Astra tilted towards Ariel, bringing its rail gun to bear on the saucer-shaped ship.

I punched my comm button. 'Don and Zack, for god's sake, please stop this. There's been enough blood shed already. The same goes for you, Ruby.'

'Oh, I can take them in a straight fight,' Ruby replied.

'I'd like to see you try,' Don said, his voice solid iron.

I cut in before Ruby could bait the flight crew more than she had already. 'Don, I can only begin to imagine how angry you are, but you have to listen to me.'

'And why should I? That craft has just butchered the rest of my wing! Who are you, anyway?'

'I'm Lauren, the woman you saved by telling your commander I needed help.'

'Oh Jesus. We wouldn't be here now if I'd ignored you.'

'But you didn't and it was the right call, Don. I heard what you and Zack said about not agreeing with your orders to target the Tic Tacs. And you're right about that too. Your superiors are the ones in the wrong here, not you. They've picked a fight with the wrong aliens, namely the Greys.'

Alice's voice cut in over the open channel. 'This is the captain of Ariel. You need to listen to Lauren extremely carefully. Everything she has just told you is the absolute truth. What your superiors should be worried about is an invasion force known as the Kimprak. They are currently on their way to destroy our world.'

'The who?'

'The Kimprak. They're a mechanised species who'll suck the life out of this planet unless we find a way to stop them,' I said. 'Alvarez and his kind are on the wrong side of history here. Please don't make the same mistake that they have. Fight for our world and not against it. This is your chance to do that.'

Alice's speech was certainly impassioned, but would Don and Zack see sense?

'Even if I believed you, and though I might not have agreed with the actions of the rest of my flight wing just now, I'm afraid I still can't let you go. I have to follow the chain of command.'

'A good soldier sometimes needs to question orders and make decisions that take pure guts,' Tom said in his fake southern accent.

There was a long pause as the radio link went quiet.

I could only begin to imagine the difficult conversation going on in the other ship. Don and Zack were good guys. They'd make the right call, I just knew it.

A sigh came over the comm link. 'I'm sorry, really,' Don said. 'But we don't have any choice in this.'

The TR-3B started to rotate its rail-gun port down towards us.

Before I could say anything, twin streams of cannon fire roared from Ariel.

'No!' I screamed.

But the rounds were already tearing into the open gun port of the triangular craft. Flames belched from it instantly as it was ripped wide open. Don's reactions were lightning fast too, though, and his TR-3B rolled away.

I leant forward, staring at my gunner's screen as Ruby poured an unrelenting stream of deadly cannon fire into the other ship, walking it across the hull to slice it open. The line of bullet holes reached one of the glowing orange lift engines. With a bellow the engine blew into a fireball that briefly engulfed the ship. As it emerged again, their Astra tipped over to its side like a listing ship and slid towards the ground, trailing smoke and plasma.

I cupped my hands over my mouth. How had it come to this?

Relief surged through me as a black sphere burst from the burning craft, hurtling away on small propellant rockets up into the sky. Seconds later the stricken TR-3B ploughed into the ground, throwing up a geyser of dirt.

I sagged back into my chair. They'd made it.

'I really didn't want to do have to do that,' Ruby said over the open channel.

'I know...' I replied.

'It shouldn't have to be like this,' Alice said. 'We should be working together, not fighting each other like wild dogs. Once again, this is all on the Overseers.'

'We can discuss the morals of this situation later, but we need to get out of here before another squadron turns up,' Tom said. 'I for one have had as much as I can deal with for one day.'

'You and me both,' I said.

'Then we'll give you a tow home,' Alice said.

'We'd certainly appreciate it,' Tom replied, casting a forlorn look at his dead controls.

I kept my eyes on the parachutes of the capsule as they floated down towards the ground a few miles away from the burning wreckage of the downed TR-3B. Then the scene was suddenly blurring away into the distance as Alice took us home.

Adrenaline slowly ebbed from me, leaving an echo of it in my blood. I tipped my head back into my seat as numbness took over. Impossibly, we'd somehow survived.

CHAPTER TWENTY-NINE

ENVELOPED BY ARIEL's gravity field, we raced back towards Eden in the stolen TR-3B. At Alice's request we'd blanked our navigation screens so we wouldn't know where we were headed. Alice had assured us there was no way the Overseers would be able to track us at long range. Thankfully, their newly developed sensor only seemed effective at very short distances.

The remaining hum of adrenaline in my bloodstream had finally started to subside. I still couldn't believe we'd managed to survive our encounter with two squadrons of TR-3Bs. Alvarez would be spitting bullets when he heard what'd happened.

'We have some time before we arrive back, so we should talk,' Alice's voice said over the comm link.

I'd been bracing myself for what I knew was coming. Alice clearly didn't want to waste any time before laying into me. She probably had Niki preparing a nice tiny cell for me back in Eden. And I deserved all of it.

'Absolutely,' I replied, jumping in before Tom could. I was going to try to get answers first. I needed to know what had happened to Ruby. 'Thank god you're alive, Ruby, but how?'

'It was a close-run thing, Lauren, with all those incoming fifty-cal rounds,' she said. 'If I were a cat, I'd probably have lost several of my nine lives, but somehow I managed to get back to our X101. Without those TR-3Bs there to pick me up I circled round in the X101 in the chaos and collected Jack and Mike just before a patrol of pursuing Humvees caught up with them. Although I had a hard time persuading Jack to leave you behind. He was absolutely frantic with worry.'

Relief surged through me to hear that Jack and Mike had made it out too. 'Well, as far as I'm concerned you made the right call.'

'Thanks, Lauren. I didn't really have much choice...' Her voice trailed away. 'But I just wanted to say that it took real guts to do what you did. Not everyone would have stayed behind so that Mike and Jack could get away.' There was a longer pause. 'You're all right, you know that, Lauren.'

There was no hint of sarcasm in Ruby's voice. Jack had been right when he'd told me she'd come round when she saw me operate in the field. 'You know what? You are too, Ruby.'

'Hey, I'll take that,' she said.

'Talking about people being worried, Tom, losing all contact with you put us all on edge,' Alice said.

'I'm very sorry about that, but needless to say it was a necessary move,' Tom said. 'After I managed to infiltrate Area 51, any attempt to make contact would have been extremely risky. I'm afraid things didn't go quite according to plan when Lauren crashed the party.'

'You were both in Area 51?' Ruby said. 'What the hell?'

'It's a long story,' I replied.

'Looking forward to hearing it all over a drink or three,' Ruby said.

'The important thing is that you're both OK, but...' Alice's tone became tense.

Tom traded a frown with me. 'Alice, is everything all right?'

'No, no, it isn't. I need to bring you both up to speed on some developments, specifically you, Lauren.'

My stomach did a slow flip. Ruby had mentioned Jack and Mike, but there was one key member of our team that hadn't been brought up yet. One who I would have expected to lead the cavalry charge to rescue us.

'Is it about Lucy?' I said in a small voice.

'I'm afraid it's bad news, Lauren,' Alice replied. 'Those TR-3B pilots who chased her managed to get in a lucky shot. Lucy crash-landed in the Everglade swamps in Florida. Moments before she crashed, she managed to radio back to us at Eden to tell us what had happened and reversed the security protocols that she'd used to lock down Eden's flight bay doors. Finally, in those last seconds before we lost contact with her, Lucy beamed us her coding back door of the military spy satellite network.'

A sudden chill rolled through my body. 'And?' I asked.

'We were able to pinpoint the exact site where she went down after replaying the footage from a military satellite over the area. The one glimmer of good news is that, despite the Overseers sending in half their air force to recover her, Niki and a security team took out an Armadillo and managed to reach the crash site deep in the swamps first. They were able to recover her micro mind ship before the Overseers arrived.'

'And the bad news is?' Tom asked, casting me a frown.

'There was significant damage to her crystal matrix and she's completely shut down. Jodie's only hope is that you can activate her self-repair function, Lauren, when you get back here.'

I swallowed, my throat suddenly tight. 'But what if I can't? What then?'

Tom turned towards me. 'Don't forget we have another part of her consciousness down in the hold. Maybe you could reboot her with that?'

I felt myself relax a fraction and nodded. 'That might actually work.'

'You mean your mission was a success, Tom?' Alice asked.

'It most certainly was. We have Lauren to thank for that,' Tom replied. 'I couldn't see a way of sneaking the micro mind off that base until she turned up.'

I stared at him and then at the speaker. 'I thought you said you didn't know where Tom was, Alice?'

'I'm afraid that was a deliberate subterfuge on both our parts,' Alice admitted. 'You see we picked up some intelligence that the Overseers had managed to recover a micro mind and had taken it back to Area 51.'

Tom nodded. 'But we weren't entirely confident in the reliability of the informant. So Alice and I decided that I should go on a lone-wolf infiltration mission. Obviously that's not what you and the rest of the team were told.'

I already knew where this was heading. 'It's the same reason why none of us knows the exact location of Eden, isn't it? So if we fell into enemy hands, we couldn't compromise your mission?'

'Exactly right,' Tom replied. 'And it was too good an opportunity to learn what the Overseers were up to at that facility. Not to mention the chance to gather intelligence about the top-secret projects going on down there, including their TR-3B development programme.' He gestured at the cockpit around us. 'Of course, even in my wildest dreams, I hadn't thought we'd end up stealing one of their ships, but this is one heck of a bonus.'

'It most certainly is,' Alice said. 'Jodie won't believe her eyes when she sees what you're bringing back for her. Tom, is there any news about the Greys the Overseers have been keeping in Area 51?'

'It's as we feared,' he replied. 'They've been actively experimenting on them.'

'More like torturing them,' I said. 'I saw them open up the

skull of the Grey they recovered from the downed Tic Tac. Talking of that, it was the Grey that showed me you, Tom – in my mind as a telepathic image. Well, not *you*, exactly, but the disguised Commander Jenson version of you. I think he was trying to let me know that you were a friend.'

'The Grey communicated with you?' Tom asked, sitting up straighter.

'Yes, Lucy mentioned that they use some sort of telepathic link. For some reason he chose me to link to – why, I've got no idea. But how did the Grey know you?'

'Well, you're not the only one it communicated with. I sneaked into the lab to see it. Like you it seemed to know I was a friend. And it showed me in my thoughts why there had been so much increased Tic Tac activity recently in our world – in the same way it obviously communicated with you.'

'Guessing it's nothing to do with an invasion?' Ruby asked over the link.

'Yes, quite the opposite, in fact. The Grey showed me an image of the Kimprak asteroid ship destroying populated planet after populated planet, and then Lucy's combined micro mind ship – accompanied by the impression that she was a friend too.'

'So they know about Lucy? That has to be significant,' Alice said.

'I agree. It suggests they must have had some prior contact with the Angelus. Anyway, the next thing the Grey showed me were their Tic Tac ships flying all over Earth. I somehow knew in that moment exactly why they were here.'

'Why?' I asked.

'To try to find the missing micro minds. They know how important Lucy is to the survival of our world too.'

It was my turn to sit up straighter. 'I don't suppose you learnt how they were planning to do this exactly?'

'Unfortunately not. But it was obvious – from this one Grey at least – that it was a big deal. I also got the impression that the Grey wanted nothing to do with the Overseers. They've tried before to warn them about the Kimprak but have had their craft shot down.'

'But why?' Ruby asked.

'I'm afraid it's a toxic combination of power and arrogance on the part of the Overseers. They honestly believe that they'll be able to take on the Kimprak ship when it arrives with their large fleet of TR-3Bs. They're planning to nuke the hell out of the Kimprak when the asteroid ship arrives in our solar system with the new shiny TR-3B fleet they're building. As for Lucy, they see her simply as a distraction, aside from thinking her technology is worthy of investigation. Of course, it far exceeds even that of the Greys' ships they've been able to recover and reverse-engineer up to now. The Overseers believe that if they harness Lucy's technology, humanity will become an unstoppable force in the universe, able to deal with any extra-terrestrial threat that we may encounter.'

'But why aren't they concentrating on forming allegiances then?' I asked. 'Working with the Greys, with us, with anyone who could help win this battle?'

'The Overseers also want to maintain absolute control. In exactly the same way their secret organisation has been able to run this world, they now want to extend that influence out to the stars and even other alien races.'

'So, this is all about cementing their position for the future?' Alice asked.

'In a word, yes,' Tom replied.

'Same old,' Ruby said.

Tom sighed. 'I'm afraid so.'

A chime came over the comm link.

'We're about thirty minutes from home,' Alice said. 'But

before we arrive, I'd just like to discuss your departure from Eden, Lauren.'

So here it came. 'I know, I know,' I said. 'I'm sorry for what I did.'

'Hey, it wasn't just you who decided to head out on an unauthorised mission,' Ruby cut in.

'Maybe, but I was the one in charge, so this is on me,' I replied.

Tom cast me a questioning look that I ignored.

'No, this isn't on you either, Lauren,' Alice said, and I blinked. 'If it's on anyone, it's on me. I should have told you the full story about Tom already being in place at Area 51 to scoop up any information about that crashed Tic Tac and the Grey.'

'You mean you already had it covered?' I said.

'We did. But I was a victim of my own secrecy, even if it was a strategy I'd already agreed with Tom. In future I think I need to be much more transparent with all of you about what we have planned.'

'I think that's an excellent idea, Alice,' Tom said. 'I was never entirely comfortable with our strategy. I also have a question I'd like to ask. How on earth did you know where to find us? I made a point of asking Lauren to make sure our transponder was turned off.'

'That was thanks to Delphi, who picked up social media posts about UFOs dogfighting over the Grand Canyon area. When we checked the surveillance footage from the military satellites and saw an Astra being pursued by a squadron of TR-3Bs that had departed Area 51, we had a very strong suspicion that it had to be you.'

I grimaced. 'You're telling me it's already on social media?'

'Like a rash,' Ruby replied. 'Photos too.'

'On the plus side the Overseers are going to have a tough time putting this incident back in the box,' Alice said. 'Mind you, knowing their track record, they will most certainly try to do so with a smear campaign claiming the photos are fake. Anyway, that's when we realised just how much trouble you were in. With Lucy out of commission there was only one ship that could get to you in time – Ariel. And I was the only pilot with any real experience of her, so I had no choice but to pilot her out there.'

'There's always a choice,' I said.

'Maybe, but let's just say I needed to do this. You can thank Ruby here for persuading me to arm Ariel with the twin Vulcan cannons. And of course there was no talking Ruby down from coming with me when she arrived back at Eden with the others in the X101.'

'Yeah, I was like a cat on a hot tin roof thinking we'd lost you,' Ruby said. 'Alice wanted to immediately head out in Ariel to find you, but I knew we'd run into a whole heap of trouble if we went straight there. So I persuaded her and Jodie to fit those bad boys to Ariel. We might lack the fancy rail gun of a TR-3B, but in a close-quarter dogfight, those Vulcan cannons can kick some serious arse, as you just saw.'

'Seems as if we have a lot to thank you for, Ruby,' Tom said.

'Aw, shucks, any time, guys.'

'So tell me about Mike – how's he doing? Is he complaining about hospital food yet?'

It was as if I'd just kit a kill switch on the mood. They both went quiet at the other end of the line.

'We need to tell her,' Ruby finally said, her tone tense.

I felt my blood run cold. 'Tell me what exactly?'

'There's no easy way to say this, Lauren,' Alice said. 'When we left, Mike was fighting for his life. Despite Jack rigging up a transfusion from himself who happened to be the same A-positive group on the flight back, by the time they arrived at Eden Mike had lost a lot of blood.'

I had to force the words out. 'You're not trying to tell me that he's dead, are you?'

'Not if Jack has anything to do with it,' Alice said. 'He and our medical team are fighting to save Mike's life right now. But I have to be honest with you, Lauren, it's touch and go.'

I covered my mouth with my hands. 'No!'

Tom unbuckled his flight harness and crossed to me as my vision suddenly blurred with tears.

CHAPTER THIRTY

WITH RUBY ADJUSTING Ariel's gravity field, she carefully lowered our stolen TR-3B on the landing pad at the bottom of the launch silo with the gentlest shudder. I felt my weight increase a fraction in the cockpit as the gravity bubble was withdrawn from around us. On my screens that'd been turned on again I saw Ariel's legs extending as she landed next to us on the adjacent pad. But only part of my mind registered our arrival back at Eden because I was focused on one thing and one thing only: Mike. And as though my anxiety levels weren't already through the roof about him, there was also the building fear about the implications if we couldn't get Lucy back online. What would happen for our world then? As soon as Tom had opened the ramp, I was on my feet and racing down it before he'd even had a chance to get up.

The first person I saw outside was a technician heading towards us, his wide gaze taking in our triangular craft. I ignored him and sprinted past, the physical exhaustion of the mission washed away by some hidden reserves of energy now coursing through my body.

The corridors blurred past me. People ducked aside to make

way for the crazy woman. Rather than wait for a lift, I took the stairs three at a time.

With almost tunnel vision, my sides burning, I skidded out of a doorway and flew through a set of double doors into the medical centre.

Time decelerated as I focused in on Jodie as she paced back and forth. Niki looked up from a seat. Jodie turned towards me, her face ashen. She almost seemed to crumple into herself at seeing me.

'How's Mike doing?' I asked between gulps of breath.

Jodie spread her hands wide, but no words came, increasing my feeling of dread. She sank into the chair next to Niki and he wrapped an arm round her, gently kissing the top of her head. Niki and Jodie were obviously far closer than I'd realised.

Niki looked over Jodie's head at me. 'They've been operating on Mike, but it's been at least ten hours now, and there's still no news.'

Ten hours... I knelt before Jodie and took her hands in mine. 'If anyone can help him it's Jack. Don't forget he managed to save my life when I got myself almost sliced in two in a lorry crash.'

'I know, but what if Jack can't? What if—'

I tightened my grip on her hands. 'You need to be strong, Jodie, to believe it will all be OK. Mike will need the person he loves to be there for him on the other side of this.'

'You think he's that into me?'

Niki jumped in before I could. 'I can tell you for a fact that he is, Jodie.'

'But how can you know that?' she asked.

'Let's just say we had a man-to-man chat about how he was treating you. I really did give him the third degree, but it was obvious to me that his intentions towards you were serious.'

She stared at him. 'Dad?'

The blindingly obvious now hit me as all the clues dropped into place. I gawped at them. 'You're related?'

Jodie dipped her chin.

'So why keep it such a big secret?'

'We've never thought it necessary to make a big deal of it,' Jodie replied. 'So we keep it quiet. Plus I prefer to be seen in my own light at Eden rather than living in the shadow of the head of security.'

'No danger of that – you've always burned too brightly to live in anyone's shadow,' Niki said, kissing the top of her head again.

I tried to wrap my mind round this new revelation. 'But you don't even have the same surname.'

'Jodie decided to take her mother's maiden name after we got divorced. Our relationship hasn't always been as good as it is now.'

'Right...' More things started to fall into place. 'No wonder you were giving Mike such a hard time.'

Niki shrugged. 'Well, you try to stand back when you see your daughter's heart being broken. Anyway, all that matters right now is Mike getting through this operation.'

Jodie chewed her lip as she lifted her eyes to the door on the other side of the room. 'I don't know what I'll do if he doesn't make it, Lauren.'

I cradled her face in my hands. 'Look, we're not there yet, not by a long way.'

My words said one thing, but my mind was flitting ahead. Just talking to Jodie was making my insides churn. If Mike died, it would leave a big gaping hole in all our lives. It was also pretty clear to me that, despite their falling out, Jodie was head over heels for Mike.

I took her hand in mine as the doors from the corridor opened and Alice wheeled herself in.

Her gaze swept over us. 'Mike's still not out of surgery?'

We shook our heads. 'I see...' She slowly nodded and took a deep breath before releasing it again. 'In that case let's get ourselves organised. Who's up for coffee?'

As I looked back at her, I felt the claws of exhaustion starting to dig in. 'Actually, coffee would be great.'

Niki shook his head.

'No, I'm good too,' Jodie replied.

She looked anything but good, I thought. I remembered seeing that same haunted look on my own face after Alvarez had murdered Aunt Lucy when he'd driven us off the road. I'd barely eaten anything for days. And no one had been there for me to help me through it. No one had encouraged me to look after myself. If Mike didn't make it, I made a silent vow that I'd do everything I could to help Jodie through this.

'I'll get you guys coffees anyway, in case you change your minds,' Alice said.

Jodie managed a shrug.

'There's a vending machine just outside in the corridor, Lauren.' Alice raised her eyebrows at me a fraction and I realised she wanted to talk to me alone.

'I'll give you a hand,' I said, standing and following her out.

'How's Jodie doing?' Alice asked as soon as the double doors had closed behind us.

'As badly as you'd expect. At least she has Niki to lean on.'

Alice tilted her head to one side. 'Does that mean you know about their relationship?'

'Niki being her dad? Yes, I do now.'

Alice nodded. 'They both like to play that close to their chests and I've always respected their decision. Talking about family, when you get back to your room, I'd like you to box up your things.'

I put my hands on my hips, heat flaring through me. Not this.

Not now. 'Oh, come on, you can't sling me out of Eden, Alice. You need me, especially now Lucy is damaged.'

She held her hand up to halt my flow of arguments. 'No, you misunderstand me. Lauren, I want you all to come back and stay with me at my house again.'

The heat instantly cooled from my blood. 'So we're not banned any more so you can have your own quality time?'

Alice grimaced. 'Yes, maybe that was not my finest moment. But I'm sure I don't need to tell you I was dealing with some serious demons back then. And, OK, I let things get out of hand. However, now more than ever, I realise that our battle to save our world starts with looking out for each other. You mean everything to me, Lauren – all of you do. You are my family now. And, like Jodie in that waiting room, I couldn't bear it if anything happened to any of you.'

I gazed at her, my eyes softening. It was the last thing I'd expected to hear and it caught me off balance. 'That means a lot, Alice, but we also have a job to do. We have to save the world. And sometimes that means we'll need to take risks and put our lives on the line.'

'Yes, I know that, or maybe I should say I remember that now. However, I can't go quite as far as condoning you sneaking out of Eden like you did. But I do understand your reasons for it.'

Her gentle tone brought a sudden lump to my throat and I slowly nodded. 'You have a point.' I gestured towards the door. 'My pig-headedness may be about to cost Mike his life. If anyone is in the wrong here, it's me.'

Alice reached out and grabbed my hands just as I'd done with Jodie. 'No, my dear friend, this isn't on you. As you said, you were trying to save our world. That's the priority here. And your heart was in the right place too, although both of us could maybe have handled the situation better. Even if you were perhaps a little *pig-*

headed, haven't you also just returned here with a micro mind? Not to mention a TR-3B that we'll be able to learn a lot from.'

'Yes, but you try telling all that to Jodie if Mike doesn't make it.'

'No, stop that right now, Lauren,' Alice told me, her tone sharpening. 'Mike volunteered to go with you on that mission. If I know anything about that man he would be the first to say we all need to keep going whatever happens to him. This is going to sound harsh with him being in surgery, but we need you to look at Lucy soon. Getting her up and running again needs to be our priority after this. I'm just praying that's possible. Apart from anything else, she may be able to give Mike extra healing time over in E8.'

I blinked. I'd been so focused on Mike that I'd barely had a chance to think about Lucy. I immediately felt a surge of guilt. So much for me starting to consider the AI a real friend, someone who'd deliberately drawn those TR-3Bs away so we might live.

'I should go to her now and see what I can do,' I said.

Alice shook her head. 'No, your place is here until we know the outcome of Mike's operation. And you must catch your breath and get some much-needed sleep. You can tackle whatever needs to be done with Lucy in the morning. Are you hearing me?'

'As Ruby might once have said to me, yes, boss.'

'That's more like it.' The smile that had been forming on Alice's face froze as a voice came from the other side of the doors.

'Lauren, Alice,' Niki called out.

We raced back into the room to see Jack looking grey and beyond exhausted. He pulled the medical mask from his face and left it dangling round his neck.

My heart clenched. His expression was like stone. In every medical drama I'd seen this was exactly the sort of expression a surgeon had before they broke awful news to the relatives with a *– we did everything we could* speech.

Jodie was already on her feet, standing before Jack. 'Just tell me already!'

Jack's expression tightened, but he nodded. 'The good news is, he's alive.'

'Oh, thank god!' Jodie said as Alice squeezed her eyes shut. I rushed to Jodie and wrapped my arms round her. 'You see, that guy is such a fighter...' Then I caught the stiffness in Jack's face and my words trailed away.

Jack took a shaky breath and met Jodie's eyes. 'I'm afraid there was a serious complication,' he said in a quiet voice that seemed shockingly loud in the small waiting room.

My heart skipped several beats as Jack dragged his hand through his hair.

'We did everything we could, but we couldn't save his leg.' Jack gently took hold of Jodie by the shoulders. 'I'm afraid in the end we had no choice but to amputate it.'

Jodie put her hands to her face. 'No...'

She, Niki and I gawped at Jack like a frozen tableau in a Renaissance painting. Alice was the only person to break the image as she wheeled her chair towards Jodie.

'As awful as this is, you need to hear me clearly right now,' she said. 'I promise you that Mike will get through this. One day he'll adjust to it. And he'll certainly receive the best medical attention in the world as he recovers in Eden. It isn't his physical wounds that I'm most worried about, it's the emotional ones, Jodie. They're something I know far too much about. But with your love and support he'll be able to get through that too. Maybe one day he'll even be stronger for all of this.'

It was such an impassioned speech, it caught me off guard. I knew that Alice was absolutely right. Mike could and would come through to the other side of this.

Jodie nodded as a tear trickled down her face.

'I mean, look at me, I'm the poster girl for this sort of life-changing event,' Alice said. 'And if I managed it, so can Mike.'

'Yes...' Jodie said with a shuddering breath before turning back to Jack. 'Can I see him now please?'

'He's in recovery and it may be some time before he wakes up. But I can think of no better medicine for him as seeing your face when he comes round.' Jack held the door open, and Jodie and Niki headed through it. But as I went to follow, Alice reached out and gently took hold of my wrist. 'Lauren, you look dead on your feet. You need some R & R. Grab yourself that sleep we talked about, now.' She nodded towards Jack. 'That goes for you too. You look as pale as my grandmother's finest bone china.'

Jack raised his chin, but didn't reply as he avoided her gaze.

'I'll take that as a yes,' Alice said. 'I'll see you both at breakfast in my kitchen tomorrow. With a new day things will seem brighter. Lauren, please fill Jack in about moving back to my house.'

'I will,' I replied as I gazed at Jack.

She nodded and then disappeared through the doors. The second she'd gone, Jack almost collapsed into a nearby chair and hung his head.

'We tried everything, but nothing worked, Lauren.'

I sat next to him, rubbing his shoulders. 'But you saved him, Jack. That's what really matters.'

He tipped his head back, resting it against the wall. All I wanted to do was take the pain away from this most wonderful, caring person.

---

ed towards Alice's house under a canopy of stars on the ceiling screens, the Milky Way impossibly bright. A razor-thin new moon hung over the house, giving it a fairy-tale look – no doubt the intended effect of whoever had designed it.

As we approached the porch, Alice's hens were gently clucking and a warm phantom summertime breeze murmured across the lake. Quite how the designer had pulled that off I had no idea, but it only helped heighten the illusion that this was a dreamy summer's night.

Jack hadn't said a thing since we'd left the medical centre. He seemed closed in, his walls up as he grappled with whatever was going on inside. I was on the outside looking in. It was killing me that he was beating himself up over what had happened to Mike.

As we stepped on to the veranda, Jack veered towards the swing seat and dropped into it. He just sat there and gazed out towards the lake.

I sat down next to him, but what could I possibly say that might help?

At last Jack spoke. 'I used to sit on a seat just like this back at my mom's house. It was one of my favourite places in the world when I was growing up.'

I angled my body towards him. 'You've never mentioned your mum before.'

'I know... She brought me up single-handedly after my dad did a flit and we never saw him again.' A sad smile filled his face. 'We lived in a small town where everyone knew each other's business. She was the go-to person whenever someone had a problem, and they all loved her for it. Mom used to sit on that old swing seat with me and get me to talk about my dreams for my life. Then she encouraged me to chase every one of them.'

'Aunt Lucy was pretty much the same for me. Your mom sounds like an amazing person. I'd love to meet her one day.'

'I'm afraid you can't. I lost her to the big C.'

'Oh god, Jack, I'm so sorry.'

He shook his head. 'It was a long time ago. It's one of the

things that prompted me to become a doctor, to try to make a difference where I could. You understand?'

'I do...and today you did as much as anyone could have possibly done for Mike. Right man, right place, right time.'

'Maybe, but it doesn't take the pain away, Lauren. I let my friend down.'

I reached out and cupped his face in my hand. 'You so didn't, Jack. He's alive. And, like Alice said, Mike will get through this, especially with our support and our love.'

'Yes, at the end of the day it all comes down to love...' His eyes looked deep into mine.

'Jack, I...'

He rested a finger on my lips. 'Enough talking.' He leant towards me, closing the distance between our faces. I found myself raising my mouth to his.

Our lips found each other. The world melted away around us as we joined as one at last and the start of our own healing began.

LINKS

Do please leave that all important review for **Earth Shout** here:
https://geni.us/EarthShout

So now you've finished **Earth Shout,** are you ready to preorder the next page-turning instalment in the series?

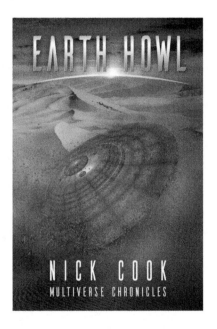

With Lucy still offline, Lauren and the others are left with no choice but to merge the micro mind they recovered from Area 51 in an attempt to reboot the AI's systems. They have only just started the procedure when the completed TREENO fleet of CubeSats detects a neutrino burst from a city straight out of myth and legend.

Ready for anything and with Ariel heavily upgraded, the team set off for the source of the signal in Mauritania region of West Africa. However, during the mission, Eden goes dark on them and isn't responding to radio transmissions. What's happened back at the base? Could it just be a technical problem or has something more sinister happened?

Soon cut off in the desert in a blinding sandstorm and without backup, Lauren and Jack encounter a micro mind that will force them to relive the natural disaster that originally destroyed the city.

You can preorder Earth Howl here: https://geni.us/Earthowl

Meanwhile, whilst you are waiting for Earth Howl, you may want to consider reading the Fractured Light trilogy which is also part of the Multiverse Chronicles. This continues the story of the AI Sentinel six years after the events covered in The Signal. A secret hidden in human DNA is about to be unlocked, but can college students Jake and his underground hacker friend Chloe solve the mystery before reality itself starts to break down?

The Fractured Light trilogy is available here: https://geni.us/FracturedLightTrilogy

OTHER BOOKS BY NICK COOK

Prequel to the Multiverse Chronicles

The Earth Song Series (The Multiverse Chronicles)

The Fractured Light Trilogy (The Multiverse Chronicles)

AUTHOR NOTES

So here we are again at the end of another book. As I write this I can't not touch on the pandemic that has swept the world, grinding it to a halt. It is one of the rare events in human history that has touched every single person on the planet, some in the most tragic of ways. For me the irony is that the rhythm of my days has pretty much continued as normal, apart from the fact I'm confined to the house as I have an underlying health condition. I feel fortunate in so many respects and my thoughts go out to everyone on the frontline, risking their lives for the rest of us, especially the health workers. I'm not forgetting the others who are helping to keep our society going, from delivery drivers and supermarket workers to postmen and women. For me you are all heroes of this heart-breaking tragedy. But as awful as this pandemic is, there have also been so many inspiring stories too. As always, the most challenging events bring out the very best in people. And now more than ever we are reminded of what really matters, namely each other, reaching out to our friends and family through phone and video calls. I suspect that this event will change the world for the better and good may actually come out of it. I certainly hope so.

If you're reading *Earth Shout* whilst the pandemic still has its grip on the world, I hope you found yourself lost in the book in a good way. Stories have always been important to me, and especially now during these difficult times when they help our imaginations to continue soaring.

You can probably tell that I had a lot of fun writing *Earth Shout*, not least when it came to imagining what it would be like to pilot a real-life flying saucer. No stranger to flying myself, the idea of controlling a craft that could change its flight direction to any angle was incredibly intriguing, especially one with little in the way of G-force to pin you into your seat.

If you've read any of my previous novels, you'll know I like to research my stories as thoroughly as possible, and *Earth Shout* was no exception. For the TR-3Bs and Ariel I obviously had to make a lot of educated guesses, including cockpit configurations that had to be radically different to those of a conventional aircraft. I have to admit I really let my imagination go wild with Ariel. A 3D-axis gimbal-mounted flight deck makes an awful lot of sense from an engineering perspective, and certainly it would be very cool. Technically the REV drive would need to rotate with the flight deck so that the gravity pull was always downwards for the crew, whatever its orientation. I can see it clearly in my mind, which is half the fun of writing about an imaginary craft like this.

I tried to come up with details that wouldn't upset the ufologists too much – or Mulder for that matter, especially in my depictions of the TR-3Bs. There is a lot of conflicting information about secret military craft out there and I did my best to wade through it to create my own interpretation. Whether TR-3Bs actually exist is open to conjecture. During my research I came across rumours that the TR-3Bs are a black-budget project and part of the US military's Aurora programme. Just to confuse things, there is also allegedly the TR-3A, another triangular-shaped but more conventional craft that's radically different in design. It has been suggested that this is part of the reason why there are conflicting reports around these craft.

As for Area 51, it is probably one of the biggest enigmas on the planet, a secret in plain sight. With a quick internet search you'll find numerous aerial photos of the airbase that show it has been considerably expanded over the years it has existed, including the addition of a second runway. But who knows whether there really is a vast underground base beneath it? Please remember that this book is a work of fiction – I have done my best to draw my descriptions from the numerous rumours that swirl around that mysterious facility, but I have no way of knowing the truth. Of course, I would love for there to be UFOs down in Area 51 that are being actively researched, but if so, I hope one day these technologies are shared with all of humanity. Can you imagine the possibilities? I know Lauren can!

I will close this by thanking the usual suspects who help to hone my books and push me hard to make them the best pieces of work they can be. Once again, I doff my imaginary hat to both my editor Catherine Coe and also Jennie Roman for catching all those pesky typos. And a shout-out to my assistant Makenna Guyler who helps me to juggle all the newsletters. I'm not sure what I'd do without her. I must also thank Karen, my wife, for helping to keep me sane during this lockdown period. She is my best friend and guiding light on the darkest of days.

It's time for me to sign off and get writing the next book in the *Earth Song* series. Will Lucy be OK and what is the significance of the red glowing micro mind? Keep an eye out for *Earth Howl*, which will continue Lauren's story and reveal more answers...

Nick Cook, April 2020

Printed in Great Britain
by Amazon